WHEN LIGHTNING STRIKES

MARY ANN BOYLE

For my children, Sam and Autumn,
and my wife, Laurie.
My love and appreciation are endless.
For my mom who taught me the value of laughter, to love
literature, and to dream of writing.
And, with tenderness, for those who have been hurt, and are
finding their way forward.

Literature can be both guide and mirror.
It provides perspective and permission.
And I know that it can be an escape, a balm.
But is that so bad?
It is not a numbing agent.
Instead, it is a room into which
one might wander seeking
shelter from the storm.
MARY ANN

INTRODUCTION

Amesville, Iowa is hot as Hades in the summertime, and 1967 wasn't any better or worse when it comes to this fact. But my story isn't about the weather. It's about my family. Mostly that means I'm gonna tell you about my little sister Annie and me. We're the only children of Daniel and Elizabeth Walker who live with us in this drafty old farmhouse.

Annie's eight and I'm eleven and it was all fine and good 'till it wasn't anymore. It's like she was swinging from a branch one minute and next thing you know she's sailing through the air with a stick in her hand. Annie fell hard. And now I'm picking up pieces of this and that trying to make sense of what went wrong and how it all happened.

Truth is that Annie was full of spit and vinegar and could find trouble in a loaf of white bread. Mama always said that someday Annie would get into a fistfight with the wrong person. But Mama was wrong. It was no fistfight that broke Annie's spirit. It was evil. Pure and simple. And it all started with a bolt of lightning in the summer sky.

CHAPTER 1

*W*ind whipped our hair and supper sloshed in our stomachs as Annie and I rushed around dragging tables and buckets and whatnot into place for the carnival we were having in the morning. We'd been planning for weeks and now that it was here, worries about the weather and kids showing up started dripping out from the palms of my hands.

I figured that if Mama could keep laundry on the line, we could lay out our goods and trust that they'd stay put and dry too. I was setting up milk bottles for bowling and horseshoes for tossing when I called out to Annie. "Annie, put the gunny sacks over there by the willow. Then lay out the hula-hoop—"

"Stop being so bossy, Ruthie. You're not in charge, you know. I'm all done with second grade, I'm a big kid too."

"Annie, school's been out for two days. That doesn't make you a big kid, yet."

"Well, I know what's what, so there!" Annie threw her hands on her hips like the Pillsbury Doughboy and stood staring at me like every word she said was the truth and nothing but the truth.

"Well, I'm better at being organized and you're...sometimes you need organizing. That's all."

"Ruth Ann Walker, I don't need you telling me what's what."

"OK, OK. Do what you want. But let's hurry up. It smells like rain."

"You're nuts, Ruthie! It smells like dog farts. I swear every time Buddy hears the thunder he farts. Or maybe...maybe thunder smells like dog farts and it isn't Buddy at all."

Annie was laughing at her joke when the wind whipped her sailor hat right off her head. "Whoa, come back here, you little devil!" She was on the chase and the storm was too. I had guessed wrong. Rain was coming fast.

And, wouldn't you know, lightning split the Iowa sky like it was a watermelon bursting with summer. Thunder rumbled without catching its breath in between the booms, and wind snatched the gunnysacks and threw them down hard in the gravel drive.

My hair whipped right out of the ponytail that was holding it, and the whole mass of long, wild curls flew in my face. I gathered it in a fist and looked up; clouds moved in on us. Buddy the Beagle sat underneath the card table with his head tipped back, sniffing. I patted his head as the sky broke open and water poured down like the Mississippi turned on its side.

"Run for cover!" I shouted at Annie, trying to be heard above the sudden downpour and howling wind. But when I turned back, she was twirling like a fool with her smiling face tipped up to the sky.

"Come on in, Ruthie! The weather's fine!" With her little hat back on her head, she laughed and danced.

"For heaven's sakes, girls! Get out of this storm at once!"

Mama's voice was nearly lost with the next clap of thunder, which finally made Annie scurry to the porch for cover.

"Hey there, Mama. It's a bit misty, aye?" Water ran down her face and her blond pixie-cut plastered to her head, as Annie repeated one of Daddy's favorite lines every time a storm felt like it might carry us away. *Away*. Why was Daddy always away? Didn't he like being home with us?

"Annie, you are soaked to the skin. Ruth Ann, run a bath for your sister. I don't know about this carnival plan, girls. You don't have the card table out there, do you?"

"I'll get it Mama!" I raced over to the table, tipped it on one side, folded up the legs, and started dragging it across the grass. Annie ran out to help. We just set it down and, *BOOM!*

"Oh, my lord!" Mama shrieked.

"Mama! What was that?" I screamed.

Annie yelled, "holy smokes! Mama, that tree got hit!"

Across the road, flames shot into the sky from the poor, lonesome tree standing off by itself just on the edge of the cornfield.

"Call the fire department, Mama! Call for help!"

"Annie, the fire department cannot be of assistance in a situation like this." Still staring across the road, she muttered, "for the love of God, Walter."

Standing underneath that tree was Grandpa. Rain soaked him to the skin and there was a lot of skin to be soaked. He was wearing nothing but an old, unbuttoned plaid shirt, a pair of Wellies, and tighty whiteys that weren't much of either. A cigarette dangled from his mouth as he looked up at the fire with his hat in his hand.

"What's Grandpa doing, Mama?" I shouted.

"Well, I imagine he is surveying the damage and confirming that the tree is the only casualty of the storm...in his underwear." Mama sounded just as disgusted as I felt seeing his underpants stick to him like Saran plastic wrap.

3

"He and your grandmother planted that tree the year your daddy was born. But why he cannot think to dress himself prior to walking out the front door, regardless of the circumstances, is beyond me."

"He should run for his life!" Annie's words bubbled out with worry.

"Annie, your grandfather has weathered many a summer storm. He will be just fine."

"Well, that tree's not gonna be *just fine*. Why doesn't he at least *try* to put out the fire?" Annie asked.

"That would be an exercise in futility, Annie. There are things in this world we do not have control over. When lightning strikes is one, and when your grandfather chooses to dress appropriately is another." Mama exhaled her words, "Right now there appears to be no danger to the house and there is no saving the tree. Sometimes all you can do is watch..." She took a deep breath and chuckled.

BOOM! BOOM! The storm shook our house and rattled my nerves. Everything that wasn't nailed down got scooped up and dropped like tiddlywinks. From inside the house Buddy howled along with a siren, and Grandpa looked to be having a fight with God. I figured the show was over when he disappeared from sight. But then he walked back towards the tree pulling a garden hose behind him and started spraying water.

"Oh, my Lord," Mama said again.

"I thought you said there was no saving that tree." I accused Mama with my words, but she didn't seem to take offense.

"There *is* no saving the tree and there may be no saving your grandfather, if he doesn't come to his senses."

Mama's words were still hanging in the air when Grandma stormed out towards Grandpa. Her housecoat flew up with every gust of wind, showing more of her than I ever did need to see. She gave it all she had trying to pull him away from flames and falling branches, but he kept right on squirting. And then he turned...his hose on her. She spun like a top and he shot her right in the backside. That housecoat stuck to her behind like papier Mache on a balloon. She waved her arms and ran for cover. That's when Grandpa's face turned our way, and I could see his mouth moving and his nasty grin.

"That crazy old man," Mama muttered.

And then Annie shouted, "look out, Grandpa!" There's no way on God's green earth he heard her above the beating of the rain and the howling winds, but he tipped his face back and saw the still burning branch falling towards him. This time he did run for his life! The branch hit the ground and sizzled.

Then, just as fast as it started, the rain stopped, and thunder crashed in the distance. And Grandpa was out of sight. And that was the first time I saw her. But I didn't know it then. I just knew an old red truck drove by and I wondered why. Who in their right mind was out for a drive on a night like this?

All three of us stared into the night listening to the burning tree crackle and thunder softening in the distance. I thought about that tree growing up surrounded by the cornfield, and my daddy playing in its shade, long before I was born. I was pushing my glasses up and shaking loose curls of hair from my face when Annie's voice startled me.

"Ruthie?"

"Yeah?"

"Will you tell me a story?"

"Ask Mama."

"She's gone."

I looked around. Annie was right. Mama was gone.

The night fell around us, and I hadn't even taken notice.

5

I'd been so busy listening to the story I was telling in my own head about the life of the burned tree, that I hadn't seen the stars that filled the sky like a million little diamonds. Sparks from the fire floated between all those stars and me. And then I realized, they weren't sparks at all. My sadness for the tree lifted.

"Look, Annie. Fireflies."

"There's millions of them!" she said in awe. "But Ruthie, can they start fires too?" Her voice trembled.

"No. Don't be silly," I said, feeling unsure.

"How am I supposed to know? How come a light flashing in the sky can make a fire and a firefly can't? That don't make any sense at all, you know."

"It's time to go in for the night, girls." Mama's voice snuck up behind me and I hadn't even heard the screen door open and shut.

"Goldarn Mama, what are you doing scaring us like that?" Annie scolded.

"Annie, I've been sitting here the whole time." Mama's voice held the softness of sleep and dreams.

"We couldn't see you. Why didn't you tell us?"

"I was quietly taking in the stillness following the storm," she said, slowly rocking herself on the porch swing.

Mama was right, the night was still, even though the tree still burned, and lightning flashed in the distant sky. Annie pushed her hands deep into the pockets of her cutoff jeans, leaned against the post, and sighed. I had just sat down beside Mama when she got up to go.

"Where are you going, Mama?" Annie asked.

"I will be back shortly. I need to put a couple of things away." When she opened the door to step inside, Buddy came out. He was one brave little beagle when it came to most things on the farm, but when it came to summer storms, well, as much as he loved Annie, he wouldn't get caught dancing with her in the rain.

He curled up with Annie on the splintery porch, as Beets the cat and I rocked beside them. "Once upon a time," I started like I did most nights, with a new chapter in the story of a little orphaned girl named Sally, who looked a lot like Annie. I was getting lost in the telling, when Mama opened the door.

"OK, girls, now it really is time for bed." She stepped to the edge of the porch. Looking through the screen at the sparkling lights of the fireflies and the glow of the burning tree, it almost looked like the sparkle and glow were coming from her. With a lonesome voice, Mama said, "my, that tree is still burning. I suppose we should consider ourselves lucky that that is the worst of it." She took a deep sigh. "And so, the story goes."

"How come you don't tell us stories, Mama?"

She turned to me and we both looked down at Annie sleeping with Buddy as her pillow.

"Hmm. I don't know. Some days it feels like the only thing I can remember is what I had for breakfast." Mama's laugh was soft, and I couldn't see her eyes to know if sadness was pooled there, like it was in her voice. "I suppose my life hasn't really been interesting enough to remember." She shook her head, like she was shaking off sleep. "Let's get you girls to bed, shall we? You will have an early morning and by the looks of that sliver of moon and the stars, it will be a fine day for your carnival."

Buddy wiggled out from under Annie's head, and she nearly clunked it on the hard-wooden slats of the front porch. "What happened to Sally?"

"You fell asleep. That's what happened," I answered. Annie's question made me wonder what *would* happen next. Sometimes I wished I could live in a world where I could write the chapters and the ending too. In that story, I'd be loved just as much as Annie. And Mama–

"It sounded to me like Sally had a grand adventure, and I do believe you missed all about the pirates and Indians and Gertrude saving Sally from disaster." Mama looked at me with a warm smile on her face, like she knew what I was dreaming. "You have the beginnings of a wonderful story. You're a far better storyteller than me."

With Annie's bath forgotten, Mama said, "now, off to bed you go. Annie, perhaps your sister will continue Sally's grand adventures tomorrow night."

We all turned and looked at Buddy. His head tipped back. Seeing through his nose. A shiver ran up my spine. The haze of smoke hung in the sky. Frogs and crickets sang. And then I heard what Buddy knew. *Howooo.* He joined in. *Howooo.* Mama pulled us closer.

"Why do coyotes howl?" I asked, wrapped up in Mama. I lost count of the heartbeats between my question and Mama's answer.

In a voice, so quiet it was almost a whisper she said, "over the course of the day they sometimes wander far from one another. And then recognizing their distance, their aloneness, they use their voices to call their family back together again with that eerie, lonely cry in the night. I suppose we all have that desire, don't we? To be family again."

Being pressed against her body I could feel Mama holding her breath. And then, when she was back to breathing, she shuddered, and I looked up. "You all right, Mama?"

"Yes, Ruth Ann. I'm fine. It's just a sound I have not yet gotten used to. I didn't hear the call of coyotes until I moved here. Sometimes it leaves me feeling both fearful and forlorn." Until her teardrop fell on my cheek, I didn't know she was crying. With my face pressed into her old cotton blouse, I gave her tear back without her knowing she'd given it to me in the first place.

Howooo. The space between Buddy and the coyotes was closing. Yipping and howling. I know Mama said they were just calling their family together and all, but it sounded to me like they were up to no good.

"Where is Beets?" The fear in Mama's voice made my hands tingle.

"She's right here." Annie moved away from us and picked her up with her engine still running.

"Get her inside. And Buddy too," Mama murmured.

I opened the door and Annie set Beets down and I gave Buddy a shove inside too then closed it. Annie looked out towards the barn and said, "How about Gertrude? Goats get scared too. Can she come inside tonight?"

"Ruth Ann, see that she's in the barn and make sure that the door is shut securely."

"Mama, do coyotes eat dogs and cats and goats?" Annie asked. "I thought they just ate chickens and gooses."

Mama didn't answer but I stood staring at the barn and the coyotes howled again. From inside the house, Buddy did too. Closer. Louder.

"Ruth Ann, go!" Mama snapped.

"Uh," I stammered.

"Here, I'll do it!" Annie chirped, as she threw open the creaky old screen door and jumped from the top step to the wet grass below. She ran for the barn without waiting for me to answer or move.

In a deep, quiet voice Mama said, "go with your sister." She sounded like water just before the boil. I was scared and didn't want to. But she wasn't giving up. "Ruth Ann, I said, go with your sister!" She shouted this time, and I flew through the door, hit the ground with a graceless thud, and took off running. There was just enough light from the moon to run without smacking into something, but I didn't need to go far because Annie was running back with Gertrude trotting beside her.

"I got her Mama!" Annie yelled all out of breath before reaching the porch.

The door to the porch flew open and Mama was framed with the light from behind. Her hair going every which way, and she looked like a wild creature herself. We stopped in our tracks. Mama shook so bad I thought she might pull that worn-out door right off its hinges. But truth be told, the one going off her hinges was Mama. Her shoulders lifted and stayed there. They sank back down again when she was calm enough to use her words.

"I didn't ask that you *get* her. I asked that you…Annie take that goat back this instant! She will be fine. Be certain that you secure the barn door. Ruth Ann, go along and double check to see that the door is properly closed."

Howooo. I didn't move.

"You'll be fine. Go ahead!" Mama held the door open and shouted from the porch. *Howooo.*

Knowing I didn't have a choice, I ran towards the barn. Annie got Gertrude back in and I slid the door shut, pulled the latch closed and we ran for dear life back to the porch. Every step of the way I felt the beady eyes of those coyotes and imagined sharp little teeth ready to rip me to pieces. I turned to look behind me. I saw the eyes I imagined. They were low to the ground. Slinking. "What in the world?" I whispered. "Get inside," Mama ordered, which was just fine by me.

"Lock the door, Ruth Ann."

"Lock the door?" I asked.

"Mama, do you think that them coyotes might be like the big, bad wolf and huff and puff and…"

10

"Enough, Annie! Just lock the door, Ruth Ann, and you two head up to bed."

I looked over at Mama as she closed windows and checked doors. She really was expecting those coyotes to come on in for a visit, and that made me wonder if they would too. I didn't say a thing about the eyes I saw. Maybe it really was my imagination.

Daddy never was around when we needed him. As I thought about it, I couldn't tell the difference between being mad and sad, but I figured either way, Mama might need to learn to howl.

CHAPTER 2

"*A*nnie, wake up. Get up."

"Knock it off, Ruthie," she groaned when I kicked the bottom of the top bunk.

"We gotta get out there and set up for the carnival." I stood on my bunk and tickled her. "Last one down's a rotten egg!" I moved out of the way as Annie landed her jump from the top bunk like a gymnast.

She raised her arms in the air, "ta-da!"

As we pulled on yesterday's clothes, sunshine peeked through our bedroom window and birds sang their brains out and Buddy was barking his head off.

"Mornin', Mama! We'll be outside getting stuff ready. Call us for breakfast!"

"For heaven's sake, Ruth Ann! Annie! Slow down. It is six-thirty. There is no need to rush about like the house is on fire and screaming like Banshees."

"Sorry. We're just excited about our day, that's all," I explained, not wanting Mama to change her mind about letting us have the carnival in the first place.

"I can certainly see that. Yes. Go along now. I will let you

12

know when breakfast is ready."

"Thanks, Mama." I raced through the door, chasing after Annie.

"Geez Louise! It's hot as Hades out here!"

Annie grabbed the wet gunny sacks and hung them over the fence to dry. From the cellar we pulled out Mama's card table and buckets and boards to put things in and set things on. We had milk bottles for bowling and Incredible Edibles for sale. There were apples for bobbing and a donkey that needed a tail pinned on. The gunny sack racecourse was set, and the hula-hoops leaned against the trunk of a tree. The fortune-telling table was hidden behind a row of shrubs so Heidi, the fortune-teller, could focus.

"So, if I'm selling my Incredible Edibles and Heidi's telling fortunes, and Merle's helping kids bob for apples, what are you gonna be doing?" Annie asked with her hands on her hips and exasperation in her voice.

"I'll be pretty busy being in charge," I answered looking around the yard at the best carnival ever.

"I can be in charge," Annie chirped back.

"No, Annie. I'm oldest. I'm in charge."

"Well, you don't get to be in charge of me." Truth is, she was right. I never really could be in charge of Annie. "I know what I'm gonna do. I'm gonna ask Mama if we can hook up the Water Wiggle so kids can cool down after the gunny sack races, 'cause right about now, I feel like I got a big 'ol wet blanket thrown over the top of me. I'm already sweating like a pig and I'm not even racing in a gunnysack. That's it! I feel like a pig-in-a-blanket!" She snorted with her laugh and spun like a top when Mama called out.

"Girls, breakfast is ready!" We bolted through the kitchen door to the smell of bacon and coffee.

"Mama, kids could be coming anytime. Would it be

13

alright if I just carry my plate out and eat while I keep an eye on things?"

"No, it certainly would not, Annabelle Rose. You sit down and eat the breakfast I have prepared for you in a proper manner. And you will rest following your breakfast to ensure that you don't get indigestion."

"But Mama…"

"Don't but Mama me, young lady. This topic is not up for discussion."

"Mama?"

"Yes, Ruth Ann?"

"How come you're not eating breakfast too? Why are you just drinking coffee and sorting the mail when breakfast is the *cornerstone of a healthy day?*"

"Do not be a smart aleck. You know very well that I have already eaten and…I have bills to take care of. Lord knows what rock I can turn over to find enough money to pay all of these."

Mama's voice faded as she sliced open envelopes in between sips of her black Folgers coffee. Annie must have noticed Mama being quiet too 'cause she looked up from her plate and said, "Mama, I know why you drink all that coffee."

"Eat your breakfast, Annie."

"*It tastes so good, you hate to put it down.*" Annie sounded just like the ad for Folgers coffee on the television.

"*That's right, George,*" I added, leaving Mama even more perturbed.

"Enough, girls. Your breakfast is getting cold."

Sitting at our gray Formica table we each had a plate filled up with scrambled eggs, toast, and two slices of fatty bacon from the Hormel factory that supplied my daddy's paycheck. Mama's homemade white bread was toasted and buttered just waiting to get all slathered up with strawberry freezer jam. Like usual, my toast started soaking up the milky puddle the eggs were resting in. I scooched it out of harm's way and reached for the jam.

"Ruthie, we need to get going. We still gotta get the wheels and apples. I'll climb up the tree and throw 'em down..."

"Tap-tap-tap-tap-tap!!!!" I nearly jumped out of my skin when I heard the banging on the glass window of the kitchen door. My back was to the door, and I looked up at Mama's face looking out. The silver metal blade in her hand stopped partway through slicing open her bill, as the door flew open. Grandpa's loud voice almost made me choke on toast and egg yolk.

"YellOW and good morning!" he shouted. "Gave you a start, did I?" He laughed, showing the brown stains on the few teeth he still had. He was wearing the same old plaid shirt and boots he had on during the storm, but I was mighty grateful he was buttoned up and wearing pants like a normal person this time. Annie jumped from her seat and into the arms of Grandpa who came in the kitchen smelling like he always did: stale tobacco and old-man stink.

"Well now, how's my favorite grandbaby? You gonna go fishing with your granddaddy? Huh? We could catch us some fine catfish. What do you say, Annie?"

Grandpa hadn't even bothered to look at me or my mama, but she was looking at him. All the while he was doting on Annie, she stared cold at my daddy's daddy in his Wrangler jeans and crumpled shirt. Her annoyance with his bad manners looked like hate more often than not, if you ask me. And truth be told, that's what I felt too, when he snarled at her like she was one of his *lazy, no-good* farmhands. It wasn't just his bad manners. Grandpa gave me an icky feeling in my stomach that made no sense. I wondered if that happened to Mama too.

Finally, between her teeth she said, "good morning,

15

Walter. May I pour you a cup of coffee?" Still in the middle of slicing open envelopes, she held her letter opener just so. The morning light winked off its blade. When I looked back at Grandpa, that light landed right in the corner of his eye like a teardrop.

"Yep. Put some milk and sugar in it too," he said when he finally answered her question. Mama walked over and poured his coffee into a cup that said, *World's Best Dad*. Every time she washed that cup, she said the same thing: *Well, this certainly is a cup that holds more hope than truth*. But never mind, she added a splash of milk and two cubes of sugar, like she did every morning when he barged in to visit Annie. Somehow Mama managed to hand him his cup without looking at him.

"Grandpa, I can't go fishing. Me and Ruthie, well, we're making a carnival. It's gonna be great. You could come on over and bob for apples or race the gunny sacks or...or you could buy some Incredible Edibles from me. Right, Ruthie? We got lots."

Annie didn't wait for an answer but kept right on jibber-jabbering. And every now and then, when she did take a breath, I jumped in, making plans with her in between bites of breakfast and swallowing down my annoyance. Grandpa didn't care that this was my time with Annie. He never did take notice of what anybody needed besides himself. He was my elder, but today I didn't really care. That was neither here nor there, as Mama said.

"Well then, little missy, maybe you can come for a sleep-over tonight. Whaddaya think about that?"

Annie looked over at Mama who was still slicing open her mail. "Can I, Mama?"

"Yes, Annie?"

"See there, Annie. Your mama said yes."

16

"Pardon me, Walter. What was the question? I'm sorry Annie, I was not really listening."

"So, Annie, how 'bout I'll walk over and get you just in time for supper? You don't mind now, do you?" Grandpa looked up at Mama, and I couldn't quite tell if he was asking her a question or telling her a truth. I held my breath waiting for Mama to take a swing at him. Not with her fists, but with her words. She was real good at that.

"Walter, I will give it some thought." She kept her cool and kept her eyes down. "No promises, Annie."

"Well, I'll tell you what, Annie. If your Mama lets you come over, we'll make homemade ice cream. You'd like that wouldn't you?"

"Sure would, Grandpa. And I bet Ruthie would too. Wouldn't you, Ruthie? You'd like some homemade ice cream too."

I looked at Mama, back to Annie, and then at Grandpa through the top half of my glasses. He was leaning back in his chair scowling at me. It felt like a trap, and my own head of steam was building. I wanted Mama to flatten him, but she didn't say a thing.

Some of that steam came out in a hiss wrapped up in words. "Annie, I think we'd better get going. The kids will be here in no time. Mama, may I be excused?" I asked swallowing down both the anger and the ick that was rising.

"Yes, you may, Ruth Ann. Please clear your plate and push your chair in."

I knew Mama wasn't telling ME to push my chair in. Every time that Grandpa finished his coffee, he left drips on the table and his chair standing in the middle of the room like a dare. But she never took the bait.

"Come on, Annie. Let's go. See you later, Grandpa."

"Uh-huh. Now, Annie, I'll come by later on to get you for staying the night."

"Well…" Annie looked between Mama and him.

Before she said more, I said, "thank you for breakfast, Mama. It was real good."

Wasn't but a minute after we were looking things over when Grandpa walked by on his way home and said, "ya'll have a lot of fun now." He winked at Annie as he shuffled along the gravel drive. I looked past him to see Mama staring out the kitchen window.

"They're here! Yay, they're here!" Annie shouted and nearly danced when she saw Mrs. Hansen turn up the drive in their blue station wagon with wooden panels running along the sides. Heidi and her little sister Merle waved out the back windows and Mrs. Hansen smiled and waved too. We both ran to meet the car and it barely came to a stop before both back doors flew open and our best friends jumped out.

"You're just in time. There's lots we gotta do before the kids get here!" Annie exclaimed.

Just then Mama stepped through the kitchen door and down the two steps to the drive.

"Well, you're out bright and early." She smiled at Mrs. Hansen and the girls, as Mrs. Hansen got out and stood leaning against the car.

"Good morning, Elizabeth. I hope we're not too early. I would have called but the line was busy and…well, I couldn't keep the girls home another minute without tying them to a fencepost. They're as excited as can be about this backyard carnival."

Mama laughed and said, "yes, I am quite surprised that Ruth Ann and Annie didn't emerge from slumber even sooner. Would you like to come in for a cup of coffee, Rose?"

"Oh, I should get my errands run and head back home to get a few things done while you're kind enough to have the girls in your hair instead of mine. I seem to be having a hard time keeping up."

And then Mama finally looked at me. "What is it, Ruth Ann? Either you're terribly interested in the conversation I'm having with Mrs. Hansen or you have a question for me. I'm guessing the latter."

"I was just wondering if the girls and me can head over to Grandpa and Grandma's and get the wheels and some apples?"

"Can you first say good morning to Mrs. Hansen and thank her for bringing the girls in for this adventure?"

"Good morning, Mrs. Hansen." I looked from her to Mama and back. "Thank you." Suddenly Mrs. Hansen took ahold of Mama's arm.

"Rose, are you all right?" Mama put her hand on the top of Mrs. Hansen's and the edges of her voice grew soft. Mama's everyday way of talking was like she was taking dictation for the president, but right now she slipped her arm around Mrs. Hansen's waist to hold her steady. Mama wasn't one for touching folks, and I didn't really know what to make of it.

"I remember when we were girls, you could run a fever if you ran too fast on the playground," Mama said.

"Oh, I'm sorry. This heat is getting the best of me. I'm just a bit dizzy." She climbed back into her car. "I'll be fine. I really better get going. Thanks so much, Elizabeth. And Ruth Ann, you are so welcome. Have a delightful day with your carnival. Give me a call when it's time to pick up my girls."

"I will indeed, Rose, and stay out of this heat. Today will surely be a scorcher."

After she drove away, I asked, "what's wrong with Mrs. Hansen?"

"Oh, I'm sure she is just fine. It is a lot of work running a farm. I imagine it can get quite exhausting at times." Mama stared after Mrs. Hansen's car with a funny look on her face. I wasn't quite sure that I could believe what she was saying. And I wasn't quite sure that she did either.

"Can we go, Mama?"

"Go where?"

"To Grandpa's? The apples?"

"Right. Certainly. I'm heading back in."

"OK!" I hollered as I headed back to Annie and the girls who were already starting to fight over how stuff was laid out. "Come on! Let's go!"

Annie took hold of Merle's hand and ran ahead of Heidi and me and just as we were about to cross the road, that red truck drove by again. I couldn't take time to think on it because I was too busy thinking about best friends.

Walking along with my best friend, I couldn't quite shake seeing my mama holding on to Mrs. Hansen and the tenderness of her voice. It made me wonder if Mama's memories of Mrs. Hansen were as faded as the clothes she wore. Heidi and I were best friends, just like our mamas had been growing up in Chicago. But it was different now. I didn't know why. Whatever it was, I didn't want it to happen to Heidi and me. I wished we were family; real family. Then she'd never go away.

"What's that?" I asked, thinking I saw something moving in the shadows.

"What's what?" Heidi asked.

"Oh nothing. I think I'm seeing things." I let it go and wondered if I was. I was still spooked by last night's coyotes. "I wish we were sisters. Or cousins," I murmured out of the blue.

"What? What's got into you, Ruthie? We're best friends. Isn't that good enough?" she asked.

"I s'pose." I shook my head like an Etch-a-Sketch to clear away the sadness.

"But our mamas were friends and now they just...they just know each other. I don't want that to happen to us."

"Don't be silly. Nothing could happen to us. We're different."

I didn't know how, but I wanted it to be true. I let myself remember, piecing together memories like quilt squares, hoping they'd be enough to hold us together.

"Remember that time we played Tom Sawyer floating down the Mississippi when the ditch flooded? Your mama was so mad at you."

Heidi laughed easily, and that made my own worry drift a bit further away. Smiling at the thought, I said, "well, I don't think Mama would have been so mad if Annie hadn't jumped in the water and played like she was drowning."

"Oh, I don't know 'bout that. My mama says that sometimes she gets scared and that's what makes her most mad of all. I think your mama got real scared when Scotty ran out to the garden and told her Annie *was* drowning." She paused. "He's such a turd." She looked at me sideways and started laughing again and that's when we caught up with Annie and Merle who were each rolling one of those giant wooden spools towards us.

"Watch out, Ruthie! I might just roll right on over you if you don't get outa the way!" Annie was running and pushing and, I swear, she could barely see where she was going if she could see at all.

"Knock it off, Annie! You could hurt somebody with that thing. Slow down!" I snapped.

"Geez, Ruthie, I was just kidding. I'm not gonna kill you or nothing." Annie and Merle and Heidi all stared at me like I was the one doing something bad.

"You all right, Ruthie?" Heidi asked.

I kicked at the dirt. Without looking up, I mumbled, "sorry, Annie. I didn't mean to snap at you."

21

"That's alright, Ruthie." I lifted my eyes. "But don't let it happen again," she said, wagging her finger just like Mama scolding us. I couldn't help but smile at my little sister, and that gave her what she wanted. "Now I mean business, young lady," she went on.

"OK, OK. Let's get these spools across the road." Heidi helped Merle push hers and I followed behind Annie, who climbed up on top and rode it like she was in the Barnum and Bailey Circus.

"You know what I think?" Heidi said.

"What's that?" Looking at her I thought she was gonna say something about me being grumpy, but she said, "I think these big ol' spools look like sewing bobbins for the Jolly Green Giant!"

"Yeah, the Jolly Green Giant!" Merle laughed and started singing, and then Annie and I joined in. Rolling and running across the street we were singing at the top of our lungs.

"Ho, ho, ho, Green Giant!"

Annie and Merle took off again to pick apples when Mama came walking up with a baking sheet covered in greasy brown bags. "Where would you like your popcorn, Ruth Ann? Shall I put it on the card table?"

"Sure, Mama, that'd be swell. Thanks."

"Hello, Mrs. Walker. That smells delicious." Heidi always was good with her manners, never even needing to be told.

They chatted a bit and I was skedaddling around the yard when Annie came running back across the yard pulling her wagon filled with apples, leaving a trail of fruit bouncing on the ground behind her.

Mama looked at Annie and started to say something, but Annie cut her short. With her hands on her hips, and her head tipped back, she said, "I'm thinning the trees, Mama. Grandpa helped us decide which apples to pick, and he said me and Merle were a *great help* to him." Annie dumped apples into the tub of water just as some of the neighborhood boys rode up on their bikes.

"We're not ready yet!" she hollered.

"Annie, those are your customers arriving." Mama folded her arms across her chest. "I would suggest you be a bit more gracious."

"They're *just boys*. And we're not ready yet. We still have gobs to do."

"Perhaps the *boys* would like to give you a hand," Mama said, as she turned and headed back inside.

Annie huffed and turned to Matthew Wright, Bud and Walter, shouting again, "you can help us finish getting ready if you do what I tell you to!"

I looked over at Matthew when he asked, "how can we help, Ruth Ann?"

"Ooow. *How can I help you, Ruth Ann?*" Annie mimicked. "*Ruthie and Matthew sitting in a tree…*"

"Stop it right now, Annabelle Rose!" I hissed through clenched teeth.

"OK. You can help us!" She yelled to the boys.

Wasn't but a minute and Annie had them racing around the yard following her orders like she was a general in the army. As they worked, other kids showed up and waited on the edge of the grass. They all knew our carnival was happening, just like it did last year, right when school ended. Old bikes were lying on their sides in the gravel and new ones were standing proud on kickstands. Some kids were dropped off as their parents drove by on their way into town. Next thing I knew, Annie raced up the steps of the front porch and called out, "Welcome to the Great Walker Carnival!" She pulled her sailor hat off her head, took a bow and rang the old cowbell that hung from the front porch.

Kids bobbed for apples, raced across the yard in gunnysacks and tried out the *Wheel Ride*. Heidi told fortunes from underneath a couple of sawhorses with a sheet thrown over the top, and Merle followed Annie like a shadow.

"This is the best day ever!" I said to Heidi, when she crawled out from her 'tent'.

"Ruthie, we're all outa popcorn," Merle said, looking up at me with green eyes so bright they looked teary. "Annie said to tell you to tell your mama, so she could make us more." She looked from me to Heidi and said, "Annie said it's an *emergency*!" And then we all looked at Annie.

"Why's Annie fighting with Bud?"

"Oh, she's not fighting. She's just trying to get what she has comin' for all them Edibles. But Ruthie, the popcorn is an *emergency*!"

"OK, OK."

As I ran by Annie I shouted, "hold down the fort!"

I threw open the kitchen door and saw all our breakfast dishes drying in the drainer. Mama's half-filled coffee cup was sitting on the table with her Bic pen beside it. I ran through the house hollering for her, like it really was an emergency. The house was so still and quiet I started to worry. I thought maybe she'd be lying on the sofa, resting. But Beets was there instead, perched on the back cushion, drenched in sunshine. I stopped. She stood and stretched and jumped to the cushion releasing a cloud of dust into the stream of sunshine, just like a *Kansas City dust storm,* Mama would say if she was where she was supposed to be.

"Mama! Mama! Where are you?"

My bare feet were slick with sweat when I looked through the door to the laundry room. There she was, hunched over the ironing board. *Whoosh.* A fine mist of Niagara Spray Starch landed on my daddy's blue shirt. The hot iron sizzled. I watched as Mama slipped the shoulders onto a hanger. That shirt stood straighter than Mama.

Rounded like a curlicue, she reached into her basket, pulled out a hankie and started pressing again.

"Mama?" I whispered. With eyes red and puffy and snot hanging from the end of her nose, she turned and looked at me.

"What is it, Ruth Ann?"

"Mama, I'm sorry to interrupt you, but can me and Annie have some more popcorn, please?" I tried hard to remember my manners every time I spoke to my mama, being that manners and grammar are *virtues as great as kindness and love*. But Mama forgot all about her own, ignored me and reached into her sleeve, like a magician, and blew her nose on the wadded-up Kleenex tissue she found.

"Ruth Ann," she finally said, peering through glasses smudged with an oily film and speckled with dandruff, "can you please rephrase that question for me?"

"Mama, please. The kids are gonna go away if I don't get back out there. Please can we have some more popcorn?"

After another long pause that made my blood boil she said, "Ruth Ann, please get your sister and come up to my room. I need to speak with you about something that cannot wait."

"But Mama..." My voice trailed off as she stepped past me, left the room and started up the stairs. That iron was sitting on its heel and still plugged into the outlet. *That's how fires start little missy.* My daddy's voice sniggered in my head as I slammed through the back screen door.

"Annie! Annie!" I couldn't see her from the porch, so I raced straight away to the place where I last saw her. Instead of finding Annie I smashed into little Merle who was bent over picking at clover or popcorn or who knows what. I sent her flying face first into the apple-bobbing tub that was on the ground in front of her. "Merle, what in tarnation are you doing?!" I pulled her out and shouted, "where's Annie? I've got to find her!"

Merle stood in a puddle of confusion and apples and then started bellowing something awful. Heidi raced over to find out what happened to her little sister, and I stood like a lump, pushed my glasses up my nose, and tried to get into focus what in the world was going on.

"Ruth Ann, why were you shouting at Merle? Merle, what happened? Why are you all wet?"

"She puuushed me!" Merle wailed.

"I didn't mean to. I, uh, I dunno. I never saw her and I uh...I need to find Annie!" Stammering and stuttering, my mind was going all hazy-crazy. And then I heard the whistle.

"Oh, Lord." The whistle is NEVER blown when we're in our own yard. A cold panic set in when I realized I had no idea where Annie was, and Mama was still waiting, and the iron was still hot. I looked at Heidi and Merle and knew I had to say something but couldn't.

"I...I gotta go." I tried to breathe and to think. "Annie!! Annie, where are you?!" I turned in circles like a whirligig.

I didn't see Annie but every face I did see was pointed in the same direction.

I looked up too. The silhouette of my mama upstairs in her bedroom window was looking down at us. With the morning light I couldn't see her face, but her hair was a wild bush and light reflected off her glasses. Her whistle twinkled like a silver tongue, filling in for the scowl that I knew was there.

I don't know if I was more humiliated or terrified at the sight of her looking like a crazed woman.

Run! Find Annie!

I turned and tripped straightaway over the very same tub that Merle had tumbled into. The sting of pain, shame and fear turned to tears as I picked myself up and ran around the house shouting. I must have looked just as crazy as my mama.

This time, it was Matthew I nearly rammed into. He was all sweaty and out of breath standing in his gunnysack.

"Hey, Ruth Ann." His voice was soft. "I know where Annie is. Your grandpa came out here when you were in the house. He just walked off with her. She was saying…"

Matthew was still talking when I dashed across the road to Grandpa and Grandma's house. From the drive I could see towards the back of their property, and there was Grandpa holding Annie's hand, leading her out towards the old corn-crib. I stopped in my tracks. "Annie! Annie! Mama needs us! You gotta come right now!"

Annie dropped Grandpa's hand and ran towards me shouting, "Grandpa, I'll come back another time to see them."

"First, it's Grandpa, now it's Mama. Why can't we just have our carnival, Ruthie?"

"What were you thinking, Annie?" Her annoyance didn't nudge me from my path of self-righteousness. I was too worried even though I wasn't sure what I was worried about. "Why were you walking off with Grandpa right in the middle of things? And Mama's in a mood and needs to talk to us. I don't know what the matter is but she's acting mighty strange. Annie, you can't just go off like that!" I was mad at everybody, but I took it out on Annie.

"He made me. He said…oh, never mind. But it's not my fault. Why are you mad at me when it's Grandpa and Mama who are ruining things?" Annie huffed beside me as we threw open the screened porch door, ran to the living room door and fell against it and each other like circus clowns. I can't speak for Annie, but the thud against the door didn't hit me half as hard as the fact that it was locked.

"Why's the door locked, Ruthie? What's going on?" Annie was nearly at a whisper.

"Let's go!" We raced around the house and crashed through the back door.

"You do it," I said to Annie when my sweaty hand couldn't turn the knob of Mama's bedroom door.

"Mama?" I whispered, when Annie pushed the door open.

"Who slammed the door? Where have you been?" she asked the floor. The silver whistle rested on the arm of her pink chair and her hands were folded loosely in her lap. Her fingers moved, trading places, like a silent game of cat's cradle. When she lifted her eyes, her hands stretched out onto the arms of her chair. Her whistle clanged to the wooden floor and Mama startled like she'd been sleeping.

"What happened, Mama? Did somebody die?"

"No, Annie. No one died."

Annie tapped her foot and loosened her tongue. "Well, if nobody died, I don't know why we needed to come in now, Mama. This ain't fair. It just ain't fair."

"Now girls, I know this is hard to hear and I am not certain that it is appropriate to share with you, but I just cannot endure another day pretending. I know it is quite a load…"

"But Mama, I don't need no extra load. I'm all loaded down with just tryin' to get what I have comin' from Bud Fleeting," Annie griped.

I shot her a dirty look that she was too busy pouting to see and then turned back to Mama. "Mama, what is it that you need to say? You need to tell us. Please, it'll be OK." Fear shook my words like dried leaves rattling in the wind.

Annie drew in her breath. Ready to start again. "Shush Annie, Mama's trying to tell us something."

"Don't you shush me, Ruthie!" And then without thinking it through, I pinched her to shut her up. But it opened her up even wider instead.

"Ouch! Mama, Ruthie pinched me, and it hurt real bad."

28

"Ruth Ann, you are certainly old enough to keep your hands to yourself. My word. I am trying to...trying–. Oh." Mama's hands danced with each other while her glasses slipped down her nose. Annie dug her heels in.

"Mama, I don't think you should be tellin' us a thing. That's what I think. All our friends are gonna leave and Bud's gonna trick Merle and take the rest of my Incredible Edibles and I'll never get what's coming to me."

Mama blew her nose on her ragged ol' tissue, and mumbled, "OK. I will be OK. Fine. Just fine." It sounded to me like she was talking herself into closing out the bad thoughts just like she closed out the coyotes. "I will get to your popcorn shortly. I just need a moment." She shut her eyes. With the doorknob in my hand, her voice turned back to the color of ice. "Doors in my home will not be slammed."

"Yes, ma'am," Annie muttered, filling the space of my silence. Mama didn't often scare me, but in that moment she surely did. I wanted her to say her piece, so I could get to the other side of worrying. But that wasn't going to happen. I may have still been holding my breath when we went through the back door and stepped into the bright sun. Heidi walked towards me, and Annie bolted towards her Edibles with Merle chasing behind.

"Where'd everybody go?"

Our carnival was over.

"What's going on, Ruthie? You look like you seen a ghost."

"I dunno. I think Mama's gone kinda kooky. But I just don't know."

"Well, Annie's gonna be mad as a hornet. Bud ate every one of her Edibles. Oh, and Scotty took bites out of every single apple in the tub and that's when most of the other kids took off. Some of them who were waiting for rides walked down to the Tremble's place. Your mama has bad timing for sure. Doesn't she know how hard you and Annie worked on all this?"

"She's just sad. She didn't mean to." My mood danced and swirled faster than a Spirograph changed direction. "Don't you go talking bad about my mama, Heidi. And don't tell anybody I called her *kooky*. She's just having a bad day, that's all. Your mama has bad days too and I don't call her kooky."

"*You* called her kooky, Ruthie. Not me. I was just saying…"

"I don't need you *just saying* a thing."

"Merle! We're leaving! Now!"

"That's fine with me Heidi Hansen. But how is it you'll be leaving when your mama's not here to get you yet?" She walked away. "Heidi! Wait! I'm sorry. Don't go." Heidi turned back and eyed me like a stranger. I stepped closer, looking at her feet instead of her face. "I don't want you to be mad at me."

"I'm not mad at you, Ruthie. Sometimes–" She looked just like her mama as she searched for words. "I just…oh I don't know. Let's get cleaning up all this mess."

"Ruth Ann?" The sound of Mama's voice caught me by surprise. I was even more surprised to see her coming towards us holding a cookie sheet filled up with more brown bags of popcorn. "Where are all of your friends?" I didn't even have to get mad again. Annie did it for both of us.

"The kids went away, Mama! I told you they would." She spit her words like Mama was on fire and she was the hose.

"Stop it, Annie. Just stop it." And there I was defending Mama. Again. "Mama, I'm sorry," I muttered, not quite sure what I was sorry for.

"No, Ruth Ann. Annie's right. I'm sorry." She pushed her face into a smile and turned to Heidi and Merle. "Would you girls like some fresh buttered popcorn?"

"Yes, thank you, Mrs. Walker." Polite as could be Heidi

reached up and took a bag from the tray. Merle reached up too. "Say thank you," Heidi scolded.

"Thank you, ma'am."

"You are so welcome." Mama shuffled back across the lawn holding her tray of fresh buttered popcorn.

"I'm really sorry, Ruthie." Heidi had tears in her eyes as she looked at me. Her kindness almost undid me. *Look away! Don't cry! Stop it!* I told myself and felt like if I started crying now, I'd turn into a puddle. And then Buddy saved the day.

"Buddy!" Merle laughed at the sight of that dog scenting around the yard for dropped kernels of corn. When she called his name, he ran towards her with his tail wagging so hard it nearly threw him off course. He was still wagging when he sat in front of her staring hard at the bag in her hand.

"Merle! Stop feeding Buddy!" Annie hollered. "I can smell his farts from here!"

As soon as Annie said it, I smelled it too. I looked at Heidi. She looked at me. We busted out laughing right along with Buddy and Merle. "It's not funny!" Annie shouted.

"Let's finish cleaning, Merle. Mama could get here any minute." Heidi offered me some of her popcorn and when I tried to shove the handful in my mouth, a couple of kernels fell to the ground and Buddy jumped on them quick. I looked over at Annie to see if she was watching but she wasn't. She was looking across the road. I turned. There was Grandpa, shuffling in our direction.

"Annie!" he called out, "I've got something to show you."

"Come on, Merle! Let's go!" Annie shouted.

"Annie, you have to help us finish cleaning first," I hollered.

"You too, Merle. We're not done yet," Heidi chimed in.

"That's alright, Annie. You come over when your friend's gone home." From the edge of the property Grandpa turned and stared at the house just as the door opened. Mama stepped out.

"Girls, Mrs. Hansen will be here within the hour. Get this mess cleaned up." Mama looked at Annie and me, and then at Grandpa who was eyeing her like she was the problem.

"Walter, I believe I overheard you asking Annie about visiting today? That will not be possible, as she has other commitments."

"Is that right?" he grumbled as he turned, winked at Annie, and dragged his sorry self across the road. Out of the corner of my eye I saw it again. The wild eyes were part of a wild animal. This time I knew. It was a dog. Coyote? I wondered, never having seen one. My breath was shallow. I lifted my hand. My voice was trapped by my worry. Annie looked up and started moving in the direction I was pointing.

"No, Annie! Wait!" I shouted.

She stopped short and crouched down a few feet from the wild thing. She put her hand out and it slunk towards her. I couldn't get any words out. I watched in horror. Expecting it to attack any second.

"It's OK. Come here," she crooned. The coyote belly crawled to her and rolled over. Even from where I was standing, I could see the blood.

Heidi and Merle slowly walked towards Annie. Panic set in and I turned to run for Mama. But Mama was by my side. She had ahold of my arm, squeezing so hard I thought she'd bruise me.

"Annie, get away from that thing!" she called out half in a whisper and half in a shout.

"But, Mama, it's hurt," Annie called back. She sat in the dirt stroking it. Heidi and Merle crouched down a few feet away. "Call a doctor, Mama. She needs help."

I could almost hear tears in Annie's voice. There was no way she was stepping back no matter what Mama said.

"Ruth Ann, go call Doc Waltner. His number is in the book on the telephone stand." Mama's breath was fast and her voice firm. "Go!"

When I came back out, I said, "Doc Waltner's dead, Mama."

"Oh, yes. He is." She touched her forehead remembering that she'd forgotten. "There must be someone."

"Dr. Molly. That's what the lady on the phone said. But she can't come right now. She said to get Annie away. All of us. To get away."

Mama moved towards Annie. "Annie, the doctor will come when she can. But we must move away. Injured animals can be–"

"But Mama, we can't just–"

Annie didn't finish her sentence when the coyote got to its feet and slunk off toward the barn.

"Let it go, Annie," Mama said softly.

"You don't care about nothing!" Annie accused her and ran for the house. "You scared it off and now what's gonna happen?"

When we got in the house, I called the veterinarian's office back and told them it ran off. That was that. Or so I thought.

CHAPTER 3

Today Mama ruined our lives. And for nothing. She didn't tell us what the trouble was, but she looked like a lunatic in front of all our friends and scared everybody off. After Heidi and Merle headed home, Annie and I went to lie down in the only soft green grass that grew in the early summer heat. In the shade of the sugar maple, hiding away from Mama, we counted our money. And then she came looking.

"I thought I would find you here." Sweet as honey, Mama peered into the cool, green shade and acted like she didn't ruin our lives at all. "Would you girls like to catch a matinee?"

We did love going to the movies, but not today. We didn't need to look at each other or lift our faces. "No, thank you," we said at the very same time.

"Well then, are you hungry? We could go to Woolworth's and get a nice lunch or milkshakes, or sodas?" Her make-believe happy voice was thinning out like taffy stretched too far. I just knew it would break any minute.

"No, thank you," we said together again, like we practiced that line all day long.

Never once did she ask why we were feeling so glum or tell us to look at the person who was speaking. And then she started muttering about flowers and shrubs in bloom and weren't they lovely. Finally, she turned around and walked away. I watched her shuffle back to the house and felt ashamed of myself. I had no right to be so hateful even if she did do a selfish thing, getting all kooky on our big day.

But there I was keeping my lips pressed together while some of the juice from my heart oozed out through my eyes. I watched her go until she was out of sight. That's when Grandpa came lumbering back along the drive. He hollered out even though he didn't know where we were. "Annie! Come on now. I got something to show you. And Grandma's gonna make your favorite supper. Get on up and get 'er going."

Slow and steady with her head hanging down, Annie pushed herself up and walked towards him like she was heading to the principal's office. I thought she'd be excited to go off with him, but I guess by this time, she wasn't excited about much of anything either.

"Tell Mama you're going," I yelled after her. If she heard me, she didn't act like it, and I didn't bother trying again. She took hold of Grandpa's hand, and I watched them cross the road. Waves of heat shimmered around their feet making it look like they were walking into a dream. The red truck drove by again. The lady driving waved. Annie lifted her hand. Grandpa pulled it down and kept walking.

Round here, folks are neighborly. It's odd seeing somebody go by who we don't know. And it's stranger still to not lift a hand in greeting. But with my grandpa there was no making sense of anything. I got back to thinking about Mama. I figured she was most likely ironing my daddy's clothes or resting in the dark.

I sat up on my elbows, and put a piece of long, sweet,

green grass in my mouth. The drapes were pulled shut and I looked at our faded old farmhouse like I'd never seen it before. It was as worn out as the old bone Buddy digs up, carries around and buries again. Chipped paint and memories wrapped around every inch of the house that my daddy's grandpa built with his bare hands and *the only carpenter he was willing to share his long days with;* that being Jesus Christ. Anyhow, that's the story my grandpa likes to tell when he's getting all high and mighty.

I saw something move out of the corner of my eye. Was it that coyote? Again? I kept looking. Nothing. I was going as looney as my mama. I shifted my eyes to what I knew to be true. Staring hard at my home got me to wondering what color it was supposed to be. I didn't know if it started out white or gray or brown or green, but it ended up being the color of watered-down pond scum. I looked back across the road, and the problem there was a different one.

Grandpa and Grandma lived in a single-story ranch house painted the color of the sky in the dead of winter when *true blue shows itself in all her glory.* That's what Grandma liked to say when anyone asked how it was that she was living in a bright blue house when most everything else in the county was a pleasing brown, a worn-out white, barn red, or, well, pond scum. Their farm was the last one on our road. Others were divvied up years back and cut into lots to hold the houses of our neighbors. With an acre a piece folks had space for gardens and chickens but stood close enough to be neighborly.

My daydreaming was interrupted when that old red truck turned down our driveway. I stood up and waved at the lady who was waving at me. She stopped her truck and got out.

"Hello!" she called to me, "I'm Dr. Molly, the new veterinarian in town."

"Hi, I'm Ruth Ann," I said, with one hand shading the sun from my eyes.

"I didn't mean to interrupt you but I'm looking for a dog that I think maybe your mama called in about."

"Oh that. It ran off. I think it was a coyote," I said, completely unsure if that was true. "I might have seen it again today; just a while ago. But I'm not sure."

"Well, if it turns up again, can you call the vet's office? There were a lot of animals that got spooked in the storm and haven't turned up yet. Just trying to piece families back together," she said with a smile.

"Families?" I asked.

"Families look lots of different ways." She smiled and cocked her head. "For some folks, their critters are as much a part of their family as children and rest of the lot." Her eyes smiled as much as her mouth when she talked. "No offense intended." She winked.

I smiled right back, not sure what I could be offended by. "Sure, I'll tell my mama you came by." I looked across the road as soon as I said it and wondered if my grandpa saw her truck pull in. I was grateful he was still gone with Annie. I didn't want him making Dr. Molly feel unwelcome to her face the way he did behind her back. She turned and drove off.

I took up my spot under the tree and thought about what Dr. Molly said about family. Did folks, besides Annie, really think their pets and cows and whatnot were family? I knew Heidi's family did with their dog, Sal. But did anybody else? I looked up the road one way and then down the other. Most folks around here had barn cats and hound dogs and I never considered that they were family. I spent more time thinking about the outside of their world than making guesses about the inside.

. . .

37

Down the way the Tremble's house was nearly new, just five years old. It was a two-storied white house with tall pillars holding the roof up and that made no sense to me whatsoever. I just knew that the next time a tornado blew through, those pillars would sail away like pick-up-sticks. But that's just my opinion and nobody asked me for it. Mama said that Mrs. Tremble fancied herself living in the White House. Well, it *was* a white house. But it surely was not THE White House.

And the Miller's farmhouse? It was a dull and faded white that stood out against their bright red barn. Being Amish, they weren't tied together with the rest of us with power lines and telephone wires. Matching their clothing was an old white mare and a buggy, black as midnight hitched up along their drive.

Never did a stitch of color catch the wind and dust blowing across the plains until the bright yellow daffodils were in bloom. That's when spring-cleaning happened around here, and folks threw open their doors and took the storm windows down.

In the springtime, the Millers had the most colorful clothesline of all. Quilt squares of every color you could dream up were sewed together in crazy patterns and blowing in the breeze like a bunch of show-offs. I think all those quilts gave my grandma's blue house a run for the money come springtime. When the quilts got taken down, the Millers were still the most colorful folks in town.

Their garden started blooming in the spring and kept right on till the first frost of winter knocked snapdragons to their knees and sent the hollyhocks face down, with the weight of winter's touch. Their garden looked just like their quilts: colors woven together that made no sense whatsoever but looked like a rainbow shooting out of the palm of God's own hand. I rode my bike in circles in front of their house just to see what popped up from the earth while I was sleeping.

The only competition they had for color was Mrs. Tremble. I don't know if she grew flowers for beauty or for winning. She looked to be in competition with the Millers, but I'd put money down that they didn't know the first thing about competing.

When I looked out beyond the houses of my neighbors, I was looking at the only sea I knew; a sea of green that traveled to the edge of my imagination. I couldn't believe that there was any body of water more beautiful than a field of corn with feathery tassels swinging and swaying in the hot summer breeze.

But when I was little, I thought summer should be all dressed up in yellow not green. Mama likes to tell the story about me getting mad as could be when she said that all those green fields were corn. I said, *No they're not! Those fields are green, and corn is yellow!*

I wasn't much of a stomper, but I stomped my foot good and hard when she said something as silly as that. She took me by the hand and led me out to the cornfield and she reached up and broke off two ears and plopped down in the cool dirt and patted the spot beside her. I sat down and watched her pull back the little green dress that yellow corn was wearing and then she did the same to the next one. I was three years old when she put that corn in my hand and took hold of hers and bit into the sweet kernels and juice ran down her chin and she smiled at me and said, *Corn, Ruthie, lots of corn.*

To this day, when the sweet corn grows high, I pull off an ear and eat it right then and there. And then I lay myself down in the shade between the rows and go to sleep. Mama says that's a holdover from my being a baby when she would put me on a blanket as she was hanging out the wash and next thing she knew I was fast asleep. I never heard of her rocking me to sleep. I guess I just grew up knowing that everything would be all right when the corn was high, and the tassels sang and danced in a pleased to be here sort of way.

I was still staring at the cornfields when I heard the call of a Flicker, and that sound brought me back to the sugar maple's soft green leaves. Looking up I saw her. She was chirping to her heart's content, and I don't believe she knew I was listening. And then I heard Annie singing.

"This little light of mine, I'm gonna let it shine..."

Across the road she waved goodbye to Grandma who was on the way to her car with a casserole. When she drove away, I remembered that being Saturday, she was off to play pinochle with ladies from church.

With Grandma out of sight, Annie was still singing, "let it shine, let it shine..."

Grandpa hurried after Annie. When he got close, he opened up the lid of the box he was carrying. I couldn't see what she pulled out, but Grandpa put his arm around her shoulder, and they walked past the burned-up lightning tree towards the back of the property. I went in search of Mama and stopped. *Who's making Annie's supper?*

THE BACK END of Mama's pink pedal pushers was staring at me when I walked through the screen door. "It's time to get cleaned up for supper, girls," she said pulling a pan from the oven.

"But Mama, it's just me. Annie's having supper with Grandpa." Still confused, I said, "Grandma just left carrying a casserole to her car, so I don't know what she'll be eating."

Mama unfolded her body and turned towards me, with a casserole dish in her hands. From the corner of her mouth, she released a hiss of breath, and a runaway curl flew from her face. "I know exactly what she is eating for supper this evening. Tuna casserole. I did not stand in front of this oven with this heat to have that man usurp my authority. Go get your sister, Ruth Ann."

"But Mama, he's fixed on having her stay–."

"Never mind. Set the table. I will get her myself." Mama marched out of the kitchen throwing her apron on the counter and slamming the screen door behind her.

Doors in my home will not be slammed...unless I do the slamming, I thought as I pulled out plates and silverware and glasses. I set the table in a flash, so I could sit on the front porch, like I was just there to enjoy the afternoon breeze and catch Mama swinging at the end of her tether. I sat down just in time to hear her holler.

"Walter, I have asked time and again that you respect my role as Annie's mother. If you think you can set the rules when it comes to my children, you shall think again!"

Mama stood in front of Grandpa's truck, with her hands on her hips yelling over the sound of his engine. Annie's head poked just above the door on the passenger side. Grandpa blasted his horn and Mama leapt so high she looked to be spring loaded.

"Annie, get out of that truck this instant!" she shouted. The passenger door opened, and Annie slid to the ground and barely had the door slammed shut when Grandpa roared the engine and spit a cloud of exhaust out behind him like a hooligan.

"He was taking me to Woolworths for supper! I was gonna have everything I wanted, even soda! So there!" Annie stomped towards home with her arms folded across her chest, and my mouth hung open like a Venus flytrap.

Mama marched home right behind her. But she didn't do it like a normal person would. She acted like she was the

Farm Queen in the Fourth of July parade. She waved hello to neighbors who were standing in front yards and fields, shading their eyes, and watching the commotion.

I hurried into the house hoping she was still too busy with the queen's wave to see me. With two sweaty hands I was holding the milk bottle, when I looked through the screen at her fixing her hair and brushing her shirt into place before she stepped inside. Annie was already sitting at the table when I started pouring.

Mama stood proud, but she shook something awful.

"Annie, please go wash your hands and face before I serve our supper. Thank you, Ruth Ann, for getting things set. You're working with particular efficiency this evening, aren't you?" Looking at me over the top of her glasses, I knew she knew. "And girls, we will be having a conversation during supper regarding the new rules when it comes to your grandfather. Annie, I asked that you clean up. Please do so."

"You wreck stuff. You do," Annie whimpered, still sitting with her arms folded. "You wrecked our carnival and now you wrecked my supper. I don't wanna wash up. I don't wanna eat your dumb food." Her bottom lip stuck out so far it looked like she'd wrestled with a hornet.

Mama sank into her chair. She picked up a paper napkin and wiped the sweat from her face. "I'm sorry that you feel that I *wreck stuff.*"

"You do," Annie muttered.

"But Annie, I am your mother and I decide what is best for you. I know very well that there are times that I am... distracted." She looked at both of us. "For that I am sorry. I am not sorry when I intervene with your grandfather. He can be...well, never mind. I will ask once more that you clean up for supper. This has been a trying day for all of us and I would like to enjoy a nice tuna casserole with my daughters. I hope that you will accept my peace offering."

Annie looked up and asked, "does it have tater tots?"

"Yes, Annie. Just the way you like it." Mama reached out and patted one of Annie's hands that was now flat on the table in front of her.

"Did you make pie?" Annie asked with a funny smile on her face.

"No, I did not make pie. Why would you ask about pie?"

"Well, I remember one time, when you didn't want Daddy to be mad at you, you made pie."

Mama gave a little laugh and said, "wash up, silly girl. There will be no pie."

"*Georgie Porgie, pudding and pie...*" I started, and Mama and Annie joined in, "*kissed the girls and made them cry.*"

"Off you go! The tuna casserole will soon be cold," Mama smiled.

"You mean the tuna tot *pie,*" Annie said with a grin on her way to the bathroom.

"Where's Daddy? I thought you said he would be home for supper," I asked.

"Your father has been delayed. He will drive home tomorrow."

"But he was supposed..."

"Ruth Ann, I have told you what I know. Please..."

The minute we all sat down at the table, Mama took one bite of tuna tot pie, put her elbows on the table, and blew out the last bit of air that kept her shoulders and neck inflated. She took off her glasses and her head fell into her hands.

"Mama, what's wrong?" I asked, not sure I wanted to know.

"*I have to remind myself to breathe...almost to remind my heart to beat,*" she muttered.

"What are you talking about?" Annie's words squished out from around the edges of tater tots and tuna.

"Emily Bronte," Mama mumbled.

43

"Oh, is she that lady with the red truck–?"

"Annie!" I scolded.

"What?" Annie stopped chewing and sat with her chipmunk cheeks drooped, staring at Mama.

"Sometimes it is all too much, too much to bear," she moaned.

"What's too much?" I asked, wanting an answer that didn't include the locked door and the pink chair, the whistle and crying, Mama going crazy, and the popcorn that nobody was around to eat. Even though my mouth asked the question, my brain was running on a wheel, *don't say it, don't say it.* It *was* too much to bear.

I felt the weight of Mama's heartache pulling me under when Annie jumped in,

"Matthew Wright said that the lady in the red truck took that dog away."

"Nobody's talking about a dog, Annie," I snapped.

"I was!" Annie shouted. "Why you so mad anyhow, Ruthie?"

"Nobody's mad, Annie," I muttered and kept eating.

"Well, somebody's something. So, anyhow, when Merle makes me mad, being that I can't hit her since she's a girl and all, I have a nice bowl of ice cream. That makes me feel better. Sometimes a banana Popsicle, or Cracker Jacks, 'cause there's always a prize inside." Annie was as pleased as punch. "All you have to do is be just like Mary Poppins, *just a spoonful of sugar…*" she started singing.

"Fine, Annie, fine." Mama patted her hand again to stop her. "Yes, just like Mary Poppins. Yes." She put her glasses back on, lifted her face and her fork and took another bite. When she was done chewing, she said, "perhaps when we finish supper, we should eat ice cream. We could go to Frostee's for a special treat."

"Sure, but first, I forgot to tell you," I said.

"The coyote wasn't a coyote at all. It was a dog," Annie chattered excitedly, not even hearing me. "It got scared in the storm and the lady in the red truck took it away. She's taking care of it. I could have if you'd have let me, Mama," Annie said.

Mama sighed. "Oh, Annie. Will there be no end?"

"But Mama," I started."

"Let's focus on ice cream, shall we? That might be more pleasant to think about," Mama said without any mind to scared dogs and red trucks, or what I had to say.

"Yup! That's it! You feel better already, don't you, Mama? Just thinking about it." For a minute anyway, Annie made us both believe that all we needed was ice cream.

IT's hard to imagine that once upon a time there were fruit orchards planted where the corn stood tall. But on the east side of Grandpa and Grandma's house there were a dozen old, gnarled apple trees where all us kids played, either climbing, tossing rotten apples, or stealing fruit and letting the warm juice run down our chins and make a sticky mess of our hands and faces.

It was on one of those summer days, a week or so after the carnival, that Annie was sitting high up on a branch in an apple tree. Scotty Tremble decided this was the moment that he was going for a ride on Annie's prize possession, a blue Schwinn stingray with a banana seat covered in huge pink and blue flowers.

"Woo hoo!" Scotty squealed like a pig as he rode past Heidi and me sitting in the shade at Grandpa's place. At first, I didn't make sense of what I was seeing when he grunted past us already out of breath and grinning like a fool. In the grass he couldn't get much speed up and Annie was coming out of that tree like her pants were on fire.

45

"Goldarn, Scotty! You best keep riding 'cause…"

Heidi and I were sitting in the shade of Grandpa's porch not sure yet what was what. We jumped to our feet, and Merle ran to our side. Annie was still five feet off the ground when she flew from that tree and hit the ground running with a broken branch in her hand.

"Scotty Tremble, you're gonna be sorry, you big, fat bully!"

When Scotty reached the pavement, he started to fly, but I had my money on Annie, who was shaking her stick and shouting, "you get back here with my bike!"

"Mama!" I hollered, running for home. It wasn't until I got to the screened porch and threw the door open that I remembered that she was at the market. I ran back to the edge of the road and watched as Annie caught up to Scotty. He dropped her bike and tried to make a run for it.

Annie was on him quicker than lightning strikes. Threatening him with her stick, she hollered before she leapt, "I swear if you ever lay your hands on my bike again…"

They both landed with a thud and were rolling around in a rainbow at the feet of Mrs. Tremble who was watering her glorious garden, including her prize, state-fair, blue ribbon-dahlias. Every kind of flower in every kind of color you could dream up was reaching for the sun with a smile on its face before Annie and Scotty showed up. The dahlias got the worst of things. But hollyhocks and snapdragons, daisies and gladiolas were jumping and twitching as those two hellions rolled around.

Finally, Scotty's mama yelled, "git! Git outa my flowers!" But before they could *git*, she had her hose in one floral garden-gloved hand and Annie in the other, held up by the collar of her shirt that Mama made with *precision and care to ensure that plaids are matched perfectly.* Boy, was Mama going to be mad!

And wouldn't you know, Mrs. Tremble was still standing there in her grass-stained peddle-pushers and sleeveless print top, with Annie swinging like a Piñata when Mama's white Chevrolet Impala drove home from Nelson's Market. I raced back across the road to the steps of our front porch, somehow believing, or hoping, that the cavalry had arrived.

"Well now, we got us a situation, indeed." Daddy's voice startled me, and I must have jumped a foot.

"You're home," I stammered.

"Sure am. And look what I came home to. I'd have left Mankato sooner if I knew there was gonna be a show starring my own wife and daughter. Yes siree."

I looked at him and wondered why he *didn't* leave Mankato sooner.

"Yes indeed. This ought to be interesting," he mumbled and stepped out from behind the screen porch and together we nudged ourselves back across the grass and right up to the edge of our property where a long row of Buck Roses protected us from the ruckus. That's when I realized that standing behind *Carefree Beauty*, *Frontier Twirl* and *Hawkeye Belle* made me feel safer than he did. They were Mama's pride and joy, and I just knew that nobody would want to get Mama's thorns in their side.

Mama blasted her horn, and my heart nearly came out of my chest. She jumped from her car and leapt like a crazy lady over the boxwood hedge that framed the Tremble lawn. As she was leaping, Annie fell to the ground with a splat. I had never in all my born days seen such a sight. Annie was just being Annie. But Mama? I was so floored by her hurdling the bushes that my breath stopped.

Daddy laughed out loud, "good Lord, look at her go."

"Annie!" Mama shouted, and her youngest child snapped to attention. And then she started in on Mrs. Tremble. "Ethel, you have no right to touch my child! I will not stand for it!"

Even though Mama didn't see what happened, she put two and two together and came up with Tremble Trouble.

"Scotty Tremble, you are a troublemaker and I'm sick and tired of it." It was Annie's turn next. She had a lopsided grin and opened her mouth to speak when Mama shouted, "shut up, Annie! You are not off scot-free, young lady." *Shut up?* That was like using the Lord's name in vain. Mama really was shaking loose from her tree. "Get your bike and get home," she snapped.

Annie ran her bike to the edge of the lawn, scooched through the only break in the hedge, and jumped on her banana seat without one bit of smart aleck smeared across her face.

"Oh boy," Daddy muttered. "We're in for it tonight." I looked at him just as Annie flew by like a tumbleweed in a tornado.

"We're not in trouble, she is," I said to Annie's back as she rode through the open barn door with Buddy following behind. "Are we?"

Daddy let his breath out with a whistle as Mama straightened herself up to full height, pushed her hair back away from her face, wiped the sweat from her forehead with the back of her hand, and turned to Mrs. Tremble to say, "good day, Ethel."

Scotty dropped to the ground wailing and carrying on as Mrs. Tremble brushed dirt from her knees. "Knock it off, Scotty," she said still holding that hose as she walked in the direction of her pillars. But then she turned and looked over at my daddy and me standing and staring and then at Heidi and Merle who were still at Grandpa and Grandma's. "What the heck is wrong with you people! Mind your own darn business!"

Mama's head swiveled around, and she saw us watching. What she didn't see was Mrs. Tremble aiming her trembling hose right at Mama's backside. But Mama jumped into her Chevy lickety-split and shot across the road before the water could reach her. She was safe and sound when I looked back over and spotted Gertrude, the goat.

She stepped out real quiet like from behind a row of sunflowers that stood between Grandma and Grandpa's property and the Trembles. Staring hard at Mrs. Tremble, she pawed at the ground and charged. Gertrude blew the feet right out from under Mrs. Tremble, who went up as the water came down making a rainbow above her flailing body.

Gertrude reared up once and then walked away with a swagger that I didn't know she had. Daddy and I burst out laughing and quick-stepped back onto the porch without saying one word to each other, but he was still chuckling when Heidi and Merle ran over. "Did you see that?" Merle exclaimed. "Your mama's a sassy pants just like Annie!" she laughed.

"I don't suppose she's going to feel like driving us home, is she?" Heidi asked, without her sister's delight.

We all stared at Mama, who stopped her car by the mailbox and sifted through envelopes like nothing out of the ordinary had happened. Before I could get my thoughts straight, Daddy spoke up, "I'll give you girls a ride home. Just a minute now, I'll get my keys." They drove past as Mama took her sweet time smelling her roses.

WATCHING Mama leap over the Tremble hedge reminded me of an old, yellowed picture of her in a photo album that I looked at about a million times. She was leaning on a car with her head thrown back laughing. In the background, there were three men dressed real fancy in suits and ties, staring at her with big old smiles on their faces. It didn't look creepy or anything; more like she was the popular girl that all the boys wanted to take to the dance. Her leaping and yelling and saying *shut up* stuck in my head just like that picture. It was a different kind of sass. But it was sass, all right. Merle was right; Mama did look a lot like Annie when she had her hands on her hips and told Mrs. Tremble what's what.

My thoughts were tied up in so many knots I felt like macramé would come out my ears. When Mama ran from her car, she was someone I didn't know. And that was a different someone from the one who blew her whistle just last week and scared me out of my gourd. And now she was just my rose-loving mama. It was like looking in those crazy mirrors at Arnold's Amusement Park. Everywhere you look, it's a different version of the same old you. I had no idea which mama would walk through the door with milk and butter and bread.

But if Mama could act like nothing at all was going on, I could too. I was going to be the happy-go-lucky big sister who was just delighted to see her mama home from the market. I opened the Skippy peanut butter jar and jammed a spoonful of goodness into my mouth right before Mama walked in with a brown grocery sack carried by two scrawny legs following behind her.

"Ruth Ann Miller, put that peanut butter away at once!"

"Tharry thmama. I wath justh…"

I was gummed up something awful.

"Sometimes, Ruth Ann…I do not have words."

Happy-go-lucky would have to wait for another day.

When Annie stepped out from behind the groceries, she managed to pull together just the right amount of sorry and shame into her slumping shoulders. Mama took one look at her and said real quiet, "thank you for your assistance, Annie. Now go to your room until supper is ready, please."

Looking as pitiful as could be, Annie whispered, "yes,

50

ma'am. If you need anything at all, you just call on me." With her walk of shame, she climbed the stairs slow and steady. And there I was staring at Annie who could change colors quicker than leaves waking up to frost.

WHEN THE FOUR of us sat down to supper, Daddy said, "there's a fellow I saw on the television set yesterday. Elizabeth, I thought you might take an interest."

Mama looked up and kept on chewing. Annie asked, "what fellow, Daddy? Why would Mama be interested in a man on the television set? She doesn't like nothing but books and roses. Right, Mama?"

"Well, that's not entirely true. I do like lemon meringue pie." With Mama's little joke, she sounded just as sweet as pie herself, and that made my brain so fuzzy I took off my glasses trying to clear the fog.

"Well, this fellow, he's teaching ladies exercises on the television. His name's Jack LaLanne."

Mama kept chewing with her eyes fixed on Daddy.

"Yes sir, I thought with a few more stretches and squats, you could go from jumping hedges to jumping fences, and, well, who knows where that might take you? Iowa State Fair and beyond." Daddy had a big ol' grin on his face, not paying one bit of attention to Mama's eyes. I knew he was just having fun, but my feet started sweating, wondering if Mama was going to go back to crying or cursing, and all I wanted was for her to stay looking sweet as pie. And then her face broke into a smile. Daddy lifted a forkful of food smiling back at her.

"Maybe I could leap a bit higher next time. I think you're right, Daniel. I'll devote a bit more time to my stretches and squats. Thank you for that suggestion." Mama winked and took another bite of her supper.

CHAPTER 4

The next day I was lying on the sofa trying to read Nancy Drew, *The Clue in the Crossword Cipher*, but getting lost in thoughts about Mama, when she asked me to help her with the dusting. I wasn't at it long, when I got tangled in my brain. How did she go from the pictures I saw in her photo album, to the leaping lady, to now: dark, curly hair, streaked with gray, and black cat-eye glasses riding just below the bridge of her nose? Her skin was browned from the sun, and the lights in her eyes were turned low, leaving the green faded away and nothing but brown showing through. Yesterday she looked like the girl in the picture. Today she looked tired.

"What is it, Ruth Ann? Why are you staring?"

"I was just wondering…"

"Do you suppose that you can wonder as you dust?"

I looked down and lifted a little metal bell by a small cross on top, gave it a ring, and before I set it down again, I noticed for the first time that there was writing on it. *Sitka.*

"Mama? What's a Sitka?"

The can of Lemon Pledge she was about to spray on the

bare-naked dining table stopped in midair. She saw the bell. Her eyes got soft and gooey, and she wore a faraway smile. And then she laughed. "Sitka is not a thing, Ruth Ann. It is a place. A place in Alaska."

"Alaska!" A dribble of spit flew out of my mouth when I shouted out the foreign land. "How did you get a bell from Alaska?"

With a sweep of her hand, Mama sprayed the table again with a fine mist.

"Mama?" I asked softly.

"Ruth Ann, that was a long time ago."

"Did you GO to Alaska?" Amazement bubbled out with my words.

The idea of her traveling outside Iowa or Illinois was not something I could even imagine. But the faraway sound of her voice made me wonder again who this lady was and what she might do next. I set the bell back in place, knowing now that it was some kind of a window into a mystery that included my mama.

"I was in Alaska for a brief period. Three years, to be exact." Mama had that same strange smile on her face while she stared at nothing that I could see, and her hand moved 'round and 'round on the table. "It was a wondrous time. Oh Ruth Ann, you cannot imagine the mountains and glaciers… the bears!"

Her eyes sparkled green. She threw her head back and laughed at a memory, with the laugh that I imagined when I looked at her old pictures. It didn't matter that in the picture, she was dressed like a model, and now she was wearing her stained and stretched out sweatshirt. But then the real surprise came.

"There was a sailor…" With the next squirt of Pledge, she disappeared, wiping the memory away when she saw her reflection in the table.

"A sailor? A sailor in Sitka? Does Daddy know?" I just knew this was it. This was when Mama would tell me about her adventures too.

Before I finished asking, she lifted her eyes. They turned back to brown. "Ruth Ann, when you are finished with your dusting, set the table please." Like flipping a page in her photo album, Mama turned and was gone.

The ringing of that bell stayed with me. I saw my mama for the very first time as a girl who had dreams and believed that life was supposed to be more exciting than casseroles and Jell-O salad. In the middle of August, with nothing but cows and Iowa corn all around, Mama slipped on a pair of wings and for a minute I saw her lift up and fly away to a place where she was happy. And it got me wondering if she was sorry that she ever did lay eyes on my daddy and pack up herself and her stuff and move from the city to the country.

I didn't want to spend anymore time wondering, so when the dusting was done, and the table was set I went back to Nancy Drew. Buddy started whining and barking but I didn't take much notice until Daddy touched me on the shoulder, and I nearly jumped off the couch. It was half past five and he was standing there with a Marshall Field's bag in his hand. His tie was pulled loose and sweat showed dark against the baby blue of his dress shirt. He had no way of knowing, and I wondered if he would even care, that on that very day Mama's spirit had soared above her sorrow.

"You're might jumpy, Ruth Ann. Why is that?"

"I was just surprised. That's all. I know I should be outside Daddy. I just lost track of time…"

He interrupted my unfinished mumble.

"It's hot as Hades out there, Ruth Ann. No need to blister your bonnet. Where's your Mama?"

"I…I don't know. I can't remember. I…"

Again, Daddy stepped on my stammering,

"That's alright, Ruthie, she'll turn up. She don't go far." The corner of his mouth turned up in a smile.

Ruthie. I couldn't remember the last time my daddy called me *Ruthie.* I looked up at him and his face was soft and kind.

"You alright, Daddy?"

And with that he snapped out of it, threw his shoulders back and stuck his chin out, like a little kid with something to prove. "Now Ruth Ann Walker, why wouldn't I be, OK? I just landed a new account that's gonna make me rich and I have here a fine new shirt and tie as my reward for my efforts."

He jiggled the bag with a smile that didn't have the oomph to make it to his eyes. After he emptied his pockets onto the coffee table, he dropped his pocket protector stuffed with pens, turned and walked away. "Yes siree, I'm just as right as a man can be. You let your mama know that I'll be washing the road off and then taking a rest before supper."

Daddy's pile was still lying where it landed when Mama spotted the pocket protector filled with her own pens lined up like little soldiers. She started yanking pens out. "Your father has utter disregard for property that is not his own. These are my pens." Her voice fell into a whisper. She gulped. "God, grant me your serenity."

I jumped up as Mama's crumpled body dropped into Daddy's recliner like somebody stuck a pin in her and all the air whooshed out. My eyes followed hers to the empty pocket protector she was staring at and realized she wasn't staring at it, but at a small, white piece of fabric, with embroidered yellow and pink daisies around the edge.

Mama was still as stone and as silent as snow. Daddy's whistling in the shower filled up the space between us. I wanted him to stop. I wanted him to go back to Mankato, Estherville, or Des Moines. Anywhere but here. But I wanted

55

him home too; home like a normal daddy who kisses his wife and twirls her around in the kitchen and makes her laugh. I wanted him to be the Buick she leaned against with her head thrown back, just as happy as sunshine. But it wasn't like that.

"What is it, Mama? What's wrong?" When she didn't answer, I looked again. It was a lady's hankie. I didn't know whose it was, but I knew it was bad. "Mama? Look!" I picked up the pens she had dropped. "All your pens are right here. Now you can balance your checkbook *to a penny.*" I repeated her own words; the ones she said every time she sat down with her checkbook and ledger.

Mama peered at me through the smeared lenses of her glasses. "Thank you, Ruth Ann. Yes, to a penny. What would I do without you," she said and took the pens from my hand and turned. I followed her into the kitchen. She sat down and sorted through bills.

"Steinberg's Fine Jewelry. For the love of God, Daniel."

Mama pushed away from the table, opened the cupboard, and Anacin rattled from the bottle into her hand. Then she gathered up her bills, set them aside, and started cutting tomatoes and lettuce for our salad. When Daddy got out of the shower and up from his nap, he whistled his way into the kitchen. I glared at him and wanted to knock that whistle right off his lips.

Mama didn't look up from the gravy she was making for the roast and vegetables. I filled water glasses and Annie washed off the stench from the river in the laundry tub on the back porch. I looked over to see Daddy give Annie a kiss on top of her head and scrunch up his face. "Pee yew! God Almighty, Annie! I think you'd best wash more than your hands and face."

"Well Daddy, Grandpa says that that there is the smell of hard work and there ain't no shame in working hard."

He acted like he didn't even hear her before he said, "now, Ruth Ann, you smell just fine. According to your grandfather, that must mean that you're not working hard at all. Is that the truth of it?" I knew Daddy was being playful, but I didn't know how to be playful back, so I just stared at the cracked linoleum. He reached out and lifted my chin. "Now Ruth Ann, you look your daddy in the eye when he's talking to you."

I was looking right at the sneer on his face, but that lady's hankie was all I saw, and I hated my daddy for it. Without another word, he marched away hollering, "what in tarnation, I forget my pocket protector one time, and somebody comes along and steals my pens while I'm hard at work putting food on this here family's table! Goldarn!"

THE VERY NEXT day Annie and I were riding bikes up and down through the empty drainage ditch that ran alongside our grandpa's farm when the red truck drove by again. Dr. Molly smiled and waved as she headed out to the main road.

"Don't wave back, Ruthie. Grandpa don't like her," Annie said.

"I met her," I said casually, like it was no big deal. "She's really nice."

"Why didn't you tell me?" Annie snapped. "You're not supposed to keep secrets, you know." She thought for a minute. "I want to meet her too," she whispered.

Annie called out to Grandpa, "hey Grandpa, what's wrong with that lady in the red truck who picks up dogs?"

"Get off that bicycle and give your ol' grandpa some lovin' young lady!" Annie dropped her bike in the dirt and ran into Grandpa's arms. He picked her up and twirled her around like she was filled with feathers instead of forty-five pounds of flesh and bones. Her scrawny legs flew out from the bottom of her hand-me-down blue shorts while the toes of her dirty bare feet curled into tight little balls.

When he set her down again, Annie's grin stretched from one sunburned ear to the next. "Who was that lady?" Annie asked again.

"She's the lady veterinarian. But she ain't no lady." Grandpa jammed a wad of chew in his mouth. "After Doc Waltner dropped dead a ways back, she turned up. Came 'round to check on the cattle. She come from the next county over. She's not one of us. I don't think much of her. She thinks she knows what's what...but...well, I dunno 'bout that."

"A lady veterinarian?" She paused and then asked, "how can a lady be a veterinarian?"

"It's a lady who don't know her place. That's what!" he said.

"Why should a lady know her place? Maybe I..." Annie started before Grandpa interrupted her.

"Don't you get any fancy ideas, tater tot. It ain't right. It just ain't right." He shot brown slime away from her feet and said, "now what you say we do some more fishing today? Would you like that?"

"I'd like to be a veter–a doctor like her. That's what I'd like, since you're asking." Annie grinned like she just won the spelling bee.

"I was asking if you want to go fishing," Grandpa grumbled and wiped his sweat with a hankie and spat again.

"Ruthie and me, well, we're riding bikes. Right, Ruthie?"

"Well sure. But you can go fishing if you want to." I was saying words I didn't mean. All I really wanted was for Annie and me to ride back to having fun and I didn't like how Grandpa was always leaving me out. And that funny feeling in my stomach came back something awful.

"You wanna come too?" Annie's kindness watered the

kernel of hurt planted by Grandpa's ignoring me; yesterday's lump started growing in my throat again.

"Well," I stammered, looking at my feet, "sure."

Grandpa walked away like Annie never asked and I never answered.

"Annie, I'll come by in just a little while and you and me, we'll head out to the river," he said.

"Ruthie?"

"Yeah."

"You OK?"

"Nah, not really." I kicked at the dirt. "Grandpa only loves you." I said the words I knew. I couldn't come up with words for the rest of what was going on. I just didn't know.

"That's not it." Her words were so tender I thought I might choke. "'member what Grandma said when Grandpa was showing me how to tie a hook to my fishing line? She said, *we got us two grandbaby girls. One likes books and the other likes hooks.*" Annie grinned like, see, that's all there is to it. "And besides, you don't even like fishing." For Annie, that settled it, and we rode off with her shouting, "Annabelle Rose Walker, Doctor of cats and dogs, cows and pigs! Dr. Annie!"

I forgot all about her going fishing until Grandpa drove up and hollered, "OK, Annie. Park that contraption and let's get us some fish."

"Last one there's a rotten egg," Annie called out and we raced home with Grandpa's truck following behind. We hit the brakes and skidded to a stop. Annie dropped her bike in the front yard, put her hands on her hips, and said, "tell Mama I've got my *Gone Fishin'* sign up." She gave a little salute, and yelled, "see you later alligator!"

"After a while crocodile," I called out and watched them drive away. I didn't want to go fishing, but I sure did want to be invited. Or have Annie at home. As I walked into the house, I was trying to make sense of feelings that didn't make sense even to me. The quiet of the kitchen distracted me. I listened. "Mama, where are you? Mama!"

"Ruth Ann, please stop your shouting." From the top of the stairs she said, "I am in my bedroom looking through some things." She disappeared again.

When I looked into her room, Mama was sitting in her pink chair with a photo album opened on her lap. "Hey, what are you looking at?"

"Possibilities," she murmured.

I sat down on the stool at her feet. "What do you mean, *possibilities?*"

"I dreamt of being the next Jane Austen. I always thought that I would write a great novel one day. I never imagined that I would be living in a drafty old farmhouse with a husband who...oh..." She shook her head like she was trying to shake off cobwebs. "It doesn't matter. Here we are, aren't we, dear, Ruth Ann?"

I wanted to ask what she was going to say about my daddy, but instead I asked, "Who's Jane...Jane who?"

"Oh dear, Jane Austen was a literary genius. When I was in school, I read every one of her books that I could get my hands on. I was just like you, always with my nose in a novel. And Jane ...well she made me believe that more was possible. That's all. I thought that I would be happy if..."

"You can write stories, Mama. You have that typewriter you used to write letters to Grandfather on. You can write now."

"The time has passed. It's only memories that I have now. And these pictures are bringing back such memories."

"What are they pictures of?" I sat on the arm of her chair and looked at the pages filled with smiles. When she turned the page, there she was with Daddy. They were holding hands and dressed up real fancy.

"What's this one? Where are you?"

"Oh, that was our honeymoon at Lake Okoboji. My, we were so young, and so hap…" Her voice and face fell.

And just like that, she flipped backwards in time and her eyes lit up again. "Oh, this is when…"

When she was happy. I sat beside her listening to stories I never heard before and touched my finger to the edges of beautiful clothes and fancy hats. Mama smoothed the front of her worn out blouse like she was making it new again.

"These photos remind me of what I believed was possible. But, oh, what a fool I was. Now it is your turn, Ruth Ann. You must follow your dreams. You must."

Mama looked at me with tears in her eyes. The life that Mama was looking at made her happy; the one that she was living made her lonesome and sad. When she lifted her face, she saw the inside of me on the outside.

"Oh Ruth Ann, you must know always that you and your sister are the best gifts I have ever been given. I wouldn't trade you for all the fancy hats and shoes in this world." The edges of her mouth lifted, but it was hardly a smile.

"I wish I could make you happy, Mama."

"Ah, Ruth Ann. You are more than a mother could ever ask for. It's not so much sadness I'm feeling, but nostalgia. We capture only gold dust in pictures. Sawdust, we sweep aside." I tilted my head, trying to understand.

"These photographs are some of the highlights of my youth. When I look back at them, I am comparing the best of my life with the dreary interims. Certainly not the best." She reached out and patted my leg. "You and your sister are the very best." And then she remembered. "Where did you say Annie was?"

"Fishing. Grandpa picked her up just before I came in. We were riding bikes, but he wanted her to go with him, so she did."

She slammed her photo album shut and steamed, "that

man is incapable of following my wishes. Time and again, I have asked that he check with me prior to absconding with my child."

"Doing what with your child?" I pushed my hurt down and pulled my notebook from my back pocket and pencil from behind my ear.

"A-B-S-C-O-N-D-I-N-G. Absconding," Mama repeated. "An attempt to leave without permission granted."

"Oh. Yeah, I guess that's what he did." But Grandpa didn't think he needed permission for anything. "Annie says she's gonna be a doctor for animals like the lady in the red truck. Can she follow her dreams even if it's a job that's mostly for boys?"

"What lady in the red truck?"

"The new veterinarian. Grandpa said that Doc Waltner's dead. Remember. You said she took the dog that got lost in the storm. The one that was hurt." I wasn't ready to hear about talking to strangers or keeping secrets, so I didn't tell Mama that I met the *lady in the red truck*.

"Why, yes, he passed. I guess I forgot about her driving a red truck. And, yes, Annie can follow her dreams, as well. Although I can imagine there might be times, along the way, where it could resemble following Alice through the looking glass."

And here I was following Mama through the looking glass when the only glass I wanted was filled with milk. I stuck my notebook back in my pocket and headed for the kitchen.

CHAPTER 5

*A*nnie and I raced ahead of Mama and Daddy, who were carrying Jell-O salad and homemade rolls to Sunday supper at Grandma and Grandpa's house. I could smell the pot roast cooking before we even had the door open, but as soon as we did, I wanted to turn around and go back home again. Mama and Daddy pushed in behind us, and for a split second the door was still standing open. Grandpa bellowed, "what are ya, born in a barn?"

Grandpa never got tired of joking about Daddy being born in a barn, being that my grandma was milking cows when her water broke and dribbled all over the stool she was sitting on. Doc Waltner happened to be there helping a little calf find her way into the world, and my daddy popped out alongside her just like Jesus in the manger.

As soon as we stepped in, they went right back to shouting over each other about the new veterinarian, Dr. Molly Hobart. "What choice do we have?" Uncle Bob grumbled. "Doc Waltner's dead and that crotchety old fool on the other side of the McAllister is a drunk. I can't be hauling every head a cattle to Timbuktu and back just to get their tits and balls..."

"For heaven's sake, Bob. Mind your manners!" Grandma scolded, as she put the roast and vegetables on the table.

"Mama, you know what I mean... for every little thing. I guess we're stuck with her."

"I'll be damned if I'll be stuck with her. Her kind don't belong with God-fearing Christians," Grandpa snorted. "Somebody needs to show her what's what, if you know what I mean." Grandma smacked him with her dishtowel and walked back into the kitchen.

For as long as I can remember, when Sunday night came, our family sat around this old wooden table covered in lace, making fun, fighting, burping, and bellowing. Tonight, was no different but tonight I worried about Annie. All this nasty talk about the lady doctor was sure to get under her skin. But I don't believe she was paying any attention to what they were saying.

"When I grow up I'm gonna be just like her." Her eyes were shining. "I'm gonna drive an old red truck and take care of every animal in the whole world."

She sat up straight and looked around the table, just as proud as could be. Silence. I sat taller too and pushed up my glasses just waiting for Mama or Daddy to jump in and say they'd be proud to have a doctor in the family, even if it is just for cows and dogs and whatnot.

"Pass the butter, son," Uncle Bob said to my cousin, like he never did hear Annie speak.

"Robert, will you lead us in prayer?" Grandma asked, putting her hand on the butter dish to keep it in place.

When the prayer was done, Daddy asked, "what do you know about a red truck?"

"Ruthie and I saw her drive by and Grandpa said she's the new Doc Waltner."

"Well, that's just fine," Daddy murmured.

"Just fine? It ain't *just fine*, son. If you had your wits about you, you'd tell your child—"

"Yes, Walter, Daniel and I will tell our child what…" Mama's voice cut through the room like a sliver of glass before Grandpa jumped in on top of her again.

"Lookie here, girl, if you don't know what I mean, well then, you need to open up the Good Book a time or two and get yourself right with the Lord. Ain't that right, Mother?" Grandma's bulging cheeks kept her from saying a word and she looked at him and right back down again.

"Don't you talk to my wife that way, and you can keep your threats and your *Good Book* to yourself. Annie's our child and we'll tell her what's what." Daddy spoke his piece and then jammed his mouth so full of pot roast he looked like his mama, and I was sure one of them would pop.

"That's where you're wrong, young man. What do you know about work and the ways of the Lord? You're Mister Fancy Pants, if you ask me."

"I wasn't asking."

"Maybe you weren't, but I've got a thing or two to tell little Annie." Food spit out of his mouth with the words he was yelling. "Annie, you listen to your grandpa now. I hear tell that that lady is a sinner of the worst sorts…the very worst sorts." Grandpa snorted. "You need to learn to be a lady and ladies know their place. That's the truth of it. She ain't no lady!"

This time it was Grandpa who shoved a forkful of supper in his mouth and shut himself up while half the folks at the table started talking at once, telling Annie what's what and how she needed to learn to cook and sew and keep house. I stared hard at Mama trying, with my eyes, to make her talk about possibilities and dreams and being a lady writer like Jane whatshername. But she didn't.

BANG! Daddy slammed his fist on the table and all the water glasses shook. "Now listen here, Annie. You damn well can do what you want!"

"Daniel!" Grandma scolded, "don't you talk that way at my table."

He didn't pay one bit of attention to his own mama and kept right on. "If you want to be doctor for animals, and you get the schooling, you can do what you want. That's that! And none of the fools at this table can tell you different!" Every scowling face was staring at him, and he stared right back.

"Look at me. I'm living in the house my great granddaddy built, across the road from my mama and daddy. Don't you think I ever had a dream? You know damn well I did. I could have stayed in the Navy and seen the world. But what did ya'll say to me? *You're looking mighty swishy in those fancy white pants. You're getting too big for your britches young man. We Walkers are land people.* Like Amesville is the center of the goldarn world," he scoffed.

"They've practically got a man walking on the moon and I ain't even walked on the streets of New York City or seen a palm tree or anything growing east of the Mississippi River or south of the state line. Don't you tell my child what she can and can't be! Don't do it!" He pushed back his chair, threw down his napkin and stomped out of the house.

"Now you tell me, how did I raise such a fool?" Grandpa laughed. "Blindfold that boy and he couldn't tell teats from tomatoes. No siree. And he never could be bothered to get his hands dirty."

"That's 'cause he's always had his head in the clouds. He never did learn to leave his dream on his pillow, now did he, Mama?" Uncle Bob laughed.

"Can't get dirty if you're in the clouds, can you, Bobby?" Grandpa snorted.

"Uncle Danny is a sissy. Uncle Danny is a sissy," little Clara started singing,

"Knock it off, Clara," I scolded.

"You leave Clara be, Ruth Ann," Aunt Wilma scolded right back.

Mama looked at Annie and me, stood up, and said, "it's time to go, girls." Not knowing what else to do, we got up and pushed in our chairs.

"Now, now. Don't be sore," Grandpa said. "Just sit back down and finish this fine supper with us." Annie and I both looked at Mama but didn't move. "Do as you're told!" Grandpa bellowed and slammed his fist on the table.

"Elizabeth, you married an ingrate, for sure." Uncle Bob pointed his fork at Mama and then at Annie and me. "Girls, you'd do well to remember who butters your bread. No good storming out after our mama here has made supper at the Lord's table. Always has thought he's too good; that's for sure." He stopped talking with a belch, loaded up his fork, and nobody said one thing about his manners.

"Sit down! Now!" Grandpa hollered again.

Annie and I sat. Mama didn't. She spat her words like gravel she couldn't swallow. "Thank you for supper, Ethel. Girls, we're leaving."

We jumped up.

"Sit down!" Grandpa roared as he shot up out of his chair.

"Ah Dad, let 'em all go. We don't need uppity company at Sunday supper."

"They can darn well do as they're told!" Grandpa yelled, clenched fists shaking with rage. "You leave here now, you'll regret it! Mark my word, Elizabeth, you'll regret disobeying me."

"We. Are. Not. Your. Charge!"

"Fine! Git outta here! Git!" Grandpa hollered.

I followed Mama out and looked back at Annie who was staring at Grandpa with tears in her eyes.

"Git out!" he shouted, and she scurried for the door behind us.

Annie ran ahead and stopped at the edge of the road. Daddy pulled his truck to the end of our drive and stopped. We looked at him and he looked at us. And then he was gone.

"Where's he going? Why's Daddy leaving us?" Annie cried and started running after him. "Daddy!"

Just as fast as her legs were flying, my tears were flowing. When his truck pulled out of sight, she plopped down in the middle of the road, and Mama took off after her. I stood alone between the spot where Grandpa cussed and spit and Daddy turned tail and ran. The weight of my worry and sorrow made it hard to breathe.

With Annie in her arms, Mama walked back towards me, looking as tall and strong as I ever did see her. She carried Annie into the house, put her in a chair, opened the freezer and took out four Banquet Turkey Potpies.

"Mama, where's Daddy going? When will he come home?" Annie whimpered.

"I have no idea, Annie. He was clearly very upset, as we all were. This behavior–" Mama took a breath. "I'm just so sorry you girls are exposed to such unkind behavior from...them."

"Why are they all so mean to Daddy?" she whimpered.

"I cannot possibly decipher the motivation for their behavior." She stared into space. "First of all, sometimes your father's family acts without thinking. They can be very disrespectful with their words. Secondly, I do not know the whereabouts of your father. I am certain that his feelings were very hurt. And I trust that he will come home."

"They laughed at Daddy." Annie's voice was soft. "They made fun of him."

"Why didn't you talk about possibilities, Mama?" My

voice shook as much as my hands did. "You didn't say a thing about dreams? Why did you just sit there? You could have told them about Jane…"

"Ruth Ann, that surely would have fallen on deaf ears."

"So what?" I accused. "Maybe Daddy would still be here if somebody stood up for him."

"The pies will be done shortly. In the meantime, Annie, please set the table and Ruth Ann, pour two glasses of milk." There was no more talk of Daddy and dreams. As she put dollops of mayonnaise on sliced tomato, she paused. "Ruth Ann, please do not speak to your father about what your grandpa and uncle said in his absence. He would be unnecessarily hurt."

"I just don't understand," I whispered, and then jumped at the ringing of the telephone.

Mama got there first.

"It's Heidi. Let her know that we are having supper and you will get back with her shortly," she said, handing me the phone.

"She just wants to know if I can go with her and her daddy. They'll be getting a load of manure tomorrow and then we can ride on top to go into town," I said, covering the mouthpiece with my hand.

"That should be fine. Please get the details."

After I hung up the telephone and sat back down, I said, "Annie, you can come along too, if you want. I know they won't mind." Annie didn't even act like she heard me.

"Annie, your sister is extending an invitation to you," Mama offered.

"Nah. I might be going fishing."

"Well, I don't think so, Annie." Mama's words sparked like fire, and I worried that the fighting would start up again.

"After that outburst, I cannot even imagine that you

69

would want to go anywhere with your grandfather. I hope that you girls do not have the impression…"

Annie jumped at the sound of the screen door opening and threw her arms around Daddy who stood there with both hands jammed in his pockets. Mama put her napkin to her mouth and wiped away invisible crumbs, and I glared at him with nothing but anger in my heart. When he was gone, I was mad at Mama, and when he was back, I was mad at him.

Annie asked in a whimper, "where did you go Daddy, when your feelings got hurt?"

"My feelings weren't hurt. I was just mad. I went for a little drive." His head dropped. "I got nowhere to go. You best finish up that supper."

"But they were so mean…"

"Annie, your father has answered your question. Eat your potpie."

Daddy reached out and gave my shoulder a squeeze. His eyes were soft, and my heart softened as he took his place at the table while Mama put the last potpie on a plate for him. There were no more questions or answers.

"BEST YOU PUT away your things and get some sleep," Daddy said when he came to the door of my room.

"OK. Night, Daddy," I said to his back as he walked away.

When I was done brushing my teeth and slid between the sheets, Mama came in to rub my back. "You are right. Dreams do matter. Even when I forget, you must not. And your father was right, too. You and Annie…you can do and be anything, absolutely anything."

"I wish you still believed too, Mama."

"Perhaps one day." Then she repeated the words I heard my whole life. "Now close your eyes and quiet your mind…"

With my eyes closed, I joined in. "Enter the world of dreams, and a treasure you will find."

"Good night, dear Ruth Ann."

"Night, Mama."

THE NEXT MORNING, Daddy was the only one around when I walked into the kitchen. "Where is everybody?" I asked.

"Well," Daddy stared down at his paper, "part of everybody is sitting right here."

"You know what I mean, Mama and Annie."

"Ah, they're at the market, miss sleepy head. They left without you."

"That's OK. I'm going with Heidi." I hesitated. "Daddy? Did you really want to see the world?"

He put down his paper and looked out the window. "Sure, I did."

"What stopped you?" I sat at the table across from him, but he looked out the window instead of at me.

"Plenty stops a person. Maybe your grandpa's right; maybe I am a good-for-nothing dreamer."

"That's not true. And he didn't say that, Daddy."

"Sure, he did. And if he didn't exactly say it, it's what he meant. I wanted to sail ships and fly planes, but all that was left for me was driving tractors and growing crops. That wasn't my dream. But my dream never did matter to anybody but me. So here I am in Amesville, working for Hormel Meats."

"Is it our fault, Daddy? Is it 'cause you had Annie and me?"

"Nah. It ain't nobody's fault but mine. I was too light on my feet to take a chance. And I never was smart like your mama. She could have done better...better than the likes of me and this falling down farmhouse." He looked around the kitchen.

71

"But Daddy, she loved you."

"That's right. She did."

We both heard the yesterday in our words.

"Ah, Ruth Ann, I'm just a country boy who had city dreams, and somehow or other, I thought the city girl could make my dreams come true. But I just made a mess of hers, instead."

"There's still time. Why, you could see the world. You and Mama could."

"I'm not gonna be made a fool chasing down rainbows with my head in the clouds. Not anymore, that is." He tried to smile. "But you and Annie? That's a different story. Annie's got the spit I never did, and you got brains like your mama." He looked down at the page. "There's leftover hotcakes keeping warm in the oven."

All the while I ate my breakfast, Daddy stared at his paper, then out the window, rubbing at the handle of his coffee cup like he was working the clay. I cleaned up the kitchen, and then climbed the stairs to get dressed. Before I was back down again, I heard Mr. Hansen honk.

"See you later, Daddy." My words followed me like a tail as I ran through the door.

"You mind your manners." He stood in the doorway. When sunshine hit his face, it was like he just stepped out of the telephone booth and right back into his confidence and cape. Clark Kent sat next to me at the table and Superman waved hello to Mr. Hansen and laughed at me climbing into the back of the truck that was filled with dried manure. "Good to see you, Arthur."

"Hey there, Danny. There's room if you want to ride along on this load of crap," Mr. Hansen joked.

"Well, that's sure kind of you," Daddy laughed.

Danny. Danny must have been the boy with dreams. I lifted my hand to block the sun. My daddy stood there with

72

his hands on his hips. A curl fell across his forehead, and he looked like he could do anything. But I knew that was just the sun in my eyes and the hope in my heart.

I climbed aboard our carriage, sat down on a burlap sack next to Heidi, and started up the road. I felt just like a princess, both of us practicing our waves and smiles like we were in a parade passing through the cheering crowds. We were busy smiling and waving, and folks honked and waved right back. I stopped worrying about Mama and Daddy's dreams and started thinking about my own. It's my turn. That's what they both said. Maybe I could be a famous writer even if Mama couldn't. I could write Mama and Daddy's story, *The Luckless Lass and her Dandy Danny*. Maybe people really would wave as I drove by, whispering, *oh, that's her, she's that famous writer*.

"Ruth Ann!"

"What?" I stammered. "Don't yell at me, Heidi."

"Yell at you? Geez. The girls were waving like crazy and it's like you didn't even see them. I must have called your name a hundred times."

I blushed. "Sorry, I was just thinking."

"Well, stop thinking and start waving." Heidi's laugh brought me back to the fun of riding through town on a soft and stinky pile of dried manure. At the edge of town, Mr. Hansen stopped at Frostee's and we got black licorice ice cream cones and were still licking away when he pulled off the road and walked towards an old red truck with its hood up. "Whose truck is that?" Heidi asked between slurps of her melting black cone.

"I don't know but I think it might be the lady veterinarian." Seeing that red truck made Grandpa's hateful words bubble up again, and I thought about all the times he turned roses into rot.

"What lady veterinarian?" Heidi asked, as we climbed to the ground, taking turns holding the cones.

"Well, look at the two of you," Mr. Hansen laughed. "Dr. Molly, these two ice-cream covered scalawags are my daughter, Heidi, and her best friend, Ruth Ann. Trust me, they don't always smell like crap, but isn't it your lucky day."

Dr. Molly smiled, and reached out her hand. "Nice to see you both. I've had the pleasure of meeting Ruth Ann after that awful storm some weeks back. Nice to see you again." She smiled at me and turned to Heidi. "I'm Dr. Molly. I take no offense; that's a smell I'm way too familiar with. And if that isn't the darkest chocolate I've ever seen."

"Oh, this isn't…" I couldn't help myself. I needed her to know the correct flavor of our ice cream. I heard my Mama's voice, *details matter, Ruth Ann.*

Heidi poked me. "She was just kidding, Ruth Ann. She knows it's not chocolate."

Making matters worse, I went to push my glasses up, somehow forgetting that I was holding a *not chocolate* ice cream cone, and nearly jumped back in surprise when that cone suddenly appeared right between my eyes. They all laughed, and I did too. Dr. Molly had her hands in the pockets of a pair of worn-out coveralls, *dressed for comfort, not for crowds,* just like Annie.

Her brown hair was pulled up messy-like on top of her head, and her eyes smiled the way Annie's did. But Annie had eyes that were as deep blue as the Iowa sky, and Dr. Molly's were the exact color of Hershey's chocolate syrup. But most especially it was Dr. Molly's smile that made me stare. She looked to be filled to the top with kindness.

"Looks to me like you might just have a wire or two that wiggled free," Mr. Hansen said as the two of them put their heads back under the hood of her truck, while I brought my attention back to myself. Black licorice ice cream dripped like candle wax down my hand.

"You're kind of a mess," Heidi said with a smile and pushed me in front of the truck's side mirror. I pulled my black lips away from my black teeth. We both doubled over laughing.

Mr. Hansen slammed shut the hood of Dr. Molly's truck and walked over laughing. "You two are quite a pair."

Dr. Molly nodded to Mr. Hansen. "Thanks for saving me beside the road." Then she included Heidi and me. "It's been a pleasure meeting you and seeing you again, Ruth Ann." She got behind the wheel, the engine roared, and she was off.

When Mr. Hansen dropped me back home, I flew through the door shouting, "Mama, guess who I saw today! Mama!" I ran through the front door and out the back and that's when I saw the red truck. My mouth dropped open, and I skidded to a stop. Mama and Dr. Molly were talking and laughing like old friends.

"Ruth Ann, you're home. Come over and say hello…what in the world is all over your face? Oh my. Well Dr. Molly, this is my oldest daughter, Ruth Ann."

Dr. Molly smiled again and said, "twice in one day, isn't this a nice surprise? Hi Ruth Ann."

I just stood there grinning like a fool.

"Ruth Ann, Dr. Molly has spoken to you." Mama fixed a smile on her face waiting for my manners to catch up with my surprise.

"It's nice to see you again, Dr. Molly."

Dr. Molly turned back to Mama. "Ruth Ann and I met on the side of the road, when most of that ice cream was still in her cone." She winked, as my big black grin went from ear to ear. But now that Mama was satisfied with my manners, she turned back to talking with Dr. Molly, without showing her hem. That's what she calls it when you keep going with polite

75

speech, not letting on that you're downright embarrassed by your filthy, stinky daughter standing beside you.

"Dr. Molly stopped by to let us know that she found the owner of that dog who was injured in the storm."

"We thought it was a coyote!" I exclaimed. "At first," I blushed.

Dr. Molly smiled. "Just a poor dog that ran off when it was frightened by the storm."

"Annie may have chosen to believe that it was more than some mongrel, but it certainly was not," Mama said in her show offy voice.

"Sometimes the story is much less interesting than we'd like it to be." Dr. Molly's smile softened in a way I couldn't read. "That poor little creature traveled miles that night and was worn to the bone."

I thought about her *piecing families back together.*

"Yes, well I've asked Dr. Molly to take a look at Buddy and Beets while she is here." Mama looked at Dr. Molly and smiled. "She has reported that all of the members of our menagerie are well."

And then Mama said, "I so appreciate you coming by today. It's such a pleasure having someone with whom to visit who knows who Jane Austen is." Mama paused. "And someone who is not born and bred within the county lines. I do appreciate a fellow interloper." Mama smiled.

"And a fellow outcast," Dr. Molly returned Mama's smile.

"I know who Jane Austen is," I interrupted. "You told me just the other day. You said that you..."

"Yes, Ruth Ann," Mama interrupted, "yes, you do, don't you?" she stammered.

"What is it, Mama? What's wrong? Are you an *outcast?*"

Before she could answer, I turned and watched Annie walking from Grandpa's truck with a string of catfish slung over her shoulder. If Grandpa saw Dr. Molly's truck, would he drag his sorry self over and make a scene? I couldn't stand the thought of it. I felt trouble creeping up my spine, just for knowing a person.

"I got some good ones, Mama." With every step she took those fish were slapping Annie's behind, swinging out and slapping again. "Grandpa said I can keep 'em all and we can have a fish fry."

"Annie," now her *hem* was showing, "this is not acceptable. You were to spend the morning with Merle and her mother. How ever did you end up fishing with your grandfather?"

"Oh that," Annie chirped like Mama had forgotten the plan. "Grandpa said you said it'd be OK. So, Mrs. Hansen said alright since it was alright by you." Annie looked at Mama, then at me, and for the first time took notice of the lady in the coveralls standing between us. She stuck out her fishy hand. "Hi, I'm Annie."

"Oh yes, dear me, this is my youngest child, Annabelle Rose. Annie, this is Dr. Molly Hobart, the lady veterinarian." Dr. Molly reached out and shook Annie's fishy, slimy hand.

"It's a pleasure to meet you, Annie. Your mother has been telling me all about you."

"When I get big, I'm gonna be just like you. I love animals more than anything in the whole world! And I love fish. Do you like fish Dr. Molly? You can stay and eat some with us if you want. I've got gobs." Annie was like a sparkler on the fourth of July. Once she got lit, there was no turning away from the sizzle and sparks.

"Oh, I am sure Dr. Molly has other plans with her family…that's very kind of you to offer, Annie…but"

"But Mama, maybe she don't have plans. Do you, Dr. Molly? I've got enough to share." And then she turned to Mama, "You taught us real good, Mama. *Share what you have because what you have was shared with you.*" Annie grinned like she won the Publisher's House Sweepstakes.

"That's so sweet of you to offer. And another time, well, that would be great. By the way, your mama said you could ride along on my rounds sometime, if you want to."

"Sure, I would! That's swell Dr. Molly. I'm ready to go right now!"

"I'm sure you've had enough adventure for one day." Mama's lips puckered up like she was sucking a sour apple candy. "Perhaps when you haven't worn yourself out with fishing, you can join Dr. Molly on her rounds." I followed Mama's eyes across the road. Grandpa was still sitting, staring, with his truck pointed right at us.

"Annie, you better wash up before you scare Dr. Molly, and she changes her mind about asking you again," I said.

"Ruthie, you're not my mom, you know. What's all over your face anyway? Why are you all black?"

I pulled my lips back in a smile and all three of them laughed and I did too, this time without blushing away the fun of it. They were still laughing when I looked back across the road. Grandpa was gone but the tickle in my stomach was still there.

CHAPTER 6

*I*t wasn't long after our black licorice and fish gut introductions, Annie started spending more and more of her summer driving around the county with Dr. Molly. And that didn't go without notice from Grandpa.

"You know, Elizabeth, I seen that red truck coming by and taking my little Annie out and God knows what might happen. That lady is a bad influence on my grandbaby. You should think about who you let Annie spend her time with. Folks talk and you best listen."

"Walter, I would appreciate it if you kept your opinions to yourself. As I said, Annie is not here and not available to join you at the river today."

"Well, you and me, we don't see eye to eye, but she is my granddaughter and it ain't right that you're keeping her from her granddaddy."

"I am not keeping her from you, Walter. She is simply otherwise engaged."

"You know what I think? I think you like having that lady around. Isn't that right? You don't care if your own child is pulled into the hands of the devil. Something's wrong with you. That's all I can say. There is something God-awful wrong with you. You'll regret it. Yes, you will."

Sitting under the sugar maple, Heidi and I listened to every word until finally Mama said, "Walter, I have work to do, and Annie is not traveling about the country with the circus, nor cavorting with the devil. Please excuse me."

"The truth about that lady is blistering tongues all over town. If you pulled your face out of your flowers, you'd know it too." Grandpa spit a stream of brown slime at Mama's feet. "The blood of the devil is on your hands. Yes siree." He turned towards home muttering, "them kinda people burn in Hell. And the flames of Hell are licking at your feet. You best start dancing now. People talk. Yes siree, people talk."

Grandpa was almost across the road when Mama kicked her bucket filled with weeds and they flew right back into the garden she'd pulled them out of. "That old fool fans the flames of hell right here in Amesville."

Flames of hell wedged into the space between Heidi and me, and I busted out with a whimper, "Mama?"

She flew around like she got stung in the butt by a bee. "Oh my. Oh, yes. Hello Heidi." She pushed her hair back and left a streak of dirt across her face. "What is it, Ruth Ann?"

"Why does Grandpa hate Dr. Molly?"

"Now Ruth Ann Walker. Shame on you! You know better than to eavesdrop in on people's conversations, especially that of adults when the meaning is unclear. So much can be misunderstood. Girls, do me a favor and pick up those weeds." She laughed in a funny way. "After all, I've already done the hard part–the pulling.

"But Mama, you swore."

"What did I just say to you? You are *not* to eavesdrop, but you *are* to clean up that mess. Please, just do as I have instructed you." Mama spun around and marched towards the house.

"Well, that's that," Heidi said.

"Sometimes she just makes me so mad I could spit!" I said.

"What's stopping you? Spit all you like." Heidi laughed and tossed a handful of weeds at me and got me laughing too. But then she looked at me again real serious like and said, "I don't understand. Dr. Molly is just so sweet. Seems like she's nice to everybody. My daddy says that folks are being unkind for no good reason. He says it's like that book we just read in school, *To Kill a Mockingbird*."

"Wow! Your daddy said that? And he read that? My daddy would never read a book like that. Or any other book far as I can tell. And your daddy knows Dr. Molly. For some reason, my daddy won't give her the time of day. He's not usually so hateful to folks." I stopped. "Not hateful. Just indifferent."

"Yeah, seems like it's your grandpa who's the bad influence. Maybe it's him who has your daddy thinking mean things."

"Maybe," I said not quite sure what I thought about Daddy but thinking more about Annie.

When we walked into the kitchen, Mama was acting like a normal person, and I took a chance on doing the same. "Mama, why do you let Annie go off with Grandpa when he can be so hateful?"

Mama didn't look up from the sink she was scrubbing when she answered me. "He is your grandfather. The fact that I have difficulties with him, at times, does not change that. And to keep Annie from him, well, that is not a fight that I can bear, not now."

"When?"

"When what?" Mama asked back.

"When is it a fight that…"

"For goodness' sake, Ruth Ann, mind your manners.

81

Speaking of private family matters in front of a guest is so uncouth."

"I'm sorry," Heidi stammered like it was her fault. "I should call my mama." She was just done speaking when we all turned at the sound of her mama's car. "Thanks for having me, Mrs. Walker," flew from her mouth as she flew for the door.

"You are more than welcome, Heidi. You are a lovely guest." Mama called after with a voice like cotton candy. Too much sweet is just too much. "Ruth Ann, walk Heidi to the car and thank Mrs. Hansen for allowing her to visit."

"She doesn't need me to..." I started.

"You could not resist eavesdropping beneath the sugar maple," she glared, "but you will mind your manners now."

As I walked out the door with Mama trailing behind me, Annie and Merle jumped out from the backseat, and ran past us, with Annie shouting, "I'm getting my stuff for a sleepover."

Mrs. Hansen slowly stepped into the heat. "Nice to see you, Elizabeth." Fanning her face and touching her hair, Mrs. Hansen said, "why do I seem to be the only one suffering the effects of soggy hair? This humidity has me looking like a Brillo pad."

Mama smiled and called out to Annie, "hurry along, the humidity seems to be getting the best of Mrs. Hansen."

"Thank you, Elizabeth, it surely is," Mrs. Hansen said as the girls raced back. "Say thank you to Mrs. Walker, Heidi."

Thank you for what? I wondered. For scaring the bejee-bers out of her and making her run for the door? But Heidi did as she was told, and all four of them drove off smiling and waving. Watching them leave got me to thinking.

I felt like my real family drove away in that station wagon and I was left with the likes of Grandpa and all the hateful people who shared his blood. We'd be better off making up a family with random jigsaw puzzle pieces. Pick and choose from a box and come up with a picture way better than the one I saw when I looked across the road or into my grandpa's face.

I knew that Mama felt it too. With Mrs. Hansen and Dr. Molly, Mama could have friends if she wasn't so determined to be miserable. Most of the time she forgot all about Alaska and bears and dreams. And when she did remember, she filled herself up with regret instead of filling up with what was possible now.

I kept my thoughts to myself, and Mama and I drove to Nelson's Market. All the way there, she stared ahead, and I stared at my feet. I wanted Mama to be happy, but I wanted her to let me be happy too. And scaring off my best friend was an awful thing to do, and I don't think she even knew she did it.

I was still staring at my feet as we walked through the aisles, and Mama acted like there was nothing more fascinating than a jar of green olives with pimentos jammed up their holes. When we got to the check-stand, she remembered aluminum foil. "Oh my, give me just a moment. Ruth Ann, you wait here."

"Ruth Ann, that's a lovely name." I looked up at the lady talking. "My middle name is Ann, Cheryl Ann." I smiled and pushed my glasses up. And then she reached into the pocket of her cashier apron and pulled out a Tootsie Pop. "Here, from one Ann to another."

I took the candy from her and saw that the kindness in her voice was a perfect match for her eyes, and her eyes were a perfect match for my Sea Green Crayola crayon.

"Well then, here we are. I would have been beside myself if I arrived home without aluminum foil," Mama chirped as she rushed back in line.

"Oh, I know what you mean. Sometimes I can't remember

what's on my own list." Cheryl laughed and winked at me as I unwrapped my sucker. "I'm so glad to have met you both while I'm still working here."

I wanted to ask what she meant, but Mama chattered on about bananas from Honduras and didn't really take notice.

"Isn't Cheryl lovely?" Mama said as we were loading the groceries into the car "She took a real interest in you, and you really should suspend your daydreaming when you are in public." Like I'm the one not paying attention. "I hate to say it, but sometimes you come across as rather addled. Do you hear me, Ruth Ann! What is on your mind?"

"I don't know. That fight you and Grandpa had…"

"Ruth Ann Walker, I told you to pay attention to your own affairs. That conversation had nothing to do with you."

"But you were talking about Dr. Molly and…"

"The point of a sucker is to suck. Just suck, Ruth Ann!" Mama shouted, and I bit that sucker and my cheek all in one chomp. I fought back tears but couldn't help myself from digging my hole even deeper.

"Why were you and Dr. Molly talking about being outcasts?" I asked.

"Ruth Ann Walker, you are riding on my last nerve," she snapped. And that ended that. For now.

SUMMER DAYS RAN TOGETHER like wet paint in a rainstorm. But when that old red truck drove up the drive, there was always cause for celebration. "Yippee, skippy! Look who's here! It's Dr. Molly! Why's she here, Mama?" Annie called out.

Mama turned from the stovetop where she was getting supper started. "I don't know. I didn't expect to see her today." She wiped her hands on her apron and walked to the door. "Molly, hello. What a pleasant surprise."

"Hi Elizabeth. Girls. I hope I'm not interrupting your supper. I was passing by and thought I'd stop to check in on Gertrude and see how she's getting on."

"Oh yes, of course. No, I mean..." Mama stuttered, and I cocked my head wondering what it was that got into her. "What I meant to say is that you are not interrupting supper, I am just getting it into the oven, and yes, how good of you to stop to check on Gertrude."

She caught her breath and said, "I imagine she's in the barn. Perhaps Annie can accompany you to examine her. When you have finished, would you like to come in for coffee?" Before Dr. Molly had a chance to answer, Mama's smile fell off her face and she sucked her invitation back through her teeth, "but of course, I understand if you'll need to be on your way." I looked where Mama did and saw Daddy's truck driving towards the house.

I know Dr. Molly was just as confused as I was, when she said, "well, sure, maybe another time. I'll just give Gertrude a quick looksee and be on my way."

Mama brushed her hands against her apron and turned back into the kitchen. Dr. Molly was headed to the barn and Daddy into the house when they passed each other. I held my breath like I was waiting for the cannon to clear the crows, but Daddy turned and called to Buddy just as he got even with Dr. Molly and she just kept walking.

"Dr. Molly's checking on Gertrude," I explained as Daddy stepped up to the kitchen door.

"I saw her," he mumbled. "Where's Annie? Is she out there in the barn too?"

"She was just here." I turned, realizing she hadn't walked out with Dr. Molly. "Annie! Where are you?"

"I'm pooping!" she hollered from the bathroom.

"Oh, for heaven's sake, must we?" Mama sighed, and then

without turning from the stovetop she said, "Daniel, supper will be another hour or so."

"Ruth Ann, put a glass of lemon-aid on the front porch, will ya. I'll be down in a bit."

At the same moment that I dropped ice into Daddy's glass, Grandpa's boots clomped across the gravel. He stepped through the door and shouted, "where's Annie?"

Dr. Molly's face peered through the door that slammed behind him. Mama turned and saw her too. "Come in, Molly, come in."

Without looking at Grandpa, Mama said, "Walter, you know Dr. Hobart, of course?" She clipped the edges of her words like she was pruning the flowers off her roses, leaving nothing but thorns.

"I'm looking for Annie. Where is she?" Grandpa grumbled.

Through clenched teeth, Mama said, "she is not available this evening, Walter." Mama turned away from Grandpa and back to Dr. Molly. "Did you find everything in order with Gertrude?"

"Goldarn! I'm talking to you, Elizabeth!" Grandpa shouted his words and slammed his fist.

"And Walter, I have answered you. I am moving on to Dr. Molly, as she is here in the care of our animals."

"I warned you!" Grandpa sneered and stomped back out of the house and down the drive.

"Well, that's that." A dark laugh rattled loose from Mama, and Dr. Molly mumbled something that didn't quite make its way to words. A cold shiver got a hold of me and shook me like it was trying to loosen my molars.

"Mama, what's Grandpa talking about? What warning?" As I asked the question, I thought about their fight beside the sugar maple. "Is this 'cause you had that fight?"

"Ruth Ann Walker, your grandfather's behavior is objectionable enough. I do not need you adding anything further." She spun away from me like I was an accident she couldn't bear to watch.

Dr. Molly said something I didn't even try to hear and touched my shoulder as she walked out the door and drove away. Spoons and pans clattered. The Anacin bottle rattled. Mama filled a glass with water. She swallowed and sighed. I walked out, sat on the step and wondered, what warning? It was hot as Hades, but a chill held me tight.

"Daddy and me are going to play catch. Wanna play?" Annie pushed past me as I sat on the stoop.

"Nah. Thanks anyhow." Daddy walked out from the front of the house. Did he drink the lemonade I poured for him? Did he hear everything and do nothing? Annie chased after pop flies he tossed in the air. Running and chasing and bending over laughing. Annie's just like an Etch-a-Sketch, I thought. All it takes is a shake, and she can make every mean, nasty picture disappear. And me? Well, I'm just shaking.

"Hey, Mama!" she called out, running toward the porch. "Can we have some more of that lemonade?" Annie's voice was as light as the seeds of a dandelion blowing in the wind, as she crashed through the kitchen door. "We're working up a real thirst out here. Can you bring us lemonade, please? Maybe Ruthie wants some too. She's sitting on the stoop." Before Mama even answered, Annie ran back outside yelling, "here I am Daddy! Throw it here! Throw it here!"

CHAPTER 7

Two weeks passed before we saw Dr. Molly again. She stopped by to check on Lizzie the lamb, the newest member of Annie's furred and feathered family. Seemed to me that Lizzie was another piece of rope that Grandpa used to try to tie Annie to him. But it kind of backfired with Dr. Molly being the one that all those creatures brought closer.

I was reading *The Secret Garden* on the front porch swing, put my book down, and hollered out to Mama. Dr. Molly waved out the window of her truck, and I must confess that I looked past her to see if Grandpa was watching. But then I heard a chickadee sing in the rosebush and decided that Grandpa's words couldn't hurt me. I waved with both arms when Mama and Annie busted through the screen door grinning so big they looked like they had a mouthful of Chiclets chewing gum lined up and standing on end.

Dr. Molly stood a few paces from me and said, "Ruth Ann Walker, a couple of weeks pass, and you look like you've grown a foot." A big grin took over the better part of my face too, and Dr. Molly turned to Mama. "I don't know what you're feeding these girls, but whatever it is has them sprouting like weeds."

"That's right, Dr. Molly. Daddy says we're like morning glory vines." Annie beamed. "He says he can see us stretching closer to the sun before he finishes his morning coffee." Her little Chiclets stood at attention and laughed.

"Molly, may we offer you a cold drink?"

"Thanks, Elizabeth." She looked from Mama to me. "No need to bother, I'll be on my way soon." Then she turned to Annie. "I just stopped by to see how Lizzie is doing. Annie, I trust that you are doing a spectacular job of doctoring. Her lease on life was a might shaky and look at her now!" Dr. Molly laughed as Lizzie bounced around the yard like a bunny rabbit, and Gertrude the goat pranced and danced like she was the proud mama.

"I know. I told Mama I could do it," Annie grinned, without saying a thing about how Mama was mad as a hornet to have Grandpa bring one more animal across the road for Annie to tend to. Mama's question popped out like she'd been holding back hiccups."Molly, would you like to join us for supper?"

"That's awfully nice, but I'm a stinky mess." She brushed her hands down the front of her brown jacket covered in spots and stains and bits of fur. "I'd love to take a rain check."

"Well then, another night. My schedule tends to be quite open." Mama wore a soft smile, but I guessed that it was the weight of loneliness pulling her face down.

"Please Dr. Molly. Please stay for supper tonight," Annie pleaded.

"Annie, Dr. Molly has indicated that another night will work better. That will give you the opportunity to make our guest feel welcome with a different scent than that of…hmm, what shall we say…?" Mama paused.

"Cow dung and chicken shit!" Annie shouted with joy.

"Annabelle Rose Walker!" Mama shouted right back without the littlest bit of joy. "That language is not at all acceptable. Where in this world are you hearing such foul speech?"

"Daddy," she grinned. "That's what he said when he was diving for the football and he stood up mad as could be after he landed in…well, he said, *that's one of the things I hate about farming, goldarn. Now I'm covered in cow dung and chicken shit! And I'm not even a farmer.*" Annie laughed and laughed before Mama caught her breath and quieted her down.

"Annie, I asked that you not use that language! And in front of our guest, of all times to be so crude!"

"Mama, you didn't ask me not to say it. You asked me where I heard it. I was just telling you…"

"Enough Annie. Molly, I am so sorry that you had to bear witness to this kerfuffle. Let's see, supper…" Dr. Molly had a smirk on her face that she tried to push off with the back of her hand. Well, that got me laughing, and now Annie really got going. She started singing *cow dung and chicken shit* over and over, like it was another verse on Old McDonald's farm. Mama finally shushed her and turned back to Dr. Molly. "Molly, I hope our inability to be civil hasn't scared you off?" Mama smiled, took off her glasses, cleaned them on her blouse and looked up again.

"I would love to. How about Thursday? Six? That would give me time to get cleaned up, so I *don't* bring the perfume of my profession to the table." She smiled at Annie and touched her head like she didn't care one bit about the cooties living there.

I was pleased as punch that Dr. Molly would be coming for supper, even though I knew that Grandpa would have a conniption fit soon as he got wind of it. But for now, Annie and I hopped on our bikes and rode alongside Dr. Molly's truck on her way down the drive. I smiled and waved, and she was just out of sight when I got a bit of a wobble. Splat! I was on the ground before I knew it with a scraped-up knee and a smile on my face. We had a friend, and she was coming for supper.

"Girls, run upstairs and get ready for Dr. Molly's visit."

"Get ready? What do you mean, Mama? I am ready."

"Oh, I don't think so Ruth Ann. Wearing raggedy shorts and a stained blouse is not being ready. And Annie, your hands are as filthy as your clothes."

"But Mama, Dr. Molly gets dirty too. I bet she even smells bad. Why, I remember the time that–"

"Annie that is not relevant. She is a guest coming to supper in our home and I intend to treat her as such."

Mama's words made their way to my brain, but my eyes caught a sight I hadn't seen before.

"You look beautiful," I said.

She was standing in the dining room arranging the table in her green sleeveless dress with a string of pearls around her neck, and clipped-on earrings that matched.

"Thank you, Ruth Ann. You think so?"

"You're the prettiest lady I've ever seen," I gushed. I knew that she was pretty in old pictures, but I didn't know that she still was. "I'll put on my blue and white polka dot sundress."

"Ruth Ann that would be lovely. That fabric brings out the blue of your eyes." Mama's compliment slipped away before I could carry it up the stairs when she said, "and please, do something about that hair."

"I know what I'll wear!" Annie hollered as she raced past me.

"Ruth Ann." Mama's voice stopped my getaway. "Look at me." I turned. "I've hurt you. That was not my intention. I'm sorry."

"That's OK," I mumbled and tried to smile.

"Come on, Ruthie. Come on!" Annie called.

"I... sometimes I am careless. You will be absolutely beautiful in your blue dress. Now, skedaddle."

By the time I walked into our room Annie's dirty clothes were in a heap on the floor and she was dressed for supper.

"Annie, don't you think that dress is getting kinda little for you? If you bend over, your underwear'll show."

"Well then, Ruthie," she said with her hands on her hips and a smirk on her face, "I won't bend over."

"But Mama made you that sundress with–"

"I like this one and it goes with my hat."

"Daddy's hat, you mean."

And that's when Mama walked in. "Annie, that old sailor hat is filthy. You can't wear that to supper."

"But Mama, it goes with my dress. I have to wear it." She huffed again like she was tired of explaining the obvious. "It's my outfit."

The kitchen timer buzzed, and Mama said, "oh Annie. Well, I need to check the roast. Brush your hair and wash your hands, if you haven't already done so...today." She looked at me, started to open her mouth, smiled and turned.

As soon as Mama went back down to the kitchen, Annie and I ran into the bathroom and turned on the tap letting the water run for a bit then looked at each other."That's enough. Let's go," I said as Annie's wet hands left brown streaks on the creamy white towel, and I shut the water off. She ran down the stairs to wait for Dr. Molly and I tried again to get my hair in a proper ponytail.

"Ruth Ann, please stop your dilly dallying and come down at once to wait with your sister and greet our guest." I flipped off the light and ran down.

No sooner was I waiting beside Annie, and Dr. Molly

turned into the drive. "Mama! She's here! She's here, Mama. I'll get the door," Annie hollered.

"Now girls, be on your best behavior. I want my family to make a good impression." She pressed her hands down the front of her dress. "Do I look alright?"

"Mama, you look real pretty. I've never seen your eyes sparkle like that." It was nice seeing her dressed up, but I wondered what made her so nervous.

"Oh, here she is. Now girls, best behavior." She pulled the door open and said, "welcome, Molly."

"It's so kind of you to have me," Dr Molly said holding an old pair of yellow boots in her hands.

"Why'd you bring your boots Dr. Molly?" Annie asked as perplexed as I was.

"I didn't actually bring MY boots, Annie. These are yours if you'd like them," she said.

"Mine?" Annie exclaimed. "I don't even own any muck about boots. Mine got too little and–" She looked up at Mama.

Before Mama could make excuses, Dr. Molly kept on. "Well, these are yours now." She set them down on the front porch. "I cleaned them up a bit, but they're not fit to come indoors," she said with a smile. I looked at those boots and knew that they'd find their way indoors and maybe even in bed if Annie had her way.

"Well, Annie, what do you say to Dr. Molly?" Mama prodded.

"Gosh, I'm ready to go right now! Thanks a bunch!" Annie's grin was ear to ear.

"Well, perhaps not now, Annie. This evening, Dr. Molly is our guest for supper." Without taking her eyes off Dr. Molly or even looking at me, she said, "Ruth Ann, will you please take Dr. Molly's coat?"

"Isn't it strange how formal it feels to have you join us

93

for supper? Dear me, I guess I'm out of the habit of entertaining. Come into the kitchen and let me get you a nice, cold drink."

"Mama, I already asked Dr. Molly if she'd like a nice, cold glass of milk. Isn't that right Dr. Molly? And we made celery with peanut butter too. That goes real good with milk. Right, Mama?"

"Yes, Annie. They go very well together. Well, not good, Annie."

"Well…I think they're good. I bet you will too, Dr. Molly." Annie grinned, and Mama shook her head.

Mama talked more while she got supper ready than she did the rest of the week. Turns out Dr. Molly and Mama were both outsiders, or so they said.

"Well, I can certainly relate," she said in response to Dr. Molly's stories. "When I first came, I thought I had landed in another culture altogether. I suppose I envisioned a different life for myself." Mama stopped talking and stirred the gravy with all her might.

"I learned to, oh how should I put it, be less visible, I suppose," Mama sighed.

"I wish," Dr. Molly said. "I stick out like a sore thumb in this town and sometimes I think…" Dr. Molly was quiet. She took a drink of her milk and said, "it's wonderful spending the evening with another sore thumb!"

I decided this was my chance to ask about outcasts. Mama wouldn't get in front of Dr. Molly, would she?

"How come you both said you were *outcasts*?" I asked like I was asking about nothing more than peas and carrots.

Mama looked like she was going to scold me, but Dr. Molly jumped right in. "Not every family is as welcoming as yours, Ruth Ann. Sometimes, we are born into families where we don't fit as well as we'd hope or live life in a way that others, let's just say, *approve*." She paused and looked at

94

Mama, who was waiting just like me, for what she would say next.

"Not everyone can see that a goat and a lamb and dogs and cats and children can all be family. It takes someone very special to appreciate that all those differences make family and love even better." Dr. Molly looked between Annie and me.

"My mother and father," Mama added, "had a vision for my life in the city. It wasn't what I chose, so they..." her words drifted off and she brought her hand to her mouth.

"It's like you were the runt of the litter," Annie chimed in.

Dr. Molly laughed and Mama's eyes smiled.

"Yes, Annie. I think your mother and I were both the runts of the litter," Dr. Molly finished.

It was funny seeing Mama so nervous and happy, both at the same time, when I didn't usually see her being either. We drifted away from talk of outcasts and runts and Dr. Molly was just as pleased as punch to jump right in helping get food on the table, in between bites of peanut butter celery and gulps of nice, cold milk with Annie beaming up at her.

"Elizabeth, what a lovely table. I feel very special indeed. I don't know when I last ate on fine china and, oh, what beautiful sterling. Your set reminds me of my grandmother's. This is such a treat!"

Standing in the kitchen, Dr. Molly smiled at Annie. "And Annie, this is a delightful hors d'oeuvre," she said lifting celery from the plate.

"Or what? It's celery, Dr. Molly." Annie crunched a too big bite. "Don't you know celery?" Annie cocked her head like Buddy does when he's confused.

"Annie. Don't talk with your mouth full. An hors d'oeuvre is a treat before the main meal." Mama said in her show-offy voice, and then looked at me and softened the edges of her words. "Ruth Ann, will you put the glasses on the table, please. Those in the hutch will be just fine."

"Surely, Mama," I said with a sly smile looking at Annie, who jumped right in with one of our favorite jokes.

"Who you calling Shirley?

Dr. Molly laughed along with the rest of us and said, "Ruth Ann, can I give you a hand with those glasses?"

"That'd be fine," I said feeling shy again. From the hutch, I handed Dr. Molly two of the fancy glasses, and carried the other two to the table. "These were my grandmother's. Just like the plates and forks and all that. She had real nice things, but Mama says she never was all too nice to her. Mama says family is complicated."

Dr. Molly let out her breath and said, "oh, don't I know it." Even though she laughed again, it was different than when she was laughing about *Shirley*.

"You all right, Dr. Molly?" The question came out of my mouth before I could stop it, and when it did, she popped back into herself.

"I am so much more than all right. I am delighted to be here with you and your family. And the food your mama's making smells wonderful."

As we were putting out the glasses, I said, "Dr. Molly, you can sit at the head of the table. That's where my daddy sits when he's home for supper. He travels 'cause he has an important job with the Hormel meat packing plant."

"Thank you, Ruth Ann. I would be honored."

Annie slid around the corner in front of us and said, "just a minute, Ruthie. Both of you, hold it right there."

She raced from the room and up the stairs, and while she was gone, I fiddled with the silverware, and wondered what made Dr. Molly's family complicated, but I wasn't about to buzz like a bee in her bonnet and give her a reason to leave us.

"Ta da!" Annie threw her arms in the air and then stuck her thumbs in the top of her pants, leaned back and said, "I'm an important man with an important job." In Daddy's big black, shiny shoes, with a checkered tie hanging all catty-wampus around her neck, she looked the part. She swept her sailor hat from her head, took a bow, (thankfully her little dress was tucked into her pants), puffed out her cheeks and said, "you see, here at Hormel, we put our cow in your cooker. Isn't that right, Ruth Ann Walker?"

"Why, that's right as rain, sir," I said with a half laugh, meaning it was half-filled with fun and half-filled with guilt for not scolding Annie when she made fun of Daddy.

"Enough girls, let's finish with the table, shall we," Mama said without even sounding mad.

Annie hustled out of Daddy's things and kicked the shoes into the corner and dropped the tie on top just as I was bringing the bottle of milk to the table. She kept her hat on as she raced back into the kitchen and reached across the sink and turned the tap on for Dr. Molly to "fill 'er up."

When I walked back into the kitchen Mama said, "Ruth Ann, I do appreciate the care you are using with our crystal glassware. Thank you."

"You're welcome, Mama." I felt so proud I imagined that feathers would shoot out of my butt like a peacock. "Since this is a special occasion, can Annie and me have Strawberry Quick in our milk with supper?"

"Yes. You *may* have strawberry milk with your supper." Even though I heard Mama fixing my words, she wasn't being mean about it. She reached into the cupboard and handed me the Quick and Annie and I hurried out to the table to stir the sugary, sweet pink goodness into our glasses. This *surely* was turning into a fine night.

"Girls, slow down. Dr. Molly will think that I don't feed you unless company comes to visit," Mama said as Annie and I shoveled food in our mouths like we had just crossed the Sahara Desert on foot.

In between bites, I said, "Mama, I can't remember when we had company for supper, except family." Even as I said it, the word *family* nearly stuck to my tongue. Here I was wishing that Dr. Molly was family.

Mama tipped her head and looked at me. "Well, I suppose I can't either, Ruth Ann. That might need to change."

And then she turned back to Dr. Molly and said, "Molly, you know that Daniel works for Hormel, and he does travel on a fairly routine basis. That can make it hard to do much in the way of entertaining."

"Mama, I thought we didn't have company 'cause Daddy don't like people."

"Annie, Daddy likes people fine," I said. "He's just tired of folks after a long day of work. It's not nice to say he doesn't like people." My face was hot and blushing, worried that we'd do something wrong and drive Dr. Molly away and that'd be the last of company for us.

"Molly, do you have family in the area?"

"I was raised in Illinois. Most of my family is still there. We're not particularly close so I don't see much of them."

I was so relieved that this ship turned away from Daddy hating on folks, that I started jibber-jabbering like no tomorrow.

"We have lots of family, and Grandma and Grandpa live across the road, and we have aunts and uncles and cousins all over the place, but mostly we don't like them much, right Annie? 'Cause they're all a little bit crazy and mean some-times, not all the time, but sometimes, and sometimes that's enough."

The more I talked the louder I got, and the louder I got,

the more I worried that I would be the one to drive Dr. Molly away, but I couldn't seem to stop myself. "Sometimes they're mean because they think my daddy thinks he's better than them, which..." Slow down. "I think he does..." Breathe. "because he says so." Stop.

"Well, aren't you a little chatterbox tonight, Ruth Ann?" Mama teased, and I knew then that nobody took offense to what I had to say.

Annie added her own part. "They're a bunch of sad sack fool farmers and Daddy's an important businessman. They're all jealous."

At that point, Mama's cup was full. "For goodness' sake, Annie. That is not at all kind."

"But Mama, that's what Daddy says."

"Now girls, we don't need to bore Dr. Molly with our family drama. Molly, my word, the potatoes didn't even make it around the table yet. Ruth Ann, please pass the potatoes to Dr. Molly."

"Thank you, Ruth Ann. I do love mashed potatoes." Dr. Molly served herself, then turned back to Mama. "Elizabeth, I attended a meeting, at the Elks Lodge, the other night and there was a very heated talk about the Hormel building plans. Do you keep up with your husband's business?"

"Honestly, I try to steer clear of that topic."

"I bet the talk at your table could get quite lively," Dr. Molly said to Mama, but I jumped in.

"We don't talk at the table. Daddy doesn't like to mix conversation and food. He says it's bad for his digestion and he could up-chuck when he hears all our girl voices mixing with his meat and potatoes."

Annie started laughing and talking with her mouth full. "That's right. I might just up-chuck myse–"

Annie stopped right in the middle of what she was saying and made a little gurgle. Her eyes bugged out and I thought,

99

oh my lord, either Mama's right, you can choke to death if you talk with your mouth full, or she just saw a ghost. Annie was staring straight ahead, and I turned around to see what she was looking at. It wasn't a ghost at all. It was my daddy. He must have snuck into the house like a fox, 'cause nobody heard him coming. And Buddy was so filled up with Annie's supper that he didn't even thump his tail.

"Oh my lord, Daniel. We weren't expecting you."

"I can see that," he muttered.

"We were just...we are...I...I invited Dr. Molly Hobart to join us for supper. She's been so kind to Annie and..." Her voice started to fade. "I thought you..."

"Mr. Walker, it's a pleasure to see you. I didn't know that I would have the opportunity tonight..." Dr. Molly stood up with her hand reaching out to shake my daddy's, and he looked right at it without looking at her and turned and walked into the kitchen. Mama hurried after him.

Dr. Molly and Annie and I all looked at each other. I reached up and touched my hair and heard Daddy's words making me feel small. And then I thought of Nancy Drew. She kept her cool, and I could too. I didn't have to be afraid of Grandpa, and I didn't have to be afraid of Daddy. So, I decided I wouldn't be.

"Daddy, I'll get you a chair," I called in the direction of the kitchen where I could hear the water running and whispering that made my mouth go dry, but I spoke up anyhow. "Annie, get Daddy some silverware. The nice stuff." I ran through the living room and opened the door under the stairs and pulled out a folding chair. I hurried back and scooched Annie's place over to make room for him.

Daddy came back and stood there with a scowl on his face.

"Here you go." I pushed the chair back from the table for Daddy. "Dr. Molly was just asking about your business, right,

Dr. Molly?" I stammered as Annie put down silverware for him. *I am brave and strong,* I told myself. I bit the inside of my cheek to keep from crying or saying anything dumb.

"I, uh, yes, I was." Even Dr. Molly looked and sounded worried, and I realized, probably too late, we best not talk at all.

Mama came back into the dining room. "Well now Molly, how nice that you can get acquainted with the whole family, after all." Her voice was as sharp as broken glass. She put an empty china plate in front of Daddy. He stared at the fancy table and the folded chair.

"Oh dear. Daniel. Girls. Annie, you trade places with your father. He can't be expected to sit on that chair."

"But Mama, why…"

"Mr. Walker, I am so sorry. I'm in your spot. Here, let's just do a bit of a switcheroo. Annie, be a dear and scooch back just for a moment…"

Molly picked up her plate and sat on the folded chair next to Annie. Mama filled Daddy's plate and he walked to his spot at the head of the table without thanking Dr. Molly for moving.

"Look Daddy. Good as new. It sure is a nice surprise to have you home for supper."

"Ruth Ann, don't prattle on. Sit down and let's resume dinner, shall we?" Mama's words stung, and I swallowed hard to not let them float up into my eyes.

"Daddy, how'd you get in so quiet. You're like a spy. I spy… Daddy!" Annie used her shiny silver napkin ring like a telescope and stared at Daddy.

"Yes siree," Daddy's voice was slow and deep, like he was standing in a well. "This is a mighty fancy supper y'all having. All the Sunday best out for show." He stared at Mama while he unfolded the yellow paper napkin that she gave him from the little rooster sitting on the kitchen table and touched it to his mouth wiping at nothing but his smirk.

"Now Annie, being that I'm a spy and all, I do believe that I spied you talkin' 'bout up-chucking. That sound about right? And Ruth Ann, let's see..." I reached up to touch my hair, hoping that magically I could still feel brave. It didn't help. "I spy you drinking strawberry milk out of a fine crystal cup. Now how in the world are you gonna manage that without an accident? Huh, Ruth Ann?"

My face was lit like fire. Why did he have to come home and be so hurtful?

"Daniel, we were just talking about the Hormel plans for expansion. Dr. Molly attended–"

"You know Elizabeth, I'm not really all that interested in knowing what your new lady friend attended. And who can tell me why my shoes and tie are in a heap in the corner of this room? Ruth Ann, would you like to explain to me who gave you permission to go into my closet and take my own possessions like you have any right to them?"

"Daddy, I..." Annie spluttered.

This time when I touched my hair, my voice came back, and I interrupted Annie to bald face lie to my daddy. "I'm sorry, Daddy. I have no right to play with your things. I'm sorry. I was wanting to play dress-up..."

"Dress-up with a man's belongings? What in tarnation is wrong with you?"

Daddy's eyes stared at me like a hawk looking down from the power line, just waiting to swoop in for the kill. Truth be told, I didn't care. Maybe I couldn't save our new friend and make her want to stay, but I would do my best to save my little sister.

"Elizabeth, do you ever stop to think that the company you keep might be a bad influence on my children? Do you ever stop to think?" He smirked again. "You sure didn't think that I might just get home in time for supper, now did you? So here we are. My family and the good DOCTOR!"

Daddy's angry spit sprayed into the light and showered the bowl of peas sitting in front of him. I know Mama saw it too because she was staring at those peas and for a minute, I thought she might scold him, but she didn't.

"Now, Daniel, isn't this fortuitous that you were able to arrive home just in time—"

"For the love of God, Elizabeth, stop your chatter and eat", Daddy scolded, even though he was the one needing the scolding.

"Well then, yes, let's finish this meal and be done with it, shall we?" Mama pushed those words through her teeth like a ventriloquist without moving her mouth.

"Mr. Walker, your girls are so lovely, and Elizabeth has made me feel so welcome. I haven't gotten to know many people in Amesville, as of yet. I understand that you work for Hormel...in sales, is it?"

Dr. Molly looked right at my daddy who looked right at the peas piled high on his fork. Him not looking didn't keep her from talking. Stop! Dr. Molly! Stop! She didn't know the rules of this family. How could she? His fork shook, and peas fell into his mashed potatoes.

Mama tried again. "Now Molly, how do you do it? You drive your truck all over Emmet County treating such a variety of animals. Your work must be..."

Mama always said that her own mama had syrup in her voice and ice in her veins when she was mad, and that's all that I could think of while I listened to Mama trying so hard to save Dr. Molly from my daddy. But Daddy wasn't having any of it and he interrupted Mama mid-sentence.

"For the love of God, Elizabeth," Daddy said to his plate. And then he turned on Dr. Molly. "What the hell do YOU know about...anything? You're a goldarn lady doing a man's job and it just ain't right. Come to think of it, missy, from what I hear, YOU ain't right."

"Mr. Walker, I don't know why…"

"My daddy don't get a lot right, but he just might be right about you!" he spat.

Oh my lord, how I wished Dr. Molly would stop talking and wiggle her nose and disappear, like Samantha on Bewitched, but it wasn't gonna happen.

Mama, who didn't seem to know better, or maybe she did, jumped in again. "Molly, I do hope that you like pot roast. I apologize that I did not even think to ask before extending an invitation to dinner."

"Thank you. It's delicious, Elizabeth." Her voice was flat. She looked down. Like she was trying to solve a mystery on her plate. I was crossing my fingers that she would just *make nice* like Mama knew how to do. But she looked up and, in a voice that sounded like velvet but fell like a hammer, she said, "Mr. Walker, you have no right…"

"No right? YOU are sitting at my table eating my food and you're…"

"None of which gives you permission to treat me with such disdain and contempt. With every word, she pounded her truth in deeper, until Daddy exploded like a firecracker buried in the cornfield.

"Oh, you can keep on using your fancy words, but I'll tell you what–"

"Elizabeth, I am so sorry but…"

Dr. Molly brought her napkin to her mouth and pushed her chair back.

"You SHOULD be sorry, acting all high and mighty at my own table and I know the truth about you…DOCTOR Molly."

"I can only guess what you think you know about me, Mr.

Walker, but let me tell you that I know my own truth and I hold no shame. NO shame, whatsoever!"

Mama opened her mouth to speak, but Daddy beat her to it.

"Yes siree, Annie. Folks should stick with what they know. There's things that are right and things that are wrong." My daddy spit his words, pretending like he was talking to Annie but glaring at Dr. Molly.

"Dr. Molly, you best stick to your business little lady, and I'll stick to mine. I don't know how in the world you think you know anything about the job I do, just 'cause you went to some meeting of fools. That's just foolish talk, right Annie?"

"Sure is Daddy. But Daddy, you can't get mad at Dr. Molly for not knowing."

Annie's smile lost its oomph, and mashed potatoes were hanging from the corners of her mouth. "Dr. Molly didn't know you don't like talk at the table, did you?"

"Annie! You are speaking with your mouth full. What will our guest think of your manners?"

"But Mama, I was just setting her straight."

I can't be the only one who wondered if Mama fell from the apple tree and landed on her head. And I made the mistake of catching her eye.

"And Ruth Ann, if I have told you once, I have told you a thousand times, please sit up straight while you are eating." She pushed up her glasses and wiped at her mouth. But that napkin couldn't take away the pucker of her lips or the sadness in her eyes.

"Oh dear, Molly, you must think my children are barbarians. I assure you I do my best and it is trying to see such poor behavior in front of a guest. Isn't that right, Daniel? Oh dear. Molly, we have stained glass Jell-O bars for dessert. Do you like Jell-O?"

"I do, Elizabeth, and I'm disappointed that I can't stay. I

really must be going. Mr. Walker, I'm sorry that my being here has been a problem for you. Elizabeth, girls, thank you for your kindness."

"Molly, I am sorry you can't stay to finish your meal. I suppose that in your line of work, you just never can..."

"Don't go, Dr. Molly. Please, don't go. You ain't even had Jell-O yet. Right Mama? There's always room for Jell-O."

Annie looked like she was trying hard to make her mouth into a smile, but the tears running down her face didn't leave room for looking happy. Watching her cry got me crying too. Daddy tossed down his paper napkin, which flew like a bird across the table, pushed back his chair, walked out of the room, and slammed the screen door.

Dr. Molly jumped out of her chair and her napkin fell to the floor. When she bent over to pick it up she smacked her head on the table and a beet, resting near the edge of my plate, jumped like a cricket, and spilled its blood on Mama's lace. Dr. Molly looked up with tears in her eyes and left without saying goodbye.

"Now girls, Dr. Molly is a very busy lady with a demanding job. If work calls her from the table, please, please...girls."

Mama's voice was as shaky as her hands when she reached up to dab at her mouth again, still trying, I suspect, to wipe this moment away. I followed her eyes to the table. When Dr. Molly first sat down with us, it all looked bright and shiny, and I was so proud of our home.

But when she left, she brushed against the windowsill. The dust that had been resting there got caught by the rays of light and fell like a curtain on my make-believe happy family. Worn out. Dingy. Mama knew it too, and the knowing pushed the air out of her body. She slid back from the table and stood, looking too small for the clothes she was wearing,

"Girls, finish your supper. I need to rest. Water. Anacin. Ruth Ann, please." She walked away.

THE FALLING sun rested for a minute in Annie's eyes. Tears spilled over her lids and made their way down her blotchy red face. Her nose dripped snot and, between the both of them, the little sailboats swimming on the front of her blue dress were being pummeled by the storm. Out the window I saw Gertrude sitting on a stump. Staring in. Watching Annie cry. I had to get Mama's Anacin.

"Annie, you wait right there. I'll be back in a flash."

In the bathroom I pulled on the string that turned on the light. The bare bulb reflected in the broken mirror; another reminder that my world was falling apart, and nobody cared enough to fix it.

But in the bright light, I saw two little white towels with flowers that I had never seen before. Hanging side by side, they looked too nice to wipe your wet hands on and seemed so out of place against the wall with paint chipped and peeling. I grabbed the Anacin bottle from the medicine cabinet and set it on the edge of the sink while I filled Mama's glass from the old white sink stained orange from iron.

As I unscrewed the metal lid, I heard the screen door squeak and the old floorboards creak. I couldn't hear his footsteps, but I imagined Daddy, like the fox, taking what was left in the henhouse. His keys jingled and then they dropped. That's when I dropped Mama's Anacin bottle and the little white pills scurried for cover, bouncing and rolling on end. I fell to my knees and stayed put listening to the house telling on him as he headed back out and was gone.

"Ruth Ann. Please bring me my Anacin!" Mama called from the living room like she never did hear Daddy making his getaway.

"I'll be right there, Mama!" I scooped up pills and pulled the bits of hair and dust bunnies free, working as fast as I could but my hands were all clammy and the fuzz and whatnot kept sticking to my skin and it felt like a million years before I got to Mama who was curled tight with a crocheted afghan pulled up to her chin even though it was hot as Hades in the living room. When I bent down to give her the Anacin and water I caught a smell coming off her. Sadness. That was the smell of sadness.

"Sorry, Mama. I didn't mean to take so long. I'm...uh... Mama, I'm sorry we didn't' eat your Jell-O windows. Would you like one? I could bring you one and..."

"Thank you, Ruth Ann. No. You and Annie finish your supper. Just let me rest."

"Mama, I think Daddy..."

"Ruth Ann, finish your supper. Please, let me rest."

I carried the drinking glass and Anacin bottle back to the bright light of the bathroom and by accident smooshed some of the pills into the cracked linoleum that I had missed cleaning up. I left them there and pulled on the string and let the darkness fall on the fancy white towels and the smooshed white pills and walked back to the dining room. Annie's chair was pushed away from the table, and her dinner plate was gone.

"Annie! Annie! Where are you?" I shouted in a whisper. "Annie, this isn't funny. This is not OK Annabelle Rose! Mama's gonna be so mad! Please Annie," I pleaded, filled with a terror that didn't make any sense being that my little sister disappeared like Houdini on a regular basis, and I didn't even take note.

I lifted the lace cloth and looked under the table first. Not there. Our bedroom? No. The bathroom? Not there! Flying down the stairs with all sorts of crazy thoughts in my head! What if she left with Daddy? What if they ran away and I never saw them again? What if he stole her and she didn't want to go? I wanted Dr. Molly to come back and fix things. I was sure she could. But she wasn't here so I raced back to the kitchen thinking I'd look in the cupboards and all the hiding places we ever used playing hide and seek. And then I saw her.

Annie sat on the stump out back where Gertrude had perched herself when she was staring in the window watching Annie cry. Buddy was licking the empty china plate Annie put on the ground and Beets was kneading Annie's lap. Gertrude was still as a statue resting right at Annie's feet. With the sun behind them, they looked like they were one. And maybe that's the truth. Maybe they're not separate at all. Annie looked up and saw me looking out. Her little sailor hat was tipped back on her head. Her smile was soft. Annie was safe. She knew where to find the love she needed.

THE NEXT MORNING the smell of coffee brought me down the stairs and Daddy was sitting at the kitchen table reading the morning paper and Mama was frying bacon.

"Good morning sleepy head," Mama said with a smile, both of them acting like it was just another day. I went along with pretending, because what choice did I have?

"I wasn't sleeping. I was writing. Where's Annie?" I asked through gritted teeth.

"You just missed her. The Hansen's dropped Merle off and the girls are out catching frogs or some such thing. Did you say good morning to your father?"

"Good morning, Daddy," I mumbled not looking at him...and how could she? What was wrong with my mama that she acted like everything was hunky dory and stand there making him breakfast when she ought to be making him pay? "Can I go out to Heidi's today, Mama?" Annie found her way out and I needed to too.

"Well, I suppose that would be fine. Daniel, what do you think?" Like he gave a rip, and like I was going to listen to what he had to say anyhow.

"Fine by me," he mumbled, probably not even knowing what question he answered.

The sound of Daddy's voice made the mask I was wearing start to itch. How much longer could I pretend? Mama was staring at the sizzling bacon. Her own mask had slipped away, and she looked just as forlorn as she did last night after Daddy broke the magic spell.

I turned to the window, so they couldn't see me cry. My breath caught. Annie's empty plate sparkled in the morning light. In the kitchen and dining room, all evidence of last night's supper was wiped clean. Last night could have been a dream, or a nightmare, if it wasn't for that plate. I wish that I could unsee it; believe that Dr. Molly's visit was around the next corner, not the last bend. I walked from the kitchen, and it wasn't long before I walked from the house too. I went to Heidi's, where I could keep on pretending that nothing was wrong.

CHAPTER 8

*H*eidi and I were sitting in the crook of an old oak tree telling stories about the boys we hated most and the books we loved best when Mr. and Mrs. Hansen drove by. Mrs. Hansen stared out the window and we hollered and waved. Sal ran alongside the car barking. Mrs. Hansen didn't look away from nothing to see the something of us. I didn't think all that much of it until they were heading into the house and Heidi said, "I think you better go. My mama doesn't look too good."

I didn't understand. I was clinging so tightly to Heidi's family being the normal one and mine being the kooky, sad one I needed her and her mama to keep on being normal. "But what about riding to town to get ice cream? I have that money from the carnival. See." I leaned back, nearly falling, as I pulled out a handful of coins to show her. She didn't see.

"It's time for you to go."

She didn't even say, 'see you later'. My heart ached as I climbed down that tree. It seemed like there was nowhere to go.

"You gonna be all right?" I was asking the question I wanted her to ask.

"Sure. Sure, Ruthie, I'm gonna be just fine. You take care, now."

My heart was heavy. I felt as lonely as a stink bug. I peddled home feeling like I needed a new best friend. But I didn't want to trade this one in for anything. I just wanted to know what I did wrong. I was hurting something awful. As much as I wanted to disappear into the folds of Heidi's family, it was pretty obvious that wasn't ever going to happen. I was stuck riding my bike home to the family that was mine and wondering what was going on with Mrs. Hansen, and when would Heidi love me again?

That night at supper Mama passed pork chops and creamed corn around the table. Annie spoke up. "I hear Mrs. Hansen is sick."

A kernel of corn flew from my mouth and knocked the little black dog pepper shaker upside the head.

"What are you talking about, Annie?" I sputtered.

"I was with Dr. Molly out at the Robinson's place, and that's what I heard."

I know Annie's mouth was still moving but I didn't hear anything else she said, until she called my name, "Ruthie, Daddy's talking to you."

"Now you don't get yourself all in a knot. People get sick every day and most every time they get well again too. Ain't that right Elizabeth?" Mama looked up but didn't say a thing. "Mrs. Hansen is as healthy as a horse and as strong as an ox. Right, Elizabeth?"

Mama's head dropped down. "Of course, Daniel. Of course." Watching her push corn and salad around her plate didn't convince me that she was sure of anything.

Finally, I asked, "sick, how?"

"Don't know. Just sick," Annie said with her mouth full of

supper. "But like Daddy said, folks get better every day." For Annie, that was that, and she asked for more bread and butter.

"Now Annie, I'm surprised you haven't turned into a loaf of bread. I think one day I'm going to open the door and all I'll see is a big hunk of bread slathered in butter standing where my youngest child used to be."

"That's what I call wonder bread!" Annie laughed and looked around the table. I tried to smile, because I knew she and Daddy were trying to make it better, but my heart sat in the bottom of my stomach like a stone. I needed Heidi's mama to be well and for everything to be OK. To be normal.

COME SATURDAY, with the sun still low in the sky, I got on my bike and started riding towards Heidi's house. Swallows dashed across the road, swooping and diving into the green fields on either side. Heat hadn't yet set its claws into the day. The air was cool and sweet, and I took comfort in the familiar cornfields and corners. Maybe this was all a mistake.

Maybe Mrs. Hansen wasn't sick at all, and Heidi would be happy to see me and sorry she sent me away. But when I rode up the long drive to her house, nothing looked quite right. The drapes were closed, and Mr. Hansen's truck was parked out front. My stomach dropped. Something really was wrong.

Quiet as could be, I walked around the house and looked through the window of the bedroom that Heidi shared with her little sister. Merle was still sleeping but there was no sign of Heidi. Her bed was neat and tidy, like she hadn't slept in it at all. Just as I was about to go, Heidi stepped into the doorway and looked straight at me looking straight at her. Without knowing it was coming, I lifted my hand and gave a little wave. She didn't move. I turned to go.

"Wait. Ruthie." I looked down at my sandals.

"Ruthie," she said again. This time I turned and looked at her. She leaned out her bedroom window. "Mama's sick."

EIGHT WEEKS LATER, well into the start of our school year, Heidi and her family buried their mama. We drove to St. John's Catholic Church in our Chevrolet Impala with the windows rolled down and the sopping wet air blowing in swirls through the car. At the edge of the parking lot Mama turned off the engine and got out without saying a word. Annie and I looked at each other and I asked, "Mama, why are you stopping here?"

"We'll walk from here. I just need a moment before we go in."

Wobbling across the gravel in black shoes that matched a black dress I didn't even know she owned, Mama still wasn't talking. Annie and I ran to keep up and she never did look back to know if we were there or not. A crowd of folks moved in the same direction, like cattle to feed. Slow and steady with heads hanging down. But there were no *hellos* or *how do you dos*.

"Ruthie?"

"Yeah?"

"Is Heidi and Merle's mama dead in there?"

"I dunno. I s'pose."

"Is Mama gonna die too?"

"Sure Annie. But not today." Even though I answered Annie's question real quick, I wasn't real sure. Having Heidi's mama just up and die made me wonder about Mama and Daddy too.

When we reached the steps of the church, kids we knew were standing around with their families. Hanging my head, I hoped nobody would see me.

"Hi Ruth Ann."

"Oh, hi, Matthew."

"It's hot."

"Yep. And humid."

"Here comes your grandpa."

Looking over my shoulder I saw him walking towards the church. "What's he doing here?" I mumbled to myself, but Matthew must have thought I was asking, so he answered.

"Well, seems like everybody in town is turning out. My daddy says that everybody loved Heidi's mama. Said she's a fine lady."

"A fine Christian lady. That's what," Grandpa bellowed making sure everybody saw him, and making me wish I could sink through the porch I was standing on. It was hard enough to worry about Heidi, I didn't need to worry what Grandpa might say or do next.

"Hello, Annie!" He called out across the steps to where Annie was standing. She looked over and gave a little wave.

Then Grandpa looked at Mama. "Where's Daniel? Out of town I suppose?"

"He's traveling on business," Mama said looking past Grandpa to the open doors we were nudging to.

"Harrumph."

"Where's Grandma?" I surprised myself by asking.

Grandpa looked at me like it was the first time he saw me. He acted like I never did ask a question, but instead looked at Matthew. "Well, lookie here. Here's my granddaughter and her boyfriend. This is a funeral for a fine Christian lady, not the roller rink. No hanky-panky now, son." Grandpa grinned showing the chew he had tucked behind his bottom lip and slapped Matthew on the back.

"Ruth Ann, get your sister and let's find a seat, shall we." Mama pushed me away from Grandpa without saying another word and left poor Matthew standing there with that ornery old man.

"Annie!" I whisper-shouted and waved her to me. She broke through the crowd and grabbed ahold of my hand. As we followed Mama towards the big wooden double doors the sound of an organ moaned its first long, sad note. Like cattle pressed against each other, we squished through the opening that was plenty big enough before the music started but was now a tight squeeze. Our eyes just got used to the dim light when Annie whispered, "is she in that box, Ruthie? Is that Merle's mama? Why is everybody looking at her if she's dead?"

"Shush. Just don't look that way. Look down at your shoes or something."

But Annie couldn't keep her eyes on her shoes, or her mouth shut. "Mama, I don't want to see a dead person. I don't want to one little bit," she whined.

"Me either Mama. I'm not going to." I felt stubborn and sure, but my hands broke into a sweat the minute I spoke up. Annie pulled her hand away from mine and wiped it on the front of her plaid jumper. She still stuck to me like glue.

I didn't even know Mama heard us until she said, "Ruth Ann, please take Annie and have a seat on the pew. Save a spot for me."

We wiggled off to the side and Mama stayed in line. Walking up to Mrs. Hansen's dead body in that box, most folks had their heads hanging down and their hands reaching up to dab a Kleenex tissue to their crying eyes and red drippy noses.

In that line of folks was Dr. Molly. She looked like every other lady waiting to pay their respects. It was the first time that I thought about how much she looked like Mrs. Hansen. Not in the features of her face, but in the way she wore her heart. Open and loving. But here in this church, she looked

116

so alone. And yet, she blended in and was dressed in the colors of dirt and despair. Here it was the funeral for Mrs. Hansen who was as bright as a garden in springtime. That didn't make any sense whatsoever.

Just as Mama was about to take her turn looking in on Mrs. Hansen, the organ music stopped with another long, drawn-out moan, and out of nowhere came a lady's voice singing. All the heads that hung down lifted up to see where that voice was coming from.

"Is it an angel, Ruthie?" Annie asked the question I was thinking. "Is that singing coming from heaven?"

"I don't know, Annie. Maybe." And that was the truth.

I looked up to spy the singing angel and noticed that all around the church there were little picture windows made of colored glass. The sun shining through them made a rainbow of light that got caught in the face of Jesus who was hanging from a cross in the front of the church. I stared into his face painted with light when a lady in a long white robe walked out from the side of the stage still singing. The angel! She lifted her hands, and I thought my heart might break with the beauty of all those voices coming together to say goodbye to Mrs. Hansen.

"I bet this is what heaven feels like, Annie."

"Maybe. But I don't like the smell of heaven one bit."

"What? Oh that." The preacher was walking up one side of the church towards the stage as Mama was walking down the other towards us. Annie and I were both watching the stinky smoke come from the box he was swinging. The music stopped right as Annie shouted, "pee-yew!"

"Hush," I scolded.

Mr. Wright, who was sitting beside us, said, "the incense is a sign of reverence for the body of Mrs. Hansen."

"Oh. Sorry, Mr. Wright. Annie didn't mean...sorry."

I was so busy looking at that preacher with his smoking

117

box I hadn't had any idea that Matthew and his family had taken seats beside us.

"You girls couldn't be expected to know, and I imagine this must be a very hard day for you." Mr. Wright smiled and touched my hand in a way that was so kind my eyes filled up with the tears I'd been holding for days. They started down my face and I worried that they might never stop. Mrs. Wright leaned over and gave me a tissue, which I was grateful for. Even though most folks around me had tears falling free, I didn't really believe it was OK if I did too. I needed to take care of Mama and Annie, and how was I going to do that if I was a mess?

But Annie didn't take notice of me crying. "Is she really dead, Ruthie?"

"She's dead," I said past the lump in my throat, knowing that there were no words I could come up with to make it different than it was. I looked around again. This wasn't heaven. It was just an old church with hard wooden benches, stinky smoke that made my eyes water, and a dead lady who left her children with nothing but memories and sorrow.

Relief grabbed at my breath when Mama got back to us. I was so grateful to have her sitting between Annie and me, I didn't even care that she stared ahead like we weren't even there. When the song faded behind the preacher's voice, I looked up to where he was standing. I didn't notice folks and their drab clothes anymore.

Flowers! It was like they suddenly sprouted up through the cracks in the wooden floor, with pictures of Mrs. Hansen and the whole family smiling and laughing in the middle of a garden in bloom. But to see it, I had to look past the back of Heidi's head. So, I scooched a little closer to Mama and made myself stare at those flowers to keep my own heart from breaking. Mrs. Hansen dying rattled me something awful and nothing that was going on made any more sense to me than her passing did.

As the service went on, folks were standing and sitting, singing and kneeling, and walking up and back again, drinking wine and eating bread. What did make sense were the kind words folks said when they walked up to share their memories, but I was mighty surprised to see my own mama take a turn.

"Hello, I am Elizabeth Walker. Rose Marie Hansen was my friend."

Was my friend. The *was* told the story of so much of my mama's life. It broke my heart to see her standing tall and speaking up *after* Mrs. Hansen died instead of claiming her place in line while Mrs. Hansen was still living.

"Rosie and I grew up together in Chicago and were best friends throughout childhood. The fact that we both ended up in Amesville seemed quite miraculous. As too often happens with time, we drifted apart. I have watched our daughters' friendships blossom and have often yearned to reconnect more deeply with Rosie. I have now missed my opportunity and regret having done so in the deepest of ways."

When she said the word 'regret', some invisible piece of twine holding her together came undone. Her voice got softer, and she got smaller. Her shoulders rolled in and her chin dropped to her chest. She stopped talking, closed her eyes, and then started up again.

"With the exception of my daughters, I do not believe that I have ever loved another soul as deeply as I loved my Rosie. All of you who have spoken have shared the truth about her. She was lovely and kind, and thoughtful and smart. But the greatest truth for me is how alive I felt in the company of my friend. She was such a bright light. And oh, my word but did we have fun. Rosie was full of life, indeed. But the candle that burns brightly burns quickly. And so it is that today I am remembering the brightest of lights. I will forever be grateful that she was my friend."

Mama's glasses fogged over, and she was trembling so bad I thought she might fall apart or fall down before she shuffled back to us. I had seen her cry more times than I could shake a stick at, but this was different. Sadness and joy fell in the same salty stream down her cheeks. People kept talking, but the only thing I heard were Mama's words over and over again.

When I lifted my eyes, the rainbow of light had moved from the face of Jesus to the face of the angel in the white robe. She lifted her arms up and tipped her head back and sang: *And He will raise you up on eagle's wings, bear you on the breath of dawn, make you to shine like the sun, and hold you in the palm of His hand.* And that sounded just fine to me.

CHAPTER 9

The next time I saw the back of Heidi's head was two weeks after the funeral. She was still missing school. And now her dog was dead. I talked Mama into letting me ride out on a Saturday to say hello. I didn't call ahead because I didn't want to have Heidi tell me not to come.

I stopped my bike at the start of the Hansen's long dirt road that cuts through the pasture. Cows stood around eating grass and, one by one, turned to look at me. A little baby cow pulled away from its mama's milk long enough for me to see its sweet brown face. Seeing her made it easier to pass by without Sal running out to greet me barking her fool head off. It was so hard knowing she never would again.

The house looked exactly like it did on the day of the funeral except that Mr. Hansen's truck was gone. It was neat and tidy, and the drapes were wide open when I walked up to the door and knocked. When no one came, I rang the bell. I knew I was pushing my luck, but I took a chance and went out back. As soon as I rounded the corner, I saw Heidi sitting on the rope swing.

"Heidi?" I said to the back of her head.

She didn't turn. I pushed up my glasses and pushed my fear down so I could keep standing.

"Sal died, you know," she finally said.

"I know. Annie told me. I'm real sorry. I'm real, real sorry."

"Probably won't get another dog. Not right away, at least." I didn't know what to say so I didn't say a thing.

"Are you hungry?" she asked when she turned and finally looked at me.

For just a minute it was summertime again and everything was the way it was supposed to be. Her mama and Sal would come around the corner with Merle any minute.

"Ruthie?" Her voice brought me back to late September and the moment we were standing in.

"Well." I thought. "Yeah, I guess I am hungry. I wanted to see you, so I just left. I guess I forgot to eat breakfast. I had to see you."

We stood grinning at each other as the swing stilled and then she walked towards me. She tipped her head back and sniffed at the air, like Buddy does when he smells a rabbit.

"That smell. Look at the sky, Ruthie."

I didn't look at the sky. I looked at the swing. "Did your mama like to swing?"

Heidi looked at me, then at the swing. It moved like a ghost was pumping her legs hard and fast.

"Don't do that, Ruthie! Don't say things like that." But she kept staring and I did too. I don't know how long we would have watched and wondered if a hankie hadn't blown free from the line and covered my face. I pulled it away and looked over at the clothesline whipping every which way.

"It's a storm coming, Ruthie. That's all. It's not my mama."

"I didn't mean to make you mad, or sad. I'm sorry I said

122

that. I just keep expecting your mama to pop out with a plate of cookies or something. I'm sorry. We should get inside."

I went to put the hankie back on the line and it was still as could be. Silent. No birds chirped, and I couldn't even hear a cricket call. The only things moving were the cows in the field that ran along the edge of the yard. They made a tight circle. That little baby was lost somewhere in the middle.

"Look over there, Ruthie." Off in the distance a lightning bolt cracked the greenish-yellow sky in two. We counted out loud, waiting for the boom. "Help me get the clothes off the line!" Heidi shouted when the thunder clapped. In wads, we stuffed shirts and pants, and socks and underwear into the basket and ran for our lives just as another clap of thunder exploded. We burst into the kitchen, letting the door bang closed behind us and dropping the laundry basket.

"Still hungry?" She smiled, breathing hard. We pulled food from the fridge as flashes lit up the kitchen like Fourth of July fireworks. My hands tingled every time the thunder exploded, but my heart was happy. Heidi was back. We were together.

"Get in the cellar! NOW!" Mr. Hansen came out of nowhere yelling. Panicked, he looked around the room. "Where's Merle?"

"She's not here. Mrs. Locket came by and took her to the schoolyard to play! What's wrong, Daddy? What is it? I thought you were in town." Heidi stuttered like she'd been hit by one of the lightning bolts.

"A tornado's coming in fast! Go! Get in the cellar!" Mr. Hansen yelled.

With bologna in one hand and mustard in the other, I started spinning in circles. STOP! My brain shouted, and my legs went weak. Another thunderous boom shook the house. I reached out for the countertop to keep myself up. The mustard shattered in an explosion of gold and glass. I fell to the ground determined to clean up my mess, tears streaming down my face.

"Leave it!" Mr. Hansen shouted again. We ran. The wind yanked and grabbed and pulled the screen door out of Heidi's hand and smacked me in the face as we bolted out of the house towards the cellar door.

"Daddy! Daddy, get in!" Heidi hollered above the storm.

"I'm going to school to find Merle. You two stay put until you KNOW, and I mean KNOW, that this thing has passed!"

With the slamming of the cellar door, darkness crashed on top of us. "Turn on the light!" I said in a panic.

"I'm trying. Got it."

In the light I saw that mustard was splattered like pox all over my feet and legs. I tried to wipe it away, but only managed to paint myself the color of jaundice. Heidi handed me an old towel. "It's on your glasses too," she said in a voice as flat as the dirt floor beneath our feet.

"I'm sorry I broke your jar," I murmured. But mostly I was sorry that Mr. Hansen came home and broke the spell. For a few minutes before he got there, I could believe that everything would be OK. But now I wasn't sure.

Heidi was gone again, and my heart hurt something awful. While the storm crashed all around us, Heidi was quiet and still. She stared out in front of her. I looked too. All around. Every wall was lined with canned goods: peaches, pears, tomatoes, and pickles. We were surrounded by all the summer's harvest in quart jars. Jams and jellies looked like little jewels in the bare bulb's light.

"Mama filled all these jars." Heidi's voice was hollow. "I thought she was just hot and tired 'cause it was summer and all. I don't know when she knew…when she knew about the cancer. Everywhere I look I see my mama. 'Cept she isn't really here at all. I wish this darn storm would take away every jar in this cellar and trade it in for my mama." Tears choked her. "It's not supposed to be this way, Ruthie. Mamas aren't supposed to leave." Another choking sob. "I miss her so much." Heidi fell to the ground and wrapped herself in a ball, choking and crying.

I bent down and rubbed her back, not knowing what to say. So, I didn't say a thing. My own eyes filled with tears, knowing that Heidi's mama would never rub her back again or fill another jar with strawberry jam. But mine would. I got so mad at her for being sad and lonely, that I forgot all about noticing the ways that she tried to be a good mama.

Finally, Heidi sat up and wiped at her face with the back of her hand. I offered her my mustard-stained towel. "Thanks," she said, as she searched for a clean corner to wipe her face and blow her nose. "We have more mustard." She smiled and pointed.

"You sure do," I smiled back. Golden glass jars were lined up and ready for service. "Your mama sure did take good care of you." I took a deep breath. "It's not fair."

"Before Mama passed, I said that too, and she said, '*it's not about being fair, it's about being good. And Heidi, it's been very, very good.*'"

We both sat in the quiet. "Listen," she said.

"I don't hear it."

"That's what I mean. I think the storm has passed. But I don't know how we'll know for sure," Heidi said and asked all at once.

"I don't know. I've never waited out a storm without my mama or daddy telling me what's what. But you're right. It sure is quiet now."

"Maybe we should wait just a little longer. Hey, are you STILL hungry?" We both laughed as she pulled an old rusty tin off the shelf: *Chicago Style Popcorn*. "Want a Twinkie?"

"A Twinkie?" I asked as she pried the lid off the old tin filled with Twinkies and Ding Dongs.

"Mama always said that Twinkies could save the day and we should keep them on hand for days that needed saving." She pulled two from the tin, put the lid back in place, and I was still scooping that pure white filling out with my finger when Mr. Hansen opened the cellar door. Merle peeked in and said, "Twinkies! I want one!"

When we climbed out, it looked like the big, bad wolf huffed and puffed and made all sorts of trouble. But Mr. Hansen said that no real damage was done. My bike was blown over and Mr. Hansen had already made up his mind that he was driving me home.

"Ruth Ann, I'm sure you'd be just fine but I'll be driving you home. No point in taking any chances with a wayward wind finding a little girl on a bicycle. Not on my watch. No siree. We'll toss that bike of yours in the back of the truck and be off."

Where the main road intersects with the river road, we saw Matthew riding towards home with his fishing pole sticking out of a basket that he had rigged up on the back. Mr. Hansen pulled up alongside. "Young man, looks like this storm caught you out at the river? Would you like a lift home?"

"Thank you, Mr. Hansen, I'll be fine. I stayed put underneath the bridge until the winds passed by. Can't say I wasn't scared. But I'm fine to ride the rest of the way."

I leaned past Mr. Hansen and shouted, "hey there, Matthew, did you see Annie at the river with my grandpa?"

"No. They weren't there today." He paused and said, "I better keep going so my mama won't worry any more than she probably already has. I hope you find Annie and that she's OK."

"All right then, son. You take care now."

It wasn't but five minutes more and I was home. "Mama! Where are you? Mama!"

"Ruth Ann, I'm right here. There is no need to shout."

I threw my arms around her, but when she pushed me away, it was hard to remember how I felt sitting in Heidi's cellar; how grateful I was for her. She pushed me right back into feeling hurt by her again.

"Oh my, Ruth Ann, what in the world has gotten into you?" And then she looked me up and down. "And what have you gotten into?"

"I was worried about you, and Annie. Did you go into the basement? Was she with you?"

"You told me that Annie was fishing with her grandfather. Is that not correct? And no, I did not go into the basement, as I did not deem it necessary. I was rolling out pie dough."

I really did want to remember how I felt in the cellar, but I just looked at her like she was crackers. "Matthew said Annie wasn't at the river."

"Now, Ruth Ann. You told me she was with your grandfather. Please do not mislead me just to get out of having her accompany you to your friend's. By the way, how are the Hansen's doing?" Mama turned to look at me, and asked again, "what in the world have you splattered all over yourself?"

"Mustard," I grumbled, just as Daddy came crashing through the front door.

"Everybody safe and sound?" he yelled. "Radio says that tornado touched down 10 miles east in Clarksville. Hey, is anybody listening to me?" he called again.

"I'm here, Daniel. I was just pulling the pie from the oven. Now, what were you saying about Clark?"

"Not Clark! For the love of God, Elizabeth! Did you get the girls into the basement?"

I didn't give Mama time to answer. I walked out of the bathroom. "She was busy. She was rolling out pie dough."

"You were with the Hansens, Ruth Ann. If you are going

127

to respond to your father, please do not mislead him," Mama scolded.

"I was at the Hansens and Mama was rolling out pie dough." I looked right at her as I said it.

"What's all over you? Is that mustard?" Daddy asked.

"Mrs. Hansen's blue-ribbon mustard." I looked from him to Mama. She didn't even look at me, but Daddy did.

"I'm sorry I wasn't here to take care of you. All of you," he said, and looked over at Mama then back at me. "Where did you say Annie is?"

"I don't know. She said she was fishing with Grandpa, but when I saw Matthew, he said they weren't at the river."

"Is she with that woman? Elizabeth, is Annie with that doctor?" He spit his words like poison. And just as he did, Annie walked in with Grandpa. "What the hell? We have a tornado warning, and you have my youngest child with you and now you show up. Where the hell were you?" When Grandpa just looked at him, he shouted again, "where were you?"

"Don't you get up in my craw, boy! Keeping your child safe during that windstorm, that's where I been. Who knows where *you* are half the time!" Grandpa hollered and slammed the door behind him.

I was rattled something awful, but Mama and Daddy paid no mind and went right into grumbling about Grandpa. It wasn't until then that I realized Annie was gone again. I looked out the window to see if she slipped away and was crossing the road with Grandpa. When I didn't see her there, I ran to our bedroom.

"What are you doing? Why are you changing your clothes?" Annie could wear the same dirty outfit for a week if Mama would let her.

"Just felt like it."

"I thought you were going fishing?" I asked.

"Nah."

"Where were you then? During the siren?"

"With Grandpa."

"Where?"

"I said I was with Grandpa. Geez, Ruthie. Leave me alone."

Here I was worried about her, and she was just as ornery and uppity as the rest of them. Our whole lives, Annie slipped in and out like a happy little garden mole, never knowing where she'd pop up next with a smile on her face. But since Mrs. Hansen died, it was different. If I didn't know better, I'd think she had a secret. But maybe it was knowing a dead person that left us both feeling like Mexican jumping beans.

By the time Mama called us to supper, I was so frustrated that I went looking for a fight. My words splattered onto the table like hot bacon grease. "I wonder where Dr. Molly was when the siren went off." I stopped chewing and stared at my daddy. "I hope she wasn't in Clarksville."

His eyes lifted from his plate and dropped back down again. "That'd be best. It's no good anyone getting caught in that kind of nonsense, even her."

Well, didn't he take the wind out of my sails? Daddy's eyes were nothing but soft and kind. I dropped my head and ate my supper.

CHAPTER 10

*T*he next morning the sound of breakfast being made floated up the stairs and pulled me out of dreaming. "Annie?" When she didn't answer, I stood on the edge of my bed and looked at her bunk above mine. She was gone, and the little bit of sleep that lingered was gone too. My stomach took a turn, and that confused me just as much as Annie keeping secrets. I went looking for her and Mama too.

"Annie, your breakfast is getting cold and you will be late for school if you dilly dally about!" When she saw it was me she said, "go check on your sister and find out what's keeping her."

I walked into the living room, then back to our bedroom. "She's not here!"

Mama stood at the bottom of the stairs and said, "Ruth Ann Walker, please do not shout throughout the house. Now tell me, where is your sister?"

"She was just here."

"For goodness' sake, Ruth Ann. There is so little that is

asked of you. And you are unable..." Mama would have kept going but I wasn't ready to keep listening.

"I'll find her." I ran to the barn, slid the heavy door to the side and looked inside. "Annie! Are you in here?" Buddy ran towards me, kicking up clouds of dust caught in the morning light that crept between the old gray boards. I walked back to the corner he came out of. Like an old Raggedy Ann doll, Annie sat hunched over, hiding something. "Annie, what are you doing out here?"

"Nothing," she whimpered.

"What do you have there?" I bent down to see what she was holding. A little gray kitten crawled up onto her shoulder and looked at me; Annie's secret. I nearly laughed at the relief I felt.

"She's mine," Annie said as she pulled it back into her lap.

"Where did you find it?" I bent down to give it a pet.

"She's a she, not an it. Her name's Shirley." Annie looked up and smiled.

"Surely, it is." I smiled back. "But where did you find *her*?"

"I can't tell. It's a secret." Ha! I knew it.

"Come on, Annie. Where'd you get her?"

"Grandpa gave her to me after Mrs. Hansen died. But she's a secret. He said I could keep her if she was just our secret. You can't tell, Ruthie. You can't," she pleaded.

"Not even Dr. Molly?" I asked.

"Nobody," she said as she lifted Shirley up for me to hold.

"Girls! Girls, are you in here?" Mama stood in the doorway with her hands on her hips.

"Shhh." Annie held one finger against her mouth.

"Mama, we're here." I stood up and started walking to her.

"Where's Annie?" Worry finally grabbed ahold of her too. I could hear it in her voice and wanted to make her feel better.

"She came out to the barn looking for Beets and there was

a little kitten. She was afraid you wouldn't let her keep it, so she kept it a secret and..." I blathered, not wanting to lie to Mama, but keep Grandpa out of the story. I didn't know why, but when I thought about him, that funny feeling came back right in the pit of my stomach.

"See." Annie walked towards Mama with the gray ball of fur snuggled tight. "Her name's Shirley, Mama." Annie pulled back her lips, but it wasn't quite a smile.

Mama looked at Shirley and asked, "you just happened to find a kitten, Annie? Did Dr. Molly have anything to do with this *find*?"

"No, Mama. Dr. Molly didn't do nothing. She doesn't even know about Shirley. She's a secret."

"A secret? That strikes me as odd, Annie, given that you have brought every animal off the Ark into our home without any one of them being a *secret*. Perhaps we need to limit your time with Dr. Molly. This *secret* business is making me uncomfortable."

"No, Mama. I swear. Dr. Molly doesn't even know." The tears in Annie's eyes ran down her face.

Mama reached out for Shirley.

"You can't know about her. You can't tell *anybody*," Annie pleaded, in a panic.

"If you're not protecting Dr. Molly from her infringement on our family, then what? This is certainly an overreaction, Annie. What is going on?"

"I don't feel good. That's all. I'm probably contagious. I need to stay home so I don't get other kids sick, too."

Mama looked down at the little kitten purring in her hands. "We won't talk further about this cat...*Shirley*...but you will go to school. Both of you, go inside, wash your hands thoroughly and eat your breakfast. You're going to be late."

Mama handed Shirley back to Annie who snuggled her

once more and put her back in an old wooden apple crate filled with straw and carefully set another empty crate upside down on top.

"I'll check in on Shirley while you're at school, Annie. There is nothing whatsoever to be concerned about. But we will continue this conversation." As Mama walked away, she mumbled, "after all, *tomorrow is another day.*"

Annie and I followed behind her and I whispered, "what's going on, Annie? Did you do something?"

"How should I know? I didn't do nothing."

"It's OK. I'm just glad your secret's out. You don't have to worry about anything. I promise." The minute I promised, I wished I hadn't. Not because I didn't want it to be true, but I had a feeling there was too much I didn't know.

Scrambled eggs, toast and bacon were loaded up on our plates and sitting on the table. Annie washed down her breakfast with orange juice and threw it all up in the kitchen sink right on top of her breakfast plate.

"Oh Annie," Mama said as she wiped the corners of Annie's mouth with a napkin and brushed her hair back. "This is one of the consequences of playing with a kitten before school. You cannot wolf down a meal and expect your digestive system to operate properly. Brush your teeth and off to school."

After Annie trudged up the stairs I turned to Mama. "Do you think something's wrong with her?"

"I do. I think she needs to slow down to eat her breakfast instead of constantly being on the run with her shenanigans and care taking of every animal on God's green earth."

"But Mama, sometimes she's sad. And that's not like Annie. I just wondered…"

"Ruth Ann Walker, please. Go brush your teeth."

"But maybe Annie's sick. Maybe she threw up 'cause she's sick. Why are you making her go to school? You said the

133

only reason we could ever miss a day was if we were throwing up, and she is." I looked at Mama as she poured herself another cup of coffee and acted like I didn't say a thing...again.

"Mama?"

"For the love of God, please!" she shouted.

"The puke, Mama." I pointed and turned to walk away.

"Ruth Ann." The edges of her anger shattered, and her quiet, scared self stood in front of me. "I'm sorry. Annie will be..."

Annie walked into the kitchen. "You ready?" she asked me. Mama picked up her cup with shaking hands and spilled coffee down the front of her housecoat.

"Almost. I just need to brush my teeth."

Mama wiped the front of herself with a tea towel when she said, "have a good day at school, girls."

As soon as we got home from school, we put our bikes in the barn, and Annie lifted Shirley out of her bed of straw and put her on the floor of the barn to play. Buddy jumped and wiggled so hard he nearly folded himself in two. He sniffed at Shirley, and she bounced like a bunny. If Annie was herself, she'd be wiggling and bouncing too.

"Look at that! Buddy and Shirley are going to be best friends. If you could be best friends with any kind of animal in the whole world..."

"Ruthie, I don't feel much like playing 'what's your favorite' today."

"What's the matter, Annie? Why are you so glum? You don't have to have a secret anymore."

"Just tired."

"How come you haven't been going around with Dr. Molly these days?"

134

"Where's my favorite grandbaby?" Grandpa's voice bellowed from the barn door.

"Hurry. I've got to hide Shirley. Ruthie, you can't know about her. Promise, Ruthie, promise," Annie pleaded in a panicked whisper.

"Your mama said you was putting your bike away. Ya'll still in there?" Grandpa's hand was shading his eyes as he tried to see into the barn.

I walked towards him. "I'm here, Grandpa. Couldn't you see me over there?"

"Now why would I be hollering if I could see you? You know the light in this broken-down barn isn't worth a hill a beans. But I ain't looking for you. Where's Annie? I thought I'd have her to supper."

"She can't. We're having a family supper tonight."

"And I'm not family? You got too much sass in that voice of yours. Keep it up, and you'll be needing a good paddling." He hacked up phlegm and spit. "Where'd you say Annie was?"

"I didn't say. I said Mama's making supper tonight, that's all. I didn't say you're not family. But Annie's not feeling so well. I'll tell her you stopped by. But I know we can't come for supper," not that I was invited, and if I was choosing *family*, I wouldn't choose him.

Grandpa put his hands on his hips. "Your mama said she was here. You say she's there. Somebody's fibbing. Are you fibbing to your grandpa, Ruth Ann?" And then in an extra loud voice he said, "you tell her she's welcome for supper. Your mama won't miss her. She feeds her every night of the week."

Buddy came running out from the corner where Annie and Shirley were hiding.

"Now look at that, will you. That old hound dog sitting in the corner of the barn all by his lonesome." He reached down to pet Buddy's head, "There's a good boy." Buddy stepped back with a low growl. "Now, what the heck is wrong with that dog? I don't know what's going on around this place, but I tell you what, I don't like it!" Just when I thought he'd go, the mew of that little kitten stopped him in his tracks. "You got yourself a kitten, do you?"

"No, Grandpa. That's just Beets. She's getting so old sometimes she sounds young. Sometimes, it happens that way. Well, I better get inside and start my homework." My mouth was dry, and my hands were wet as I slid the barn door shut and started for the house.

"Hello, Walter. I didn't realize you were still here. I came out to gather up my girls. They really must get to their homework. Can I help you with something?" The ice in Mama's voice froze me in place but didn't make one bit of difference to Grandpa.

"Is that right? You forgot to tell me that Annie's sick. My granddaughter here just told me that. Funny it slipped her mama's mind." He accused Mama of lying right to her face.

"Why yes. As a matter of fact, she did upchuck this morning." When Mama set her teeth, it looked more like a warning than a smile. "I am hoping that she feels well enough to enjoy a nice family supper tonight." Buddy sidled up to Mama with another low growl aimed at Grandpa. Finally, he spit again and left.

"Well, that's that," she said and pushed up her glasses. "Ruth Ann, perhaps you, or Annie, will be kind enough to tell me why she is hiding from her grandfather, but, in the meantime, please tell her that the coast is clear and to join you in setting the table."

MAMA STOOD STARING out the window above the kitchen sink, waiting for my daddy's truck to pull up to the house. Finally, at half past five, she said, "we're eating now girls."

"I thought we were having a family supper," I said as the three of us sat down.

"I thought so as well. So, here we are. Family. Supper." Mama looked from Annie to me, and asked, "now Annie, tell me if you would, why did you hide from your grandfather?" Annie pushed tuna noodle casserole around her plate. "Annie? I've asked you a question." Mama slathered butter on her biscuit and I put a scoop of mayonnaise on my tomato, but Annie kept right on staring down.

Then she mumbled into her plate, "Shirley's a secret."

"What secret, Annie? What is surely a secret?"

"Mama, she doesn't mean *surely*. She means *Shirley*, the kitten. Right, Annie?"

Annie nodded, took a bite of casserole, chewed for a minute and said, "I'm full. Can I go to bed?"

Mama put down her fork and reached across the table. "Annie, no, you may not be excused until you eat your supper. Please take a slice of that nice red tomato. Help me to understand."

"Grandpa said I could have Shirley, but she would be our secret. I'm not supposed to tell. She's my special present. Just mine."

"For goodness sake, Annie, you have an entire menagerie of animals who treat you as their pied piper. Why does… *Shirley*…need to be any different? Your grandfather is an odd man. *Surely*, you know that."

"Mama?"

"Yes, Ruth Ann."

"Could Annie maybe just eat a few more bites? It's not good to fill yourself up when your tummy's upset."

"I suppose." I don't know what pin poked her, but the air in Mama seeped out with a sigh and she took off her glasses, rubbed her eyes, and said, "so much for our family supper."

I helped Mama clean up the kitchen and she put a plate of

food in the oven to keep warm for Daddy. "Ruth Ann, I know that you are concerned about Annie. I am, as well. But I trust that this too will pass. Now that Shirley is no longer a secret, Annie should be feeling much better.

Secrets lead to shame, Ruth Ann. Remember that. Secrets and shame are a heavy burden to bear." With that she walked back into the living room with a glass of iced tea and a plate of store-bought gingersnaps, and I started my homework on the kitchen table.

It wasn't but a minute later and Daddy wandered in like he didn't have a care in the world. He mumbled hello on his way past me. Next thing I knew, Mama slammed her gingersnaps and iced tea on the counter, opened the oven door and tossed Daddy's supper into the trash bin, plate and all. "Ouch," was all she said as she ran cold water on her burned fingertips.

"Are you finished reading?" I squeaked like a mouse.

"I'm finished, alright!" she shouted back.

THE NEXT DAY, the only words that passed between Mama and Daddy were cross. "I don't need no primary school teacher telling me what's what. I'm telling you that right here and now. Ruth Ann, pass me that there jelly."

Facing the stovetop. Mama mumbled, "jam."

"What'd you say to me, Elizabeth? If you're talking to me, turn around and talk to ME, goldarn it!" As he was stuffing his face full of breakfast he said, "Annie, if you're fighting at school, you best take your disputes away from the school yard. Those sissies can't let a child settle their own troubles."

And to no one in particular he said, "that's half the trouble right there. People can't seem to stay outa other people's business. Just like that lady veterinarian, she can't stay well enough away from my family. It's humiliating. That's what it is. Humiliating."

Mama turned from the stovetop and started talking slow and steady. "Daniel, Miss Barnes did not say that Annie was fighting at school. She said that Annie was having difficulty completing her work on time, as she is frequently distracted and sullen. Miss Barnes is concerned as to why the problems have arisen now."

"I'm telling you, Elizabeth." Daddy turned to me. "Ruth Ann, you take your little sister in the other room. I need to talk to your mama."

"But Daddy, I was just asking Mama..."

"Ruth Ann, my asking you to go means you're all done asking. Do you hear me? Now git."

When we left the kitchen, Annie said, "we should go out to the barn. We can see if Beets or Buddy or Gertrude want to play with Shirley. Wanna come?"

"Not yet, Annie. I'll just be getting...I'll be there soon."

"You know it ain't right, Ruthie, to be eavesdropping," Annie scolded me.

"I'm not eavesdropping. I'm just waiting to ask Mama my question. Now go." I shooed Annie away and did exactly what Annie accused me of.

"I think it's time that Annie spent her time a little closer to home. I'm not gonna abide by her following that lady around the countryside. People like that can't be trusted, Elizabeth. You don't know enough about the world to know this. If you did, you'd know." Daddy was talking so loud I was afraid Annie might hear him from the barn. But she didn't even get that far.

She shot past me and ran back into the kitchen. "You can't do that, Daddy! She's my friend!"

Daddy looked at me and shouted, "Ruth Ann, I told you to take your sister out of here! When I tell you to do something… And Annie, I'm your daddy and you will do as I say." Annie ran from the room and slammed our bedroom door so hard Daddy stopped hollering for a minute and looked confused. And then he yelled, "I will not have my child traipsing about in the company of…her. Lord knows what that lady might do to our child, Elizabeth."

I ran after Annie. She was crouched on our bedroom floor. I dropped down beside her and through the vent in the floor, we listened. Finally, Mama spoke again, "*to thine own self be true.*"

"What in tarnation's wrong with you? Have you finally lost your mind? I don't give a ding bat's tit what you've got to say."

Without raising her voice one little bit, Mama said, "Daniel, Dr. Molly has been a true friend to me and she means a great deal to Annie. I cannot imagine…"

Daddy shouted, "now Elizabeth, that's all there is to it. Case closed."

We didn't hear footsteps or slamming doors. But we heard Mama. "Daniel, this case is not closed and I am not done speaking."

With her voice cold and clear, but shaking like aspen leaves, she kept right on. "Molly Hobart is a fine lady and both Annie and I will continue our friendships with her. I am sorry that you have a problem with her…persuasion. It has no bearing on our family and should not be a factor in our decision making around the welfare of our youngest child."

Annie turned her teary face up to me and said, "I hate daddy."

"I will not stand by with my youngest child acting like a pervert in this town because of that lady!" Daddy hollered again.

"Daniel, Annie is having difficulties. Some of her drawings in art can be construed as, well, let's just say inappropriate. Disturbing. However, we have no reason to pin this on Dr. Molly, who has been nothing but kind to this family..."

"As far as you know. But you're not out there while them two are driving over hill and dale," Daddy said.

"Well, there is very little hill or dale."

"Goldarn, Elizabeth, you know what I'm saying."

"And Daniel if you had attended the meeting with Miss Barnes, you would be aware that..."

"That primary school teacher doesn't know more than Jim Dolver, who was talking to me after our Lion's Club meeting today. Little Jimmy told his daddy that Annie's making a fool of herself. I won't have her acting like a pervert!"

Annie pushed herself up off the floor.

"Where you going?" I asked.

"Nowhere," she said as she opened the window and took hold of the rope we had hanging there. I was barely on my feet when she slithered halfway down, hit the ground and ran.

"Annie! Stop! Wait!" I yelled out the window.

I ran down the stairs yelling, "Mama! Annie's run off!"

"For heaven's sake, stop shouting." Mama was so exasperated she was spitting, then took a breath and asked, "now what are you saying?"

"Annie's gone."

"What do you mean, *gone*?" Daddy asked.

"She took off running when you called her a pervert," I accused. "Can't you see she's sad? What's wrong with you? And now she's run off," I cried.

"Where'd she go?" Daddy asked.

"How should I know? I've got to find her." Worry churned my stomach and I thought I'd be the next one puking.

"Listen here," Daddy said softly, lifting my chin. "There are things you don't know about yet. Nasty things I wish you never did need to know. Now, I'm sorry you girls heard me talking. But it ain't no coinkydink that she's been trailing that doctor around hill and..." he looked at Mama, "...all over tarnation same time as she's been acting strange."

"Stop Daniel. Rumor and innuendo have caused enough trouble."

But he wouldn't be stopped. "I'm not trying to be mean. I'm just saying what I know. And a lot of other folks know it, too. You gotta stay away from her, Ruthie. And keep Annie close. My own daddy warned me 'bout this nonsense. He told me he didn't like the sight of her, but I didn't pay him no mind."

The whole time he talked he clenched his fists and worked his jaw like he was chewing a piece of tough steak. "Sometimes listening to your daddy is the right thing to do. Now, where did Annie run off to?"

"I told you. I don't know. She shimmied down the rope and took off running."

"Elizabeth, give your whistle a blow and let's see if we can flush her out without running all over creation."

Mama pulled her silver whistle off the hook by the back door and blew like she was calling in the cavalry. Buddy came running with Gertrude and Lizzie trotting behind him. No Annie. Beets, who had been lazing on the porch, stood up and stretched. All four of them stood by the door, like they were waiting for Annie to come crashing through it.

"Now, Ruth Ann, you don't need to worry yourself. Annie's got fire in her britches but she'll turn up before long." I wasn't convinced, and I don't think he was either.

"Ruth Ann, help me pick up the house, please. I am going to get started with a huckleberry pie. Your grandparents are joining us for dessert and cards later this evening."

"But Mama, what about Annie? Don't you want to go searching for her?" I whined.

"This is not a Nancy Drew mystery to be solved, Ruth Ann. Your sister's tantrums are not entirely unprecedented." Mama took off her glasses, rubbed her eyes, and said, "all of this nonsense is giving me a headache." She opened the cupboard next to the stove, took two Anacin, closed her eyes, and said, "relief. I just need a bit of relief." And then she muttered, "*to rise up...relief*".

Mama's relief came from her bottle of Anacin, but mine didn't come at all. I felt like an udder that needed milking: pulled tight and in pain waiting. Mama and Daddy said to stay put. They said she'd turn up. Finally. She did.

Annie looked just like Huck Finn walking down the road in front of our house with her shoes in one hand and a string of catfish slung over her shoulder. I could hear her singing *Yankee Doodle Dandy* even before I saw her. I dropped my book on the porch swing and ran out to meet her. "Annie, where have you been? You've been gone for two hours!" I shouted.

"Fishing." She smiled. "By myself. I got a ride to the lake." She looked like she swallowed a rainbow and was bright with the color of it.

"What do you mean, you got a ride? With a stranger?"

"Nah, a kid from my class. You don't know him. Him and his mama were going to the lake to catch catfish." She lifted up the slimy fish. "They loaned me a pole."

"That's not by yourself."

"Sure, it was. They put their lines in, so I took my pole down the way and caught more than they did." She was as proud as a peach in a pie, and I was just as happy to have my little sister back again. But still–

"You can't run off like that, Annie. It's not right. I got real worried." We didn't say anything more until we were standing outside the kitchen door.

"I smell pie. Are we having pie? I'm so hungry I was half

ready to rub sticks together and cook up one of my catfish," she laughed.

"Mama made a huckleberry pie. Who's this kid from school?"

"I told you, a boy from my class named Peter."

"That poor kid? The one with all those patches on his pants and holes in his shoes?"

"Yeah. But Ruthie, he's nice. He doesn't have a daddy 'cause he died. I gave them some of my fish. They put 'em in the deep freeze for the winter. And they pick berries in the woods and they know lots of stuff you can eat out there. Him and his mama, that's all the family they got. You know what, Ruthie?"

"What?"

"You can't tell by the outside what's on the inside."

She was right. To folks in town, the outside of our family didn't look at all like it felt to be on the inside.

CHAPTER 11

When we walked in the door, Mama called out, "Annie?" She came running into the kitchen and hugged her like she'd walked home from Timbuktu. "Annie, I have been so worried. Where were you?" she asked with tears standing in the corner of her eyes.

"Fishing." Annie said and pointed to the string of fish she dropped into the kitchen sink.

"Oh my land! Look at you!" I was so happy to see her that I didn't really see her. Muddy blue jeans were rolled up to her knees, and fish guts and blood were wiped down the front of her checkered blue shirt with mud spattered on her face. Her hair was tangled with bits of twig standing out every which way. "Annabelle Rose, where are your shoes?"

"They're on the porch. I didn't want them to get wet and muddy." Annie smiled, figuring she did a good thing. "Peter was barefoot too. He said the fish like it better that way."

"Peter? Who's Peter?"

"A kid in my class."

"You went fishing with a stranger!"

"He's not a stranger. He's in my class."

"I understand that you think you know him. But Annie, you can't always know what a person's intention is. You are far too trusting. Anything could have happened to you, and we would not have known where to begin looking. Was there an adult present?"

"Sure. His mama was fishing with us. She's not all that good, but she won't let Peter go without her. He says that's on account of his daddy dying. His mama likes to keep him close. She said Peter's all she's got."

Mama pulled Annie into a hug again and said, "be that as it may, I cannot have you traipsing about the countryside with str...people I do not know the first thing about. I know nothing of their family."

As far as I could tell, Mama didn't know much about her own family. But I kept my mouth shut and she kept on. "And, oh dear, you really must get into a bath. Your grandparents are coming for pie and cards after supper this evening. "Ruth Ann, please run a bath for your sister."

A gray cloud passed by and the rainbow in Annie's eyes disappeared. "Mama, I'm pretty tuckered out from all this fishing. I think maybe I'll just need to go to bed after supper. I might be coming down with something."

"If you are well enough to spend two hours fishing, with this Peter person, you can certainly spend an hour or so with family. Now off. Get into the tub. And look at me! I need to change now too," Mama laughed.

"But Mama..." Annie whined.

"No buts little miss Rapunzel." Mama touched Annie's filthy cheek with her fingertips.

Annie pointed to the sink. "What about those?"

"I'll wrap them in Saran and perhaps we can have fried catfish for tomorrow night's supper."

During supper Annie spoke when spoken to, and that was it. When supper was done and cleaned up she sat holding

146

that table down like she expected spirits of the dead to lift it up like a Ouija board.

"What are you doing?" I asked.

"Just waiting," she said without looking up.

"Annie, I will insist that you help serve the pie." Mama's voice came from the back of her head while she was putting coffee in the percolator.

"Let's see here," Daddy said as he walked in. "Last I remembered that spot is mine." He looked over at Annie and winked.

"I know. I'm just feeling kinda poorly and thought if I sat here I could get up and go if I need to lie down or something." The back door flew open and Annie nearly flew out of her chair. Her face turned white and she looked like she saw a ghost for sure. Grandpa and Grandma walked in and something made me feel off too. Maybe Annie was contagious.

"Well, what do we have here? I smell pie but I see trouble." Grandma smiled.

"Hello, Mother," Daddy said and kissed her on the cheek.

"There's my Annie," Grandpa started. "I been coming by to get you for fishing and where have you been? Nowhere. That's where." Annie was looking down as he walked towards her. "Come on now, give your Grandpa some loving."

Grandpa was almost to Annie when Daddy stepped between them and said, "alright there, Dad. Annie's a little under the weather. Best if you give her some space tonight." And then he looked at Annie. "But you do need to give your mama a hand with that pie." Daddy gave Annie a little push away from Grandpa.

"So what's this about, you under the weather? I saw you walk past the place with a string of fish swinging and swaying. You were singing at the top of your lungs," Grandma said.

"What? You were fishing without me?" Grandpa's face turned red and he glared at Annie.

"Walter! Calm down. The girl can fish without her grand-father, now and then." Grandma laughed and said, "my good-ness, you are the most devoted grandfather a child could ask for." She patted his arm. "But dear, all little sparrows do fly from the nest eventually."

"Shut up, Eleanor," Grandpa snapped.

"Let's eat, shall we," Mama said like she never heard the ruckus and handed Annie and me pieces of pie to serve as she poured coffee.

"Elizabeth, you forgot the ice cream," Daddy said with a bite of pie already in his mouth.

"Oh yes, perhaps you can get it for us, Ruth Ann. It is in the deep freeze."

"I'll get it, Mama," Annie said.

Grandpa started to get up, "I can give you a hand with that, squirt."

Daddy put his hand on his shoulder. "Annie will be just fine, Dad. You stay where you are." Grandpa tried again to *give her a hand* when she opened up the ice cream and Daddy said, "I got it," and gave everybody a scoop.

Annie took one bite of pie and said, "Mama, I'm a bit woozy. Maybe my tub was too hot or too full or something. I think I ought to go to bed."

Mama looked over at Annie and asked, "woozy?"

"Yeah, Mama."

"Well, you know what happens when you wolf down your food. Remember to chew and let's see how you feel."

After she took about three more bites of pie she asked to be excused, "how 'bout now?"

"OK, off to bed and there will be no shenanigans. No getting up and down," Mama said as she started dealing cards. "Sleep well. I'll check in on you before I go to bed."

She wasn't gone but a couple of minutes and Grandpa excused himself. I thought he was headed to the toilet, but when he didn't come back right away, Grandma said, "now don't you think for one minute that you can keep him from his precious grandbaby." She laughed and smiled.

We finished up dessert as we waited for him. About ten minutes after Grandpa sat back down, we could hear Annie run for the bathroom. Her retching sounded like the roar of thunder on a hot August night. Mama, calm as could be said, "well now, I guess Annie was feeling a bit *woozy*, after all. Hold the game, I will be back in a jiff."

I pushed my chair back and said, "I'll go Mama. I'll probably lose anyhow."

"That would be lovely. Let me know if you need me," Mama said, back to staring at her cards.

"Go away," Annie said, when I knocked on the locked door.

"Annie. Open up. Let me help you clean up and then I can read you a chapter of Tom Sawyer or the Boxcar Children. Wouldn't you like that?"

On the other side of the door, I could hear Annie whimpering. With a bobby pin from my hair, I popped the door open.

"Annie!" I gasped. She was standing in her shirt and socks with a washcloth wadded in her hand that was covering up her private parts. Purple puke was in her hair, and down her chin and shirt.

"Do you have a case of the runs, too?"

Looking down at her feet she said, "I told you I was fine."

"Annie, you don't look too fine. You don't have anything to be ashamed of. Everybody gets the pukes and the runs sometimes. I'll go get your jammies for you. You wait right here."

A worry I couldn't find a place for wrapped itself around

149

me when I went to get Annie's pajamas. I saw her underwear in the trash and went to pull them out. "Annie, you can't throw your underwear away. Mama won't like that one bit."

"No!" she shouted just as I was about to touch them. "Leave 'em be. They're no good anymore. Just leave 'em, Ruthie."

"But Annie…"

"I don't like that pair. I got enough. I don't want 'em." Sorrow broke her face open, and she slid down the wall and landed in a puddle of tears.

"Girls, open this door. What's going on in there?" Mama's voice on the other side of the door surprised us both. "Why is this door locked?" Without even knowing I'd done it; I had locked the door behind me.

"Just a minute, Mama," I stalled.

Annie hiccuped and slurped her tears back in and whispered, "don't tell, Ruthie."

I pulled Annie off the floor and handed her jammies to her. She slipped the bottoms on as Mama rapped on the door again. When I opened the door she looked at Annie and then at me.

"Annie, I'm sorry. You really are ill, aren't you?" To me she said, "thank you, Ruth Ann, for attending to your sister. Your grandparents have left. Here, let's get that filthy shirt off. And let's get that up-chuck off your face. In fact, perhaps you should take another bath. Your hair was evidently hit by the assault."

"I don't want to take another bath," Annie whimpered.

"Mama, I can wash it out of her hair. Annie, you want me to wash it in the sink for you?"

"First things first. Let me dampen this cloth again and give your face a good washing."

"No!" We both shouted.

"Not that washcloth," I said.

"Why, Ruth Ann, this looks perfectly fine."

"But, Mama," I said, "Annie had the runs too."

"Oh. Oh dear. I really have been negligent. I'm sorry, Annie. Are you sure this is the cloth you used. It certainly does not appear to have any sign of...feces. No matter."

When Annie was all cleaned up, Mama offered, "let's get you into bed and snuggle up and read a story. What do you think of that? I just need to finish getting the kitchen set to order and then I can make myself available."

"But I want Ruthie to read to me. She already said she would and she uses all the right voices."

"Oh. Yes. Well, as you wish." I could hear the hurt in Mama's voice but she turned away and started picking up Annie's dirty clothes and towel and said, "Annie, why in the world is your underwear in the trash?" She turned. "Annie?"

"They're dirty," Annie muttered.

"That's where the clothes hamper comes into service, not the trash bin." Mama fished them out and left with all the dirty laundry.

Annie and I snuggled up together and I did my best to use all the right voices and keep my own steady. I felt sad and afraid because I didn't know what to do to keep Annie safe, because I didn't know what was hurting her. It was like the wind. You could see it moving the trees, but you never could catch sight of it. But I sure was going to try.

As soon as school let out on Monday I rode my bike to the Emmett County Veterinary Hospital, knowing that if anybody could help me sort out the trouble with Annie, it would be Dr. Molly. My nerves got the best of me as I pulled and pulled on the front door before I saw the sign that said push. I wanted to push myself right back out that door when the smell of cat pee smacked me in the face.

"Good afternoon. I'll be with you in a flash," said a lady who was on her hands and knees, mopping up the floor.

"I am so sorry. Tinkerbell is such a little pistol. This is what he does every time, and I do mean EVERY time he doesn't get his way. Roger thinks we should change his name to Tinklebell, but I think that's an affront to his masculinity," the lady holding the cat's leash said.

The lady doing the mopping looked up at me and smiled. "It won't be but a minute." She got to her feet and carried her bucket and rags through a swinging door.

"Mrs. Rhodes, Dr. Molly will be finished in a jiff. It'd be helpful if you could keep Tinkle...Tinkerbell in his box, while you're waiting." Even though she didn't make a fuss about the cat pee, she walked over and pushed the window open. When she got back behind the desk, she said, "now honey, what can I do for you?"

"Yes ma'am, I'm looking for Dr. Molly. I need to speak with her about a private matter, if I could, please." I looked up. It was her. She was the lady who worked at Nelson's Market and gave me the sucker.

"I'm sure she would be happy to visit with you, honey. Right now, she's with a patient and has one more waiting on her. She'll see you just as soon as she can spare a minute. If you'd like to wait, I have cocoa and cookies you might like."

"Well ma'am, I do think I might wait here if that'd be all right by you. But you don't have to give me treats. Thank you very much though." My stomach was rumbling and tumbling and swallowing my own spit was all that I could manage.

"You know, honey, you look awfully familiar to me. Don't I know you from Nelson's? I believe I saw you there on my last day of employment. I was handing out suckers and I specifically remember you shopping with your mama."

"Yes, ma'am." Jiminy Christmas! I just wanted to sink into

the floor. I didn't want her to remember me and remember my mama who chattered like a fool.

"Well, I'll be. You have the most beautiful eyes. It's a shame you don't give people a chance to see much of them."

She spoke to me with nothing but kindness, but it made me feel so uncomfortable I wanted to get out of there. When she looked at me then, and when she looked at me now, it was like she could see right through me.

"Well, I should probably be going. Maybe another time I can stop by to say *hey* to Dr. Molly. It wasn't all that important really."

Right as I finished lying, the swinging door swung open and there she was. Dr. Molly walked out, and a dog as big as a lion walked a tiny little lady out beside her.

"Make sure and let me know if Rufus isn't any better by the end of the week. He should be back to his rambunctious self as long as you keep him on his pills for the next couple of weeks. And Esther, cut down on his snacks a bit. Donut holes are not a dog's best friend."

Dr. Molly smiled and touched the lady's shoulder just as Rufus started pulling poor Esther across that linoleum floor in the direction of Tinkerbell. "Let me give you a hand," Dr. Molly said as she took Rufus by the collar and led him to the door. "Let's have Rufus wait in the car while you settle up your bill," Dr. Molly said, calm as could be.

Right when she opened the door for Rufus, she spotted me. "Well now, what a nice surprise this is. Ruth Ann, what in the world brings you in?"

Don't cry. Don't cry, I said to myself while I was chewing on the inside of my cheek and looking down.

"Well, let's see. I have one more patient I need to take a look at." She looked over at Mrs. Rhodes. "How about you wait for a bit in my office and then we'll have a chat?"

"Cheryl, can you get Mrs. Rhodes set and I'll be right in?

Thanks." She smiled at Cheryl as we walked back through the swinging doors into a small office with a window flooded with the last of the day's sunshine. "Ruth Ann, make yourself at home, and I'll be back just as quickly as I can. I am so glad that you tracked me down."

"I don't want to bother you. Maybe I shouldn't have come. I just..."

"You are not a bother. I just need a minute to finish things up. Your timing's just right. Make yourself at home."

She was rummaging through a stack of papers while I looked around. Her office was as neat as a pin with plaques and pictures on the walls. There was one of an old dairy farm with cows all around and a little girl standing by herself in knee boots, flowered shorts, a striped shirt and a cowboy hat.

"Is that you, Dr. Molly?"

"Sure is. That picture pretty well sums things up for me. *All spit, no style.* That's what my mama said to me every time I tumbled down the stairs to start my day."

Cheryl popped her head in and said, "Molly, Mrs. Rhodes and Tinkerbell are ready for you."

When Dr. Molly rushed from the room, I walked over to that picture and stared at the little girl. She reminded me so much of Annie with the way she was standing, the look on her face, and her mismatched clothes.

Maybe that's why Dr. Molly took such a shine to my little sister. I sat down to wait when there was a tap on the door. Cheryl walked in with a plate of cookies and a mug of hot cocoa. I jumped to my feet.

"You're fine. Now honey, I know you didn't actually *say* you wanted a snack, and if you really don't, that's fine, but I thought I'd give you a chance to change your mind." She smiled and left the room.

I sipped on cocoa and ate a cookie, not sure what it was I would say when the door flew open.

"Well, I see Cheryl's given you an after-school snack," she smiled. What's on your mind? Everything OK at home?"

I didn't know how to start slow. "Dr. Molly, there's something wrong with Annie. I don't know what, but I think it's bad."

"Bad, huh? Start from the beginning, Ruth Ann. I have noticed that she's a bit more bashful some days, but bad? I haven't noticed anything that's bad. What do you know?"

"I'm sorry. I really shouldn't have come. I just didn't know..." I started to get up.

"No, no, no. Let's just talk for a bit and see what we might bump into by way of explaining things." Dr. Molly's voice was soft. She reached out to touch my hand. "Just catch your breath." Her hand squeezed mine and stopped it from shaking. She waited.

"Annie cried in her sleep and threw up her breakfast and her pie. And she tried to throw away her underpants, but Mama saw them and pulled them out of the trash." Words spattered out of my mouth like grease from the fryer. I was done talking before I knew that I had tears running down my face and dropping on Dr. Molly's desk like rain on the sidewalk.

Without saying a thing, she gave me a tissue and then pulled me into a hug when I started to sob. After I calmed down, Dr. Molly took hold of my shoulders and held me out in front of her and said, "Ruth Ann, tell me what you know. I can't help if I don't know what's going on."

"The only thing I know," I sputtered, "is that Grandpa gave her a new kitty named Shirley. She's a secret."

"A secret?" Dr. Molly tipped her head to one side.

"Yeah. She didn't want us to know and gets real scared when she thinks that one of us will say something to Grandpa."

"That is a puzzle, isn't it? Well, Annie does love her animals."

"But Dr. Molly, that's the thing. She feeds Shirley and holds her some, but the rest of 'em stand by the door staring in, waiting for her to come play and, sometimes, she's just like Mama, resting."

"Hmm. Maybe she has a bug. Has your mama taken her to the doctor?"

"I dunno. I don't think that's it." I didn't know what it was, but something told me what it wasn't.

"Has she spoken with your grandfather? Would he know what's bothering Annie?" Dr. Molly stared at me and I stared at the floor.

"Ruth Ann?"

"I don't think that's such a good idea. He doesn't like my mama and she doesn't like him. And he made Annie keep that secret and all...so, I don't think so."

"OK, well I'll trust you on that one. Let me give this some thought. Could you stop again tomorrow after school so we can talk a bit more? That'll give us each a pillow to think on."

"A pillow?" I asked.

Dr. Molly smiled. "That's what my mama said when a problem stumped her. And right now, I'm stumped."

"I'll try to come by, but..."

"If it's going to be a problem at all, please don't. I don't want to add to the burden on your shoulders. But for now, let's get you home. It's starting to get dark out there. Can I toss your bike in the back of my truck and drive you home? Maybe then I can talk to your mama and see that little scalawag with a broken wing."

"That's OK." I rushed for the door, not ready for Mama or Annie to know I'd been 'hanging our dirty linen' around town.

CHAPTER 12

The house was still when I got there. I crept through the kitchen and started up the stairs when Mama called out, "Ruth Ann, is that you?"

"Yes, Mama," I hollered back, still hoping she would let me be, and I could just go to my room.

"What have I told you about talking to me from the other room? Please come into the living room to have a conversation."

She was settled on the sofa with one of her library books and an afghan. An empty coffee cup sat on the table beside her with one store-bought ginger snap cookie left on the saucer. I wanted to tell her about the cocoa and the home-made cookies, but I knew that I'd have some explaining to do.

"Hey there, Mama," I said.

"Hello, Ruth Ann. Could you be a dear and get me another cup of coffee. The pot is still on. Aren't you running a bit late today?"

Just as I was twisting my brain between my choices of

telling a big fat whopping lie or telling the truth, she saved me by not bothering to wait for my answer.

"Now run along and let me read, will you please? Oh, and we will be having fried catfish this evening. Supper will be in approximately one hour. But first, my coffee?"

When I walked into our room, Annie wasn't there. She was shouting and running in the yard with Buddy and Gertrude and Lilly. Maybe it had been a bug. Maybe it was my imagination.

WHEN WE SAT down to supper, Mama said, "I thought it might be nice to play a game together after we finish eating and clean the kitchen. Would you girls like that?" Mama asked when the three of us sat down to supper.

Annie's face lit up. "Why do you want to play a game, Mama? You never want to play. Are you feeling bad about something?"

"Now, Annie, I love to play board games. I suppose I've just gotten out of the habit. I thought it would be nice for us to, well, act more like a family. But if it's not something—"

"No, Mama, that's not it. I wanna play. I was just surprised. How about Chinese Checkers? I'll get it!"

Annie charged from the room. *Like family*, I thought. Why couldn't *family* be what we made instead of what we got? I wondered. I thought about Cheryl's cocoa and blurted out, "could we have cocoa while we play?"

As soon as I asked the question, I was washed over with sadness. I wanted normal to be that we drank cocoa and played games, and that Daddy was with us too. But it wasn't like that.

Mama answered without hearing the sorrow I felt. "Certainly, but I don't think we have any in the house just now. I can add it to my shopping list, if you would like."

"Sure, that'll be OK," I mumbled.

"I've got it!" Annie had the box in her hands and a smile on her face, and I just knew that I was making a big deal out of nothing. Maybe the family we got really was good enough. I'd been feeling scared and worried for so long that I didn't trust my own eyes.

"Annie, let's help Mama get cleaned up so we can play."

"Thank you, Ruth Ann." Mama's voice was soft and kind. "Annie, you may give Buddy the scraps from our plates, if you would like."

IT WASN'T long before we were all settled down playing, and there was a knock on the kitchen door. "Oh my! Who might that be at this hour?" Mama's voice shook, which didn't make any sense to me. Who could be at our kitchen door that she needed to be afraid of? Her being scared scared me too, but not Annie.

"I'll get it!" Annie jumped up from the table and threw the door open before Mama could even think to stop her.

"Well now Annie, I'm happy to find you up and about. I heard a rumor that you were under the weather." Dr. Molly was holding a plate of cookies in one hand and a green plaid Thermos in the other.

"Dr. Molly!" Annie shouted and jumped up and down like a bunny rabbit. "You're here! You're here!" She threw her arms around her so fast and hard I thought she might topple her right over.

"That's what they call, *jumping for joy*," Mama said smiling at Dr. Molly and Annie.

I was a little worried that Dr. Molly would talk about me stopping by, so I sat back quiet.

"Well, how about you, Ruth Ann? Can I get a hug from

you?" The minute Dr. Molly said it I knew my secret was safe. And this was a secret I felt good keeping.

"Isn't this a nice surprise, Molly? And perfect timing too. It's just the three of us and we are about to play Chinese Checkers. Would you like to join us?" Mama looked as happy to see Dr. Molly as Annie and I were.

"Well, I sure don't want to be in the way. I probably should have called first but…" Dr. Molly acted shy, like she didn't quite know what to do now that she was here.

"Nonsense! We are delighted to have you. And what a coincidence, Ruth Ann was just telling me that she was craving hot cocoa. How very thoughtful and how apropos. Molly, you really must join us. Don't you agree, girls?"

"Yes, Dr. Molly. Please stay," I begged, and Annie already decided it was so and ran to the cupboard to get cups for the cocoa. It didn't take but a few minutes eating Dr. Molly's treats and laughing at her stories to feel like she belonged at our family table just as much as salt and pepper.

"Molly, I would love to get your sugar cookie recipe. I rarely take the time to make cookies and the girls clearly enjoyed them." I hoped this wouldn't be the time that Dr. Molly slipped and said how I was eating those cookies for the second time in a day.

"Sure. My best friend, and well, my business partner Cheryl made them. And the cocoa too. I'm sure she won't mind sharing."

"Well, yes, that was delicious also. You must thank her for us. I have not considered making cocoa from anything but a package of Swiss Miss for years. I almost forgot that it could be done. Now tell me, is your friend Cheryl a veterinarian also? I thought that you were the only show in town?"

"No, no. She runs the office." Dr. Molly looked thoughtful. "You may have seen her at Nelson's. She worked there for several years. I convinced her to join me after I got settled into the practice. The prior office manager wasn't, well, she decided it wasn't the right fit to stay on after Doctor Waltner's untimely passing. Cheryl does a fair bit of hand holding when I'm tied up with patients."

"Ha ha! That's funny, Dr. Molly," Annie snickered.

"Annie, don't be rude," I scolded. The sweetness of the cookies and cocoa turned sour in my mouth. Until that minute, I didn't know how afraid I was that the goodness wouldn't last. I didn't want Annie spoiling it by laughing at Dr. Molly when nothing was funny. But she kept right on, not caring one bit what I had to say.

"You said," she looked at Dr. Molly, "tied up with patients. I don't think that's such a good idea. How are you gonna get your work done if you're all tied up?"

Annie slapped the table. Her laugh was just as contagious as a yawn, and Dr. Molly and Mama joined in and then I did too. It was good to trade the knot in my stomach for tears in my eyes from laughing. But before I knew it, we were hugging good night and making promises to laugh and play again soon.

"That was fun," I said to Mama after Annie headed up the stairs to bed. She looked at me. It was like a cloud covered up the stars. "What's wrong?"

"I don't know what to do or what to think. I trust that she is a wonderful influence on both you and Annie. But what will people say? And what will your father say?"

My words sloshed out like ice-cold water. "I don't know what you're talking about. Everything is good. I don't know why you can't just let it be good, Mama."

The cold splashed against her face. While she felt the sting of my words, I was washed in the shame of them. Mama was scared, but I was cruel. I was fed up, but I knew that being mean was wrong.

"I'm sorry I hurt you. I just don't want Dr. Molly to leave

us. I don't understand what all the fuss about her is anyhow. She's good and kind. Isn't that what we're supposed to be?"

"It's not that simple. I wish it were," Mama whispered.

"But maybe it is. Maybe…" and then I remembered. "Remember that time when you told me about that sailor from Sitka?" She fell against the counter like a gust of wind pushed her back.

"I asked you how you knew if you should stay in Alaska or come home again. Remember?" She nodded like a child listening to a story. "You said, *Ruth Ann, always remember* that *the only compass that can keep you on your path is the one in your own pocket.* You said it doesn't matter what other people think if you keep ahold of your own compass. I think you forgot your own words, Mama."

She pushed away from the counter and hugged me tight. "You are wise beyond your years." With the tissue tucked up her sleeve, she blew her nose. "Of course, it does matter what your father thinks. But we will cross that bridge when we get there. In the meantime, we will accept the friendship that Molly offers. We certainly can use a little more kindness. Thank you for reminding me that I still have a compass in my pocket. Off you go."

I walked a few steps away and turned. "Night, Mama."

"Good night, dear Ruth Ann. Sweet dreams. I love you."

I can't remember the last time Mama told me that she loved me without me feeling like it was another knot in the rope she was tying to keep me within sight of her needs. But tonight, was different. Tonight, it truly did feel like love.

"GOOD MORNING SLEEPY HEAD. Is your sister up yet?" Mama asked while I stood there in my jammies rubbing my eyes.

"Yeah. She's using the toilet. It stinks."

"Please do not be so crass. But I am glad to have a moment alone with you. I have given more thought to our conversation last night. While I do want to maintain our friendship with Molly, I also need to keep the peace with your father." She paused and smiled. "And I need to keep ahold of my compass."

I just wanted breakfast and to forget all about the time between Dr. Molly walking out the door and me walking up to bed, but she kept on talking.

"I will try to be thoughtful as I navigate these waters and do my best to support each of our friendships with Molly."

"Dr. Molly's MY friend! She can be your friend a little bit, but mostly she's MINE!" Annie stood in the doorway shouting.

"Annie, calm down. No one is taking Dr. Molly from you. And you mustn't get yourself worked up and sick again," Mama soothed. "But there might be times that I ask that you curtail some of your time spent with her."

"I knew it! You just want her for your friend 'cause you're lonesome. You don't want her to be my friend." Annie's lower lip shot out like a frog about to ribbit.

"That is not what I said," Mama pouted right back.

"That's what cut tail means. It means cut it off. Even I know that 'cause it happens sometimes. Sometimes..."

"For heaven's sake, Annie. Curtail is to reduce. I did not, nor would I say, cut tail." I couldn't tell if Mama was annoyed or amused as she tried to make Annie understand.

"Oh. Well, I don't want to curt the tail at all. I think it's just fine the way it is. And Dr. Molly told me last night that she wants to start seeing more of me. But she said it's gotta be alright with you. Is it? Is it alright with you?"

"Let's take it day by day, shall we? I thought perhaps you and I could have a special outing after school?" Mama looked like she was trying to squeeze through the fence without getting caught on the barbed wire. But Annie wasn't having it and slid to the floor in a puddle of tears.

"What's wrong, Annie? Mama's not taking Dr. Molly away from you."

"It's not that," Annie cried.

I raced from one corner of my brain to another, searching for clues as to what it was. I landed on Shirley. "Is this about Shirley again? We're not telling anybody, if that's what you're afraid of." Annie kept crying without saying if I was right or wrong.

"I cannot imagine why a kitten should be a secret and why this secret should lead to such...shame." At least Mama thought I might be right. And there the three of us were, poured out like a puddle on the floor. And there Grandpa was, staring in through the kitchen window.

Without being invited, he walked in coughing. "Who made my Annie cry?" he bellowed and coughed again.

"Walter, I would appreciate it if you..."

"What's going on here? I saw that red truck come 'round last night. Trouble follows that lady like flies to cow pies. You hear me?" We all heard him and nothing else. "Annie, is she giving you grief? I'm looking for a reason to get her outa here. She don't belong around good families!"

He looked at my mama and shouted, "you don't have the sense that comes with change from a dollar, Elizabeth! If you did, you'd lock your doors when she drives up. Look here at my grandbaby. That pervert riles her up!"

"Walter! I forbid you to use that language in my home! Please leave and let me get my daughters ready for school. To some of us, an education is of value."

"You and your uppity ways. You good for nothin'..."

"Grandpa! Stop! Don't you be mean to my mama. And Dr.

164

Molly is not the problem! Seems to me, you rile Annie up!" I shouted and shook.

"Stop it, Ruthie! Stop it!" Annie ran from the room sobbing.

Grandpa spit! Right on Mama's kitchen floor. He looked at me, "You're just like your mama; too big for your own britches. Somebody's gonna show you how it is, little missy, and that somebody might just be your good ol' grandpa standing here trying to make things right. But no, you don't see help when it's served up with a side of fries! You're just like your good for nothin' mama!"

"GET OUT!" Mama screamed at the top of her lungs.

Freeze. Don't make anything worse. Don't move a muscle. Be invisible. Get out. Get out.

Time passed. I don't know how much.

"Ruthie?"

Turn head. Stand still. Like a statue. Look at Annie.

"Wanna come for treats with us after school?"

"Nah. I don't think so. Thanks." It was all I could come up with. My brain was stuck in the goo of Grandpa's spit and Mama's head exploding. But what scared me most was Annie acting like nothing at all just happened. If it wasn't for Mama on her hands and knees scrubbing the spit spot, I would have wondered if I made the whole thing up.

"Alright then. Ruthie, you best get ready for school. We're runnin' late. And Mama?"

"Yes, Annie."

"I think it'd be just fine to get us some ice cream from Frostee's after school. Just you and me, Mama. A special treat." Annie was as calm as a pond froze over in winter.

"Surely," Mama said from the floor. She got up, washed her hands, and served Annie's breakfast without even knowing that the bread never toasted and the bacon was burnt to a crisp. But Annie sat right down and ate every bite like it was all just fine.

I stumbled up the stairs wondering how a family puts itself back together when it's been smashed to smithereens.

"See you later, Mama! Come on, Ruthie! Let's go!" Annie yelled as she raced past me on the way to the barn to get our bikes. I smelled Grandpa's cigarette. If she smelled it, she didn't let on. I didn't know where he was, but I knew he was watching. I was on my bike when I heard him cough. Annie was out in front and I raced to catch up. I never looked back.

AFTER SCHOOL, Annie and I rode our bikes home. As we pulled up our drive, I felt a ghost run his fingers up my spine. My body recognized being scared before my brain did. My eyes darted around looking for Grandpa. I inhaled and didn't smell anything but the dry leaves that crunched under the tires of my bike. That wasn't enough to keep my hands from dripping sweat onto my handlebars. As Annie ran ahead of me to the house, I kept looking around, like I expected him to jump out of the bushes.

"See you later alligator!" Annie called out.

"We won't be too long, Ruth Ann. You can fix yourself a snack of peanut butter and celery if you'd like," Mama said.

As soon as they drove away, I wanted to be with them. I never was scared being home alone. Not until now. I ran from the house. Too late. They were gone.

I rushed to the barn, jumped on my bike and rode to town.

Mr. Hansen was parked in front of the Woolworth's. If he was there, maybe Heidi was too. I was so relieved I nearly bashed into old Mrs. Bluster as I ran through the door. My feet stopped but my heart jumped out in front of me when

Heidi looked up from the booth where she was having shakes with three girls from school.

"Ruthie. Oh, there you are. I was…I didn't know…" Heidi stammered.

The other girls concentrated on sucking down their shakes. I just stood there staring at them like I was sinking into quicksand.

"Come on, Ruthie. I'll share my shake with you. Scoot over Hannah," Heidi tried again.

My heart was back in my body, but now it was all jammed up in my throat and I couldn't push words past it, so I turned and walked away. Heidi's voice was like the intercom in the store; I could hear sounds, but they didn't turn into words.

Maybe I shouldn't have been so broken hearted, but I was. It's not like Heidi can't have other friends, but today I needed her. Finding Mama and Annie, or being alone, none of it mattered anymore.

I headed home with tears running down my face, and my luck going from bad to worse.

Matthew was walking along the side of the road out in front of me. He jumped something awful when I caught up with him and he turned his startled face to me. That's when I could see that he was crying too. When he turned away, I wiped at my own tears, and slowed up beside him.

"Hey Matthew, how're you doing?" It wasn't the right question, but I didn't know how else to begin. His shoulders shrugged and his chin dropped down further. Most of my life, I knew Matthew Wright, but I never saw him cry…until now. I hopped off my bike and pushed it alongside him. My own hurt feelings didn't seem very important.

"Sage is hurt. It's bad."

"Matthew, I…"

"Some idiot, going too fast, too late…" his voice dropped away. "Was a truck…like your Grandpa's." We both startled at

167

his words. "I didn't mean it was him. Mrs. Court said it was a blue pickup. But she didn't see it 'till it was almost out of sight."

I ran from one corner of my brain to another, trying to think up another blue pickup truck. "I'm just hoping that Sage'll be alright," he sniffed.

"I'm sorry," I whispered, ashamed at feeling sorry for myself, and ashamed that my grandpa owned a blue truck.

"Dr. Molly'll fix her up real good," I said, hoping it was true. And then my thoughts wandered to Annie, and I hoped that Dr. Molly would fix her up too. It was like Matthew read my mind.

"Ruth Ann?"

"Yeah."

"Sometimes I see Annie fishing with your grandpa."

"So?"

"Well...I dunno," he stammered.

"What?" My stomach felt funny...again.

He stopped walking and kicked at the rocks on the side of the road. He pulled the cap off his head and pushed his hair back and then flattened it out again before he spoke up. "I don't think Annie much likes going fishing with your grandpa."

"Is that all? If she didn't like fishing, she wouldn't go." I wondered if this were true, but I plowed ahead like it was gospel fact. "But I, for one, know she loves fishing. Why, just the other day she was fishing with Peter and his mama. She had a fine time."

"It's not that. It's not fishing," he said fidgeting with his hat in his hand.

"You're not making sense," I accused, forgetting all about feeling bad for him and feeling mad and scared instead.

"Sometimes Annie just doesn't seem like herself down

there. I watch her. I just thought you might want to know since your mama and daddy seem pretty busy these days."

"She has been sick, you know."

"Yeah, probably so," Matthew said in a faraway voice.

"It's not *probably* Matthew! It's true. Grandpa's ornery but he loves Annie best. I think he'd know if she didn't want to go fishing." Every word coming out of my mouth sounded like a lie, even to me. What Matthew had to say landed in a spot that felt true and that's why it shook me up, but I blathered on anyhow. "Mama always tells her not to eat chokecherries when she's out in the woods, but she does it anyways."

"Uh huh," he said.

Matthew and I each had a hand on the handlebars of my bike and steered our way home without another word about Sage, Annie, or Grandpa. When we got to my house, he looked over. "I'm not saying–I just wanted you to know. But I'm real sorry I made you feel so sad."

"I hope Sage feels better real soon," I sniffed, and turned to go, walking my bike to the barn not knowing how to make sense of what Matthew had to say.

THE TELEPHONE WAS RINGING when I walked into the house.

"Ruthie, I'm sorry your feelings got hurt," Heidi said. "You've just been so busy. And you haven't even been waiting at the bus with me so when…are you still there?"

"I'm still here. I'm not feeling too well. I better go." Without waiting for her goodbye, I hung up and ran to the bathroom.

"You been fishing, Ruthie?" I didn't hear Annie until she spoke. White as a ghost, she stood in the doorway. Tears stood in her eyes.

"Fishing? Why would you ask me that?" Still hanging over the toilet bowl, I spit the last of the puke out of my mouth.

With eyes half open, she waited for an answer.

"No." I flushed the toilet and wiped my mouth on toilet paper.

"Did Grandpa show you where Ninny had her kittens?"

"No. I didn't even see Grandpa. I walked home with Matthew. What's got into you? Annie, Matthew said he saw you at the river. He said he's been watching you."

"He didn't see anything! He's lying!" she shouted. Blood rushed to her face painting her fire engine red.

"Annie, you're not in trouble. I'm worried about you. You've gotta tell me what's going on."

"I don't have nothing to say. I don't know what you're needing to talk about, but I'm just fine and Matthew Wright is a big fat liar!"

"Annie, you're not just fine!" I shouted back, and then simmered down. "I know there's something, and you gotta tell me what it is."

"I ain't telling you nothing 'cause there's nothing to tell! That's what. There ain't nothing to tell! NOTHING!"

Annie ran from the bathroom and out the back door. Buddy ran too, like they were playing chase.

"Girls, what is all this commotion?" Mama came out of her sewing room. "Ruth Ann, what is going on? Why on earth have you been crying?" She pushed up her glasses and stared at me, waiting.

"Matthew's dog got hit by a car." What I said was true but wasn't the point.

"Matthew Wright?" she asked like there was another.

"Yeah, his dog Sage. Remember, she's that big ol' mutt with a blue eye and a brown one?"

"Oh. Oh dear. Well, that is unfortunate. But I don't under-stand how that is related to the commotion I just heard between you and your sister, or why you would be crying over the Wright's dog."

"She's hurt bad."

"Well, yes. Being struck by any motor vehicle will certainly leave an animal *badly* hurt."

I tried not to pay attention to her fixing my words.

"Yes, there is no getting around that fact. But to the matter at hand, what provoked Annie to run out of the house? You didn't give her details of this accident, did you? She will be entirely undone if she is left to imagine any living thing hurt..."

"I didn't tell. Maybe she just went out to play. That's what Buddy thought. I'll go see."

"By the sound of things, I did not get the impression she was headed out to play. But never mind, do see if you can find her."

I'd never find her if she didn't want me to, but I walked outside to get away from Mama and back to my own thoughts and worries. The kitchen door slammed, and I turned and ran, knowing that if I had to, I'd grab Annie to keep her from running again and she would tell me what's what even if I had to hold her down.

"Whoa there, pony!" Daddy said right before I smashed into him. He stumbled back and smacked into a lamp while I crashed to the floor.

"By gum, Ruth Ann Walker, if you ain't the clumsiest klutz I ever did see, well then I never did see a klutz!" He looked down at me lying in a heap on the floor, and walked away. "You clean up that mess you're busy making and you best know that you'll be paying the repair bill for that lamp you done broke."

"*You done broke.* What an ignorant fool," I mumbled. Like a hot air balloon with fire in my belly, I was lifted right up the stairs behind my daddy's trail of perfume.

"You don't know what the heck is going on around here, 'cause you're never here. You don't know that you got a little daughter puking her lights out 'cause something, well, something's wrong. You don't know, or maybe you just don't care that Mama cries every day of the year 'cause you're chasing down ways to feel better about yourself 'cause you didn't chase your own dream, and you don't have the time of day for her. You don't know nothing about nothing, Daddy. And I am not a klutz! I am not stupid! I am not some dirty piece of laundry you can just step over. And I did not break that lamp, you did! I want to love you Daddy, but it's real hard when you're so darn busy being mean to me for breathing."

By the time I was done, I was screaming and crying and carrying on, and Daddy just stood there with his mouth hanging open like a porcupine that lost its quills. As soon as I turned to go I was sorry for every word I said 'cause I knew that there was no way he would ever love me again.

And he wasn't even the reason I was screaming and crying. I was scared and sad and didn't know what else to do. I shook with every step I took down the stairs and Mama was standing at the bottom looking up at me. "What on earth?" were the only words that came out of her mouth.

I CARRIED my piggy bank down to the kitchen table to ask Mama if she thought I had enough to fix the lamp. For the longest time she stood staring out the window above the sink.

"Mama?" I asked.

"Take your money back to your room. It was an accident. Accidents happen."

"I'm sorry."

"I am as well," she murmured. "Run along and then help me get supper on the table."

The three of us sat down to supper without knowing where Annie was or when she'd be home. Worry took up so much space in my throat it was hard to get food past the lump it made.

"Annie!" I gulped when she breezed in halfway through eating. Mama told her to wash up and Daddy twirled spaghetti on his fork, acting like it was all just fine. But it wasn't fine with me. "Where were you?" I shouted.

She ignored me and turned to Daddy. "How come *you're* home?"

He looked up but before he could say anything Mama did. "Now Annie, that is not a very kind thing to say to your father."

"But Mama, you said Daddy would be gone all week so we could have fish sticks and stuff. And you said maybe I could go to Dr. Molly's and…"

"Hush, Annie. Wash your hands and face and sit down to supper. Your father's plans changed and, well, here we are." I wanted to shake the truth out of Annie, but I also wanted her to know how scared I was that she ran off like that.

She looked to have forgotten all about the afternoon's upset and looked up at Daddy with a mouthful of food and asked, "Daddy, how come you don't like fish sticks? When Dr. Molly came for supper…"

"For heaven's sake Annie, you know what I have said about speaking with a mouth full of food," Mama scolded and then slurped up noodles like there was a prize for the first clean plate.

"Mama, you look *famished!*" Annie looked around and smiled at every one of us. And then she looked at Daddy and said, "that means starving to death." She was still smiling when Mama started coughing and choking.

Daddy kept right on chewing.

"May I please be excused?" I asked.

173

"Me too?" Annie asked.

Mama had her napkin to her face and her eyes were still watery from all that coughing. When she found her own words, she said, "clean up your plates first, and then you may leave the table. Ruth Ann, did you tell your father that you picked up the mess from the lamp debacle?" She looked at Daddy. "It was only the bulb that broke. The lamp is fine, and Ruth Ann took responsibility for her mess."

Now that Annie was safe at home, I shifted my worry to Daddy. He was so quiet that it made the palms of my hands itch. Then finally he had something to say.

"Elizabeth, this here is a fine supper. I'm sorry I interrupted your fish sticks and all, but I do appreciate you cooking a fine meal. And I'm sorry I don't always tell you that. I think I'll just step out on the porch now." He carried his dishes to the sink too. For the first time ever that I saw.

I was holding my breath as he passed by me. "Ruth Ann, maybe you can give your mama a hand and help out with these dishes. And Annie, any of your creatures have a new trick you wanna show me?"

The clock on the wall ticked and tocked while all three of us stared at him. "You all right, Daddy?" Annie finally whispered.

"Never mind, I think I'll just go for a drive."

"No, Daddy, no. I got something to show you. I got a secret. Come on." She grabbed his hand and pulled him out.

Mama and I were doing the dishes when we heard the scream. She threw the kitchen door open and listened, not sure where that sound came from.

"Was that Annie?" I whispered into her shoulder.

"I have never heard such a thing." Mama's words sent a shiver through me. "Check the front porch and see if your sister and daddy are there."

I ran. No one. Back. "They're gone."

"Wait here," she ordered.

I couldn't. I took her hand. She didn't argue. We walked towards the barn. Barely out of the house, we heard the wailing. We ran.

"I'm scared, Mama."

"Quiet."

She'd been breathing hard and now she wasn't breathing at all. She slid the door open. Dim light. Daddy on the floor. Leaning against a post. Annie in his arms. Wailing. Sobbing.

"Daniel, for the love of God, what has happened?"

She dropped my hand and ran to them. In the corner, Buddy whined.

"Lizbeth, you best take this girl."

Mama slid to the ground. Daddy lifted Annie from his own lap to Mama's. Annie shook and sobbed. Daddy moved slowly towards Buddy. When he got close, Buddy tipped his head back and howled the most lonesome sound I ever did hear.

"Daddy? What is it? What happened?"

I couldn't tell if he heard me or not. And then Mama called out.

"Ruth Ann, help me for a moment, please. Let your father attend to things here. Please, help me lift Annie."

Limp like an old raggedy doll, I tried to pull Annie up. We got her to her knees. Mama stood. Finally, Annie stood beside her.

"What happened, Mama?" I asked.

"No, no, no, no, no! Don't say it!" Annie cried.

"Give your father a hand if he needs it. I'll get Annie in." Mama picked Annie up and carried her out of the barn.

When I turned back to Daddy, he was holding Shirley.

"Daddy? What happened?"

"Seems that Annie had a secret little gray kitty. Shirley was her name."

Until now I had never seen my daddy cry. In one hand he cradled Shirley's tiny body, in the other a shovel. I walked beside him to the spot where he dug the grave.

"She'll have good company here. She can romp and play with the others that little Annie does her best to save." His words ended with a whistle that slid between his teeth, as he let out the breath he was holding. He looked around like he might find an answer hiding in the shadows that grew longer as the moments passed.

CHAPTER 13

When Daddy and I finally got into the house, Mama had Annie cradled like a baby. Back and forth they rocked. I had questions and worries, but we all sat quiet while Annie whimpered and wept. I was as scared as I was sad. If it could happen to Shirley, couldn't it happen to any of the pets? Could it happen to us?

"We best get some sleep. The morning comes whether we like it or not." Daddy lifted Annie from Mama and carried her up the stairs. She was just as limp as Shirley, and that made me shiver. He put her in my bed and I crawled in beside her. During the night she shivered and cried, with her sweaty body pressed against me until Mama found us in the morning.

"Time to get up." Mama brushed Annie's damp hair back from her face. As soon as she felt Mama's hand, Annie whimpered like a baby doll whose batteries were nearly used up.

"Ruth Ann, if you feel as though you can concentrate today, I would like you to get ready for school. I will care for Annie."

Annie came out from under the covers and put her head on Mama's lap.

"Oh Annie. Dear, little Annie," Mama said as she rubbed her back.

After I finished up in the bathroom, Annie was back under the covers and Mama was in the kitchen serving up my breakfast.

"Mama?"

"Hmm?"

"What happened to Shirley?"

Mama's face twisted, "Her neck was broken. Perhaps she fell." Her voice was as flat as the land we lived on.

I couldn't breathe.

"I'm sorry. I wanted to answer your question and I don't know of an easier way to say it," she said.

"She didn't fall. She could climb anything. And how could she fall into that corner? That doesn't make sense." I wanted her to tell me why I was wrong. But she couldn't.

"I cannot explain it. Please do not discuss these details with your sister."

"But she found her. She knows where she was. She…"

"Ruth Ann, our minds are tricksters," Mama interrupted but didn't sound cross. "Sometimes they protect us from knowing the truth, if we're not ready to confront it."

I couldn't tell if Mama was talking to me, or to herself. I shivered, and my mind wandered back to the barn. I couldn't stop seeing little Shirley–breathless and still. Mama wiped at her face as she put my breakfast on the table. "Let's just move forward, shall we." She walked to the cupboard, pulled out her Anacin, shook them into her hand and sighed.

When I got to school, Heidi was all lovey-dovey. "Hey there Ruthie! Wait for me! Don't be mad. You look real nice today. My daddy says it'd be alright if I go home with you today. Then he'll pick me up later on. Maybe I could even stay and have supper," she rattled on like she was selling cattle at the auction.

"I don't know. I have stuff I'm supposed to do. Probably another day would be better." As I walked away my loneliness stuck like dung on my shoe. All the while she talked, I thought about how lonely I felt. I wanted to tell her everything, but I couldn't tell her anything. Shirley was still a secret. I remembered Mama saying that secrets and shame can kill a person and I felt like I was dying.

When school ended, I hopped on my bike and rode to the river, wondering if maybe I'd find Annie there. But then I remembered Grandpa spitting on Mama's kitchen floor and figured she'd never let her go with him again.

One minute he was doting on Annie like she was queen of the Sahara, and the next he was huffing and puffing and blowing the house down. He could change color faster than I could change socks. Just thinking about my grandpa sent a shiver up my spine.

As I crossed the bridge, I spotted a rusty old blue bike leaning against one of the posts that holds the bridge up: Matthew. But he was nowhere to be seen. Leaning my bike by the other post, I fumbled my way down the bank through bushes and stickers before I saw a trail that could have saved me a lot of pokes.

The river's edge was muddy and made me think about how Annie always came home from fishing looking like she'd been rolling around in a pigsty. When out of the corner of my eye I saw a brown lump, I startled and gasped. Just the broken limb of a tree. Not Shirley. This was a bad idea. I don't know what brought me here.

I had the creeps and didn't want to be alone. All the bad feelings wrapped around me like a Water Wiggle on the end of the hose: chasing and grabbing and getting tighter and tighter. If Dr. Molly or Heidi or Matthew was here, I knew

179

everything would be OK. I found a dry spot to sit, knowing that if Matthew spied Annie, maybe he would spy on me too and come and sit beside me.

I heard a rustle in the bushes. I jumped up and looked around. Nothing. I tossed a rock into the river. Blue birds, swallows and herons swooped and soared and called out while water tumbled over rocks, making baby waterfalls. Maybe being alone here wasn't so bad after all.

There it was again! Someone was coming. Or something? Just when I decided to get out of there, I remembered Matthew's bike and knew he must have seen me crossing the bridge. His footsteps came closer. I decided to fix a *happy to see you* look on my face. But I didn't want him to think I was *too* happy. *Crunch.* I stared ahead. *Throw your rock.* I couldn't let him know I was scared. *Throw another.* Branch breaks under his feet. *Stop being such a baby!*

"Hey there, honey." I spun around and there he was. Grandpa! "Don't often find you down by the crick."

"Geez! You scared me half to death!" I turned away. Another rock. *Don't cry!* My *happy to see you* face splashed with the last rock. I panicked. I looked everywhere for a little white sailor hat. "Where's Annie? Is Annie here too? What'd you do to Annie?" I spit my words and shook like I was half frozen.

"Simmer down there, Ruth Ann. Annie didn't feel like fishing today. She's a little under the weather. Thought you might know that."

"Where is she?"

"Well, I reckon she's still at home. I went by and your mama said she was resting. No need to be so prickly now."

"Oh. Well, I should be getting home to check on her. I was just getting ready to go, anyway."

"Now, now. Sit beside me for a spell. No need to rush off.

We never do spend time together the way Annie and me do. Just stay a spell."

He lowered himself down. With liquor and tobacco on his breath, he offered me a horehound drop, the most god-awful candy ever.

"No thanks." *Mind your manners*, I heard Mama say. "I don't think I do care for a sweet just now." *Be nice.* "Aren't you fishing today?"

"No. Now sometimes I like to just sit a spell. And ain't this a nice surprise seeing my grandbaby sitting by the river on this fine day. Ain't this a fine day, honey?" he asked around the edges of his candy.

"Yes, Grandpa, it's fine all right." *Get outa here! Get outa here!*

"Well then, why are you looking all hang dog? A pretty young girl ought be out chasing boys. Where's that boyfriend I seen you with? That Wright boy?"

"Nah, he's not my boyfriend. I guess I'm not so interested right now."

"Not interested? Now what kinda girl is not interested in a little loving from a boy?" And then he laughed and said, "I was your age when I met your grandma. I was courting her when I taught her to fish. Yes siree. Your granny was the sweetest girl in town. And I'll tell you what, it's time you started thinking about boys."

All I was thinking about was riding home as fast as I could. But then when I looked back down at the broken branch, I wanted to ask him why he made Annie keep Shirley a secret? But I didn't. I couldn't. I picked up a rock and tossed it at the river. It hit another rock and bounced right back and hit Grandpa in the front of his leg. It wasn't even hard.

"What the hell is that about?" I froze. "You ever throw a rock at me again and I swear I'll…" Spit flew from his mouth and I jumped up ready to run for it. He grabbed my ankle. The minute he had a hold, he stopped yelling. "Now Ruthie, let's you and me be friends. Whatcha say?" His thumb moved on my ankle. "Come on now, sit on down beside your grandpa."

I sat. And shook. He talked. "I know your daddy does a lot of traveling and all so maybe he doesn't take the time you need to learn about being around boys. And your mama, well maybe she's just too shy to teach you 'bout the birds and the bees. You know, when you got questions, you can always come to me. I'll take real good care of you. You being my grandbaby and all."

"Thanks, Grandpa." I squeezed the words out even though I could just barely get air in.

"No thanks needed, honey. What's a grandpa for?"

We sat as quiet and still as the bed of rocks we rested on. He started fiddling with a stick and said, "I was just a boy when I first started coming to the river. I don't know how the hell I got so old when it seems like just yesterday I was a young boy not any older than you. My grandpa used to bring us boys fishing every Sunday after church in the summertime. He was a helluva man. But my daddy? Well, that's a different story. He was one mean son-of-a-gun. He'd whup us boys if we didn't do exactly what he told us exactly when he told us. I remember one time going to school and I couldn't sit down on my chair being that my behind was so sore." His eyes were closed, and his head tipped back. "He was a son-of-a gun."

I half heard his story but mostly I was fixed on slipping a little further from him and every time I did, he knew it. He'd reach out and touch my leg, letting me know that even though his eyes were closed, he saw every move I made.

"Grandpa, I'm sorry to interrupt you but I really need to get home. Mama's gonna start to worry."

"One of the times he beat me was 'cause I was trying to save a litter of kittens that he was fixing on drowning."

The only way I knew he heard me was that his grip on my leg tightened.

"He didn't like that one bit and he whupped me bad. I was just a little tyke when he started beating me. But that didn't stop me from saving critters just like Annie."

With the mention of Annie's name, I thought about what Matthew said, and shivered.

"When your granny and I started courting, I used to bring her to the crick and we'd talk 'till the sun went down. She was nice to me just like my grandpa was. And she didn't seem to mind one little bit that I was saving critters anytime I could. She thought I was just fine for a long time. And then she had them babies and well, it was all different then."

Grandpa opened his eyes and caught me looking at him. "What the hell are you looking at? I don't know why you're prying into my business. Little Annie doesn't do no prying. She's a good girl. She loves her grandpa!"

"I wasn't prying. I was just listening. That's all."

I stared at the river, and he stared at me. Then he put his arm around my shoulder and pulled me close.

"Why ya'll shaky Ruth Ann? You cold? I'll warm you up real good. I think you and I just need to get to know each other. Maybe you can come to the river with me and I can teach you to fish. Would you like that?"

"Sure, I guess so," I lied.

"Well, I know sometimes I spoil Annie but that don't mean me and you can't get better acquainted now does it? Well, we should be heading back before it gets much later. Your old granny's gonna be wondering where I've gone off to."

I wiggled out from under Grandpa's arm and jumped up. I wanted to run. I stayed put. Grandpa rolled to his knees and pushed himself up from all fours. Together, we started up the trail. Through the bushes I saw a flash of blue. While grandpa watched where he put his feet, I watched Matthew creep out of sight.

"I parked on the other side of the bridge. Didn't you see my truck when you came on down here?"

"Nope. I didn't see it," I said, trying to keep my eyes fixed in front of me and not look around for Matthew.

"Now honey, you just wait over there with your bike and I'll pull up, pitch it in the back of the truck and you can ride on home with your grandpa. How's that sound to you?"

"Thanks, but I think I'll just go ahead and ride. It won't take me any time at all. But thanks a lot."

"Now honey, you listen here. You best just hop in the truck. I won't be taking no for an answer." Through my wall of hair hanging in front of my face I saw that he meant it. I headed for the bridge.

On the bridge, I sat on my bike waiting for Grandpa to pull up in his truck.

"Hey there, Ruth Ann."

"God almighty, Matthew!" I hollered. "You scared the living daylights out of me. Don't go sneaking up on a person like that."

"I thought you might like to ride home with me," he said, like he was reading my mind.

"I can't. I'm waiting for my grandpa." I kicked at the dirt. "But you knew that, didn't you?"

"I guess if I was waiting by the river, and somebody came sneaking up on me I'd be pretty scared too. You alright?"

"I'm alright," I muttered dropping my chin to my chest and feeling embarrassed about what he might have seen and heard.

"Let's ride home," he offered.

184

"My grandpa wants me to wait so he can give me a ride in his truck."

"Well, seems to me, maybe your grandpa would think it's just fine if you were riding home with your *boyfriend*."

I could hear his worry without even seeing it. "Matthew Wright, you were listening to everything that nasty old man said to me, weren't you?"

"I just thought I'd keep you company. I didn't want to find you–puking in the bushes."

I didn't know what to think but I knew what to do.

"Let's go home, Matthew."

We had just started peddling when Grandpa pulled up beside us blowing smoke and hollered, "I told you I'd be driving you on home."

I didn't even have a chance to answer before Matthew called out, "hey there Mr. Walker, I came along and asked Ruth Ann if she'd go for a bike ride with me, seeing that we're both headed to the same street and all. I hope you don't mind." A big ol' grin took up most of his face, just like he was pleased as punch to be speaking to my grandpa.

"Well, no now son, I don't mind at all. I was just telling Ruth Ann that what she needs is a boyfriend and lookie here, she's got herself one, quick as all that." He snickered. "No son. That's just fine. Ruth Ann, I'll be seeing you real soon. Maybe next time we can do us some fishing." Grandpa headed towards home right down the middle of the river road until a car coming towards him laid on their horn and he swerved over to his own side just in time.

When I walked into the kitchen, Mama spun around like a wooden top. "Ruth Ann Walker, where have you been?"

"I, uh, the river, and then Heidi, forgot, I–well, Matthew–and then Grandpa."

Daddy looked up from the newspaper like he was about to say something, but Mama jumped in. "After the incident yesterday, I need to have you close to home. Heidi indicated that she expected you to spend the afternoon with her. We have enough to worry about with Annie."

"Well, I was going to. Is Annie home? See, I thought I'd be, well, I went to the river..." Mama dropped her head and I stared at the streak of silver parting the black waves of her hair. She turned away from me, and her shoulders slouched with worry and defeat. It was Daddy who spoke next.

"Girlie, did you develop a stutter today? You aren't making one lick of sense. God almighty! What in tarnation were you doing at the river? Good God!"

"Daniel, please! Enough of that language!" Mama moaned.

"I'm sorry. I didn't mean to make you worry. I didn't think you would notice." The edge of my own hurt and worry sliced the air. I wanted to tell them what Matthew said. I wanted them to know how Grandpa made me feel. But mostly I wanted them to keep Annie safe.

"Mama?"

"Yes, Ruth Ann. What is it?" She turned to face me.

"Is Annie still feeling poorly?"

"She is. But I encouraged her to accept Merle's invitation to play. Your father drove her over after he got home from work. That was how I learned that you were not with Heidi. Why do you ask?"

"I don't know. I just wondered." I held my breath but let my words tumble out like water over the McAllister Falls. "I wondered if she'd be fishing with Grandpa anymore?"

Mama put her hands on her hips and Daddy folded up his newspaper. "Your grandpa has temper tantrums. Always has. Always will. He's been a spitter my whole life. But he's still my daddy and your grandpa. There's no changing that."

I wiped my sweaty palms on my jeans and knew that they

might punish me for saying what was on my mind, but I was saying it anyhow.

"I don't want Annie fishing with him anymore. I don't want you to let her." *I don't want him to be my family anymore,* were the words I didn't say.

Even though I never saw her wet them, Mama dried her hands on her apron, and chewed on her lip, while Daddy chewed on me. "When you're the mama, you get to decide!" he hollered. "But, for now, it's not up to you. You stay out of it!" Daddy said, rolling up his newspaper like he was fixing to swat at something. Mama kept wiping and chewing. But neither one of them could hush me up.

"No. It's just not right! You know Grandpa acts crazy sometimes. Why does everybody pretend that it's not true?"

"Now you just simmer down, Ruth Ann. You got to learn to mind your p's and q's. Yesterday's all done and paid for. Your mama and me will be taking care of things with your sister."

"Enough of this!" Mama spit. "I don't know why we are even talking about your grandfather. Annie is with Merle. You are home. Please get cleaned up for supper." Mama straightened up, smoothed her apron, and went back to cooking.

"Why did you say you have *enough to worry about with Annie?*" I asked like I hadn't been dismissed.

Mama exhaled hard, spun around again to face me, pushed up her glasses, and stared.

"Ruth Ann Walker, if we wanted you to be a part of the conversation we were having in your absence, we would not have had the conversation…in your absence. Quite frankly, it is none of your concern."

"Annie is my concern! I worry about her too, you know!" Tears shot out of my eyes like a popped blister.

Daddy's chair squealed as he pushed back from the table,

stood up, and came at me. His shiny black shoes moved slow and steady the four or five steps between us. I was shaking like salt but couldn't talk myself into looking up to see if he really was coming my way or walking past on his way to the toilet. I squeezed my tears back and my butt cheeks tight.

And then he wrapped around me and whispered, "ah Ruthie, you let your mama and me take care of little Annie. No need for you to be sloshing through a trough of tears."

The stubble on his face caught my hair as he raised his head, "Elizabeth, why don't you come over here and give this girl some lovin'?" He opened up one arm and Mama came into his hug too. The three of us stood there until the oven timer went off and Mama peeled off like the skin of an onion. What was left, just Daddy and me, felt tender and raw.

"Now sport, no need to keep the faucets running." He stepped back, pulled out his hankie, and wiped my tears.

"Thank you, Daddy."

"Actually Ruth Ann, the faucet that does need to be turned on is the one in the tub," Mama said. "Supper will be ready in about thirty minutes; just enough time for you to wash off your encounter with the river. Annie will be home at that time as well. Toddle along."

I was drying off when Annie knocked on the door. "I'll be out in a minute," I called, thinking she could use the toilet downstairs and let me be. Wrapped in my towel, I opened the door. She looked at me like she was looking at a ghost.

"What's wrong? What happened now?" My mind raced around to Buddy and Beats and Gertrude or Lilly. Was another one of our pets...I couldn't even finish the thought in my own head. "You're scaring me with that look on your face."

"Mama said you went fishing." Her words dribbled out like the last of the ketchup that wants to stay put in the bottle.

"I was at the river, but I wasn't fishing," I corrected, holding my towel around me with one hand.

Now she was the one who looked like a ghost. "Then why were you at the river–" Her eyes and her voice dropped, "with him?"

"Girls! Supper's ready!" Mama called.

Without looking up, Annie backed away. With my free hand I tried to grab her, but she was gone.

"This is a quiet bunch," Daddy said, even though every other night of my life that's what he wanted. "Annie, what kind of trouble did you and Merle get into today?" he winked.

"We didn't do nothing, Daddy, I swear," she answered like he meant it.

"Now, now, Annie, I was just making fun." He reached across the table and touched her shoulder. "I know, sport, I know."

After that, Daddy seemed to lose interest in his supper too and left the three of us pushing food around our plates. Annie put down her fork, picked up her plate and started for the sink without even asking if she could be excused.

"Annie, sit back, please."

But she just kept walking.

"Annie! I have asked that you retake your place at the table," Mama said in that way she had of shouting without raising her voice.

Annie stopped walking but didn't turn back. And that's when I just couldn't keep my mouth shut. "It's just not fair! I don't know what's going on with Annie. I can't ask about Shirley. Grandpa spit on the kitchen floor and everybody's trying to act like it didn't happen! Mama, you said secrets lead to shame and this house is nothing but secrets so I figure we must all be filled up with shame too!"

CRASH!!! China and mashed potatoes exploded as Annie dropped her plate. She didn't move. But Mama did.

"For the love of God, Annie! What are you thinking?" But when she rushed over and took Annie by the shoulders, she pulled her close. Mama held her as I watched the pile of potatoes at her feet change color. Quiet as could be, I pushed back from the table and walked closer.

"Mama, Annie's bleeding."

They both looked down and Annie got so wobbly Mama just barely caught her before she toppled over. "It hurts, Mama. It hurts real bad," Annie cried out.

"Ruth Ann, call Dr. White at once."

"No! Not him. Not him. Can't Dr. Molly help? Please, Mama," Annie begged.

"Mama, Annie doesn't like Dr. White. Don't you thi–"

"Just do it!" she shouted as she scooped Annie up and put her on the counter with her feet in the sink. That's when Daddy walked in.

"What in tarnation!" he said.

I ran to the hall and called Dr. Molly, without even thinking about what I was asking for or what Mama or Daddy would have to say. She picked up the phone and hearing her voice made me forget my own.

"Hello? Who's there?" she asked.

"Uh, Dr. Molly. Is that you? It's me. Ruth Ann Walker. Uh…"

"What's wrong, Ruth Ann? Are you OK?"

"Annie's feet are bleeding and–uh–Shirley died."

"Oh my land! Has there been an accident? Who's Shirley? Have you called the police?"

"No, it was a plate of potatoes." I couldn't even hear her breathing. "Dr. Molly? Are you still there?"

"I must have misunderstood. I thought you said a plate of potatoes?" She sounded just as confused and scared as I was feeling. That's when Mama grabbed the phone away from me.

"Hello, Dr. White? Oh, Molly, how did–? Well, yes. No, no. Shirley was a kitten. Another time. Yes, her feet. Well, Ruth Ann was instructed–of course–that would be helpful, yes. Surely. No, not Shirley. Right. Thank you so."

"Is she coming? How bad is it?"

"How dare you place me in this position! I clearly instructed you to...oh, what were you thinking? You have made a difficult situation worse, Ruth Ann! We will be discussing this further. And what am I to say to your father? And yes, she is coming. Although she is not the appropriate person for the job, I hope that Molly can assure us that there is nothing broken."

"Something is broken," I said.

"For heaven's sake, Ruth Ann. You know what I am referring to."

"I'm sorry I didn't do like you said. It's just that–"

"It is just like nothing!" Mama stormed off.

I went back into the kitchen where Annie was lying with her back on the counter and her head on a stack of potholders. Daddy had both her feet in the air pressing on them with a towel soaked with blood.

"Hey Annie, you feeling alright?" I smoothed her hair back and rubbed her head. Her eyes were closed.

"Daddy, is she OK?" I choked.

"She'll be fine, Ruthie. Won't you Annie? You'll be good as new."

I shuddered. I pictured Shirley. Daddy carrying her out of the barn. Even though he tried to make me believe that Annie would be OK, my head spun with worry. She was as limp as that poor little kitty.

"Here Daniel. Try this." Mama handed Daddy ice cubes wrapped in a clean white cloth.

191

He took it from her, looked down and said, "just a minute. Trade me places, Elizabeth."

Annie opened her eyes when Mama took her feet. "Don't leave me Daddy. Don't go away again."

"Hey there, sport. I'll be back in a flash."

"Where are you going, Daddy?" Annie's worry echoed in my brain, but the door slammed behind him, and if he said anything, I couldn't hear it. Once outside, twin beams of light flooded him as if he had walked onto the stage of a play. He stopped and looked towards Dr. Molly's truck, and then disappeared into the glove of night.

"Molly, thank you for coming," Mama whispered.

"Well, look at you," Dr. Molly said to Annie who looked so woozy that I was surprised she could lift her head.

"Dr. Molly, you're here, you're here," Annie murmured. "I was worried that–"

"Hush, Annie. Just let Dr. Molly–" Mama's words were pushed to the side when Daddy pushed the door open.

"Here you be, Annie. Crushed ice is gonna feel a might better than sharp edged cubes poking into your soreness."

"Daniel, it's nice to see you," Dr. Molly tried.

"Harrumph," Daddy grunted back. "I thought Doc White was on his way."

"I'm only here to help. I can leave–" Dr. Molly drew in her breath and looked right at my daddy.

"I called her, Daddy. Annie doesn't feel comfortable with–"

"You best do as you're told," he grumbled without looking at me.

"Daniel, I will address this issue with Ruth Ann at another time. Now is the time to allow Dr. Molly to take a look at Annie's injury."

"Now Annie, I'll just be out here on the porch." Daddy jammed his hands in his pockets, "Don't you worry. Just making space for the...uh..." he backed away, "...doctor to take a look at them cuts. Holler out if you need anything." His eyes traveled from Annie to me. "You come outside where you can't stir up any more trouble."

Annie pulled me down and whispered, "Don't let him go, Ruthie. Don't let him leave us."

"You don't need to worry about a thing. Daddy and me, we'll be on the porch." Trying to not let Annie's real worry drift into the light, my voice broke the quiet like Daddy's hammer to ice. But when we got outside, my own troubles spilled into the night with a whisper, "Daddy, I'm sorry for misbehaving and for the things I said to you..."

"You need to learn to do as you're told. That's the truth of it. As for that business of you breaking the lamp and cursing at me, well, that fish is fried. We can't put it back in the river so, no point in, well, that's just how it is." He put his hands deep into his pockets and looked out at the stars sparkling in the sky like diamonds dancing. "I didn't hear how it was that Annie got hurt?"

"Well, it was almost like she forgot she was holding her plate, and poof! It dropped."

"Hmm. That don't seem right."

His words drifted into the background while my brain picked at a scab.

"Hey Daddy, talking about things that don't seem right; what happened to Shirley?"

He pulled both hands out of his pockets, dropped his head down and pushed his hair up. But then he shoved them back in and said, "well, her neck broke."

"But how?"

"That's the thing. It was almost like...oh, I don't know."

"Almost like what?"

"Well, when I was a kid, if there were too many kittens, well, sometimes...I can't say Ruth Ann. It's bad business.

193

It's..." I could hear him swallow, or choke back tears, I'm not sure.

"My daddy, he was a mean son of a gun. I couldn't make like I cared 'cause that seemed to be enough for him to–"

"Did he kill the kittens, Daddy?" My voice trembled as I asked a question I didn't want the answer to.

"Now I can't say what happened to Shirley. Nobody saw. I just know it wasn't right. T'wasn't right at all."

"I didn't mean Shirley." My breath caught. Tears filled my eyes.

"It's bad business, Ruthie. It's bad business." His voice drifted away. My mind did too. I felt sick to my stomach. I thought about Grandpa beside the river...*just like Annie...* that's what he said. *Saving critters anytime I could.* Was it just one more lie? I shivered. Daddy draped his arm over my shoulder. Without saying a thing, he pulled me close.

"Daniel, Ruth Ann, Annie is back among the living," Mama said through the screen.

"Well, that's fine. Yes siree."

He turned away and we turned the page. No more talk about Shirley or dying kittens. When we went back into the kitchen, Annie was sitting on the edge of the counter, slurping on a banana Popsicle and Dr. Molly was closing up her bag.

"It's all fixed up. Look, Ruthie." Annie held up her bandaged foot. "And I didn't even scream."

"That's fine, just fine," Daddy mumbled. "Now there, uh, I want to thank you for, uh, helping out this little squirt." He shuffled from one foot to the other like he was asking a girl to dance. "I do appreciate all that you, uh, that you done for my here family...kind of you."

"I'm glad I could help." Dr. Molly reached over and touched Annie's head. "Now, no more clumsy plate dropping from you, young lady." She winked at Annie and then looked over at my mama who was rinsing out rags in the sink.

"Elizabeth, probably would be good to take a looksee at Annie in a day or two just to make sure everything's healing up nicely.

"That'd be fine, just fine," Daddy answered for her.

Mama looked at him and asked, "Daniel, perhaps I can take the girls over to Molly's one day this week to follow up?"

"Like I said, that'd be fine." And then he turned to Annie. "Squirt, did you bleed on all the food or just your own plate? All this hullaballoo has worked up my appetite."

"Oh, I only bled on my potatoes, Daddy. That's just ketchup on the meatloaf."

While they laughed with Annie, my mind raced around the farm like a hen running from a hatchet. If I couldn't keep Annie safe from herself, how could I keep anybody safe?

CHAPTER 14

"Brrr, Ruth Ann, are you bringing the cold in with you?" Cheryl smiled at the three of us and said, "you must be Elizabeth. I've heard so many wonderful things about you."

"And you must be Cheryl of hot cocoa and cookie fame." Mama smiled right back.

Dr. Molly came out. "My last patient of the day, and my favorite one to boot. It won't take but a minute to take a look and make sure I didn't miss any broken bones or bits of mashed potatoes that snuck in through the cracks."

"Yeah, maybe a new potato is gonna sprout right out of my foot!" Annie moved around the room like she was dragging roots behind her.

"You are being very silly, Annie." Mama's voice was soft and warm, but she wasn't one to overstay her welcome. "Let Dr. Molly examine your foot, potato and all, so she and Cheryl can close up the office."

"Elizabeth, if you and the girls are free this evening, would you like to drive over to the lake and have supper with us?" Dr. Molly kept talking, but my mind got caught on the *us* I was trying to make sense of.

"Daniel is out of town but..." Mama said, answering a question I didn't hear.

"Please, Mama, please," we started but her *stop it now* look worked and we turned to stone, caught in the act of begging.

"We cannot, as I have committed to setting the girl's grandmother's hair after supper. She is a stickler for routine, so I am afraid it is not a good night for us. But thank you so much for your kindness."

"But what about us, Mama? We're not putting pins and curls in Grandma's hair. Can we go?" Annie asked, hopping up and down on one foot. After a good amount of pitiful pleading and promises, Mama agreed, and Dr. Molly said she'd be happy to drive us back home after supper.

The question of *us* got answered when we climbed into the backseat of Cheryl's car and waved to Mama as she drove towards home and we drove away on our adventure. The narrow, winding road crossed over the McAllister River and took more twists and turns than any other strip of pavement in Emmett County.

When we finally pulled up to the little yellow house sitting on the edge of Squam Lake, I half expected to see Dorothy clicking her ruby red slippers with Toto in her arms. We were that far away.

"Dr. Molly, is this where you live?" Annie asked in amazement. "Is that your very own beach? I never saw anybody's house on a beach before. Have you, Ruthie?"

"'Course not. How could I if you didn't?" The look on Annie's face made me realize how snotty I sounded. But Annie shook it off like a nasty flea and ran to Dr. Molly.

"Can we touch the water, please, pretty please?"

They both smiled and laughed, and Dr. Molly answered, "sure, but don't get your foot wet!" When we were at the water's edge she called out, "there will be no wild horses on the beach tonight with that foot healing, Miss Annie!" We stopped and looked back at the two of them.

They were looking into the sun that was just about to drop into the lake and shading their eyes. Annie lifted her hand, gave them a quick salute, and laughed as she turned back around. We were tossing rocks when Dr. Molly walked down and scooped up her own to throw. "Come July and August this is a fine lake for swimming. Cheryl and I swim most days of the summer."

"Does Cheryl live nearby?" I asked.

Dr. Molly blinked her eyes, looked over at Cheryl, and opened her mouth to speak, but Annie's words came out first.

"Shirley died." Dr. Molly scooped Annie up and held her. When she put her down, she knelt in front of her and waited.

"She was a secret. Grandpa said so. And then she died. She was mine."

My eyes filled with tears as Annie choked on her own. "Why did she die, Dr. Molly? I wish you could have saved her."

"Ah sweet, little Annie. I am so sorry. I wish I could've too." Dr. Molly looked at me and back at Annie. She held both her hands when she asked, "why was she a secret?"

"She just was." Annie stepped away from Dr. Molly and threw another rock into the water. "I'm hungry."

"But Annie, why did Grandpa tell you to keep her a secret? Maybe you didn't hear him right. Grandpa says all kinds of crazy things he doesn't mean," I tried.

She threw another rock and Dr. Molly looked at me and shook her head and I knew it wasn't the time to ask more questions.

"Well girls, what do you think about our lake?"

"I like it fine. Can we come back in the summertime and go for a swim? We like to swim, don't we, Annie?"

Annie scooched down sorting through the rocks and sand.

"Wouldn't it be nice to swim, Annie?" I asked again.

"Well, I can tell you this, when I was a young girl, I never dreamed that someday I would be living with a lake as my neighbor and jumping in any time I pleased," Dr. Molly said into the space that Annie left open.

Annie thought for another minute before she said, "I can imagine just fine living here in a house just like this one and eating barbecue and going swimming and not having nobody telling me what to do." She stopped for a minute and looked up. "Hey, Dr. Molly?"

"Yes, Annie."

"We're not eating fish for our supper, are we?"

"Why no, we're having Cheryl's special lasagna with garlic bread and salad. That alright by you?"

"Yeah. That's just fine," she mumbled into the ground.

"Honey, what's wrong?" Dr. Molly asked in a whisper as she knelt back down again.

"Nothing. I just hate fish, that's all."

"That's not true, Annie–" I didn't need Dr. Molly to shush me this time. I closed my mouth, but questions about Shirley and Cheryl and Grandpa bubbled over like lava inside my brain.

"No fish for you, little bambina!" Dr. Molly announced with an accent and a pinch of Annie's cheek.

"Oh, I see Molly's practicing her Italian." Cheryl laughed and surprised us all. "What a beautiful sunset this is going to be!" She smiled into the setting sun. "I hate to interrupt but supper is ready."

"Good, I'm hungry," I said as Cheryl reached out her hand

to Annie. Walking behind with Dr. Molly, I got to wondering what it would take to make things better. Three dogs with smiles on their faces wiggled and whined the minute we stepped inside. That answered my question. For now.

WITH A MOUTHFUL OF LASAGNA, I asked, "Cheryl, are you I-talian?"

"No. I just happen to love good Italian food. In Chicago there's lots of places to get it but here in Squam Lake, it's just the pizza parlor. So we make what we can here at home."

"Our grandpa says you can't trust the I-talians," Annie added, "he says they're just like the Jews. They'll steal–"

"Shush, Annie!" A little bit of red sauce came out with my *shush* and I was so upset by that itty bity dot of red on the white tablecloth that I nearly forgot all about Annie 'till she started up again.

"But, Ruthie, you know it's true–"

"OK, girls. Let's enjoy supper. Now who wants to tell me what the fastest animal in the whole world is?" Cheryl asked.

Both Annie and I shot our hands in the air like we were sitting in school. For the rest of supper, we talked about all the different kinds of animals that Dr. Molly helped out when she was working for the zoo in Chicago before she came to Amesville. That got us through supper without any more talk about who Grandpa hates and why.

"Thank you for a delicious supper, Cheryl," Dr. Molly said and volunteered the two of us for kitchen cleanup which was fine by me.

While we started cleaning, Cheryl asked Annie, "how 'bout we take these wild beasts for a walk while the girls get their job done?"

"Really? All of them?" Annie squealed like she was a blue-ribbon winner at the county fair.

Cheryl warned her before they left, "now Annie, walking three dogs at once is tricky business. One of us has to take two at a time."

Annie squealed again, "I'll take two, Miss Cheryl. I could take the little ones and you take the big one."

"Alright then, Scotty and Sam are all yours and I'll take Wilbur."

Annie laughed and asked, "how come you got a dog named Wilbur?"

With a grin on her face and eyes that twinkled, Cheryl said, "because silly, Wilbur was the runt of the litter and Charlotte's Web is my very favorite story." She puffed up in a funny sort of way and Dr. Molly laughed and went across the room to hug her.

Annie stood there thinking. Then she blurted out, "but Cheryl, that's a little kid's book. Why is a little kid's book your favorite? Our mama reads lots of books but they're big fat books for grownups"

When nobody answered Annie's question, she asked, "is that a bad question too?"

"It's not a *bad* question. But the answer is way too long for a short walk. Let's say you and I get these dogs out of here before they twist themselves in two?"

Cheryl brushed some crumbs of truth away the way that Mama does and that got me wondering. After they left, I asked Dr. Molly if it really was OK with Cheryl that we were there for supper. I knew something seemed wrong, but I didn't know what it could be.

"Cheryl's just as pleased as can be that you and Annie are here. Her story is a complicated one. Well, I suppose all our lives have complications, don't they? Back in Illinois, she has loads of family. But they have a hard time with...well, they aren't any too interested in visiting us here in Iowa."

"Do they think it's too far to drive?" I asked.

"Hmm, no, but let's talk about you, Ruth Ann. How are things going at home? Can you tell me more about Shirley? I still haven't gotten the story straight."

I looked at Dr. Molly like she was asking me to tell her about the sun. What's there to say? It's up. It's down. But pretty soon words tumbled out that I didn't even know were in me.

"Well, I guess Grandpa gave Annie a kitten and told her not to tell. But she did tell Mama and me. And then she was just about to show her to Daddy and that's when–"

"Oh honey, you don't have to say more about the end. But do you know why she was a secret?"

"No. But Grandpa's, well, he's–well, Mama says he's complicated. He can be nice as pie one minute and then... well, sometimes he's scary. He spit on Mama's kitchen floor."

"Oh my!" Dr. Molly said and she stopped washing and stared at me with her mouth hanging open. "We do seem to be going from one bad story to the next, don't we?"

I felt like a combine in the field with chaff and grain spewing out almost faster than I could keep up. I wasn't out of words, but I was out of steam. Catching my breath, I asked, "could you tell me about when you and Cheryl first knew you'd be living here on the lake?"

Dr. Molly had just opened her mouth when the front door burst open and all three dogs ran in, looking like Dasher, Dancer and Rudolph, pulling Annie like she was steering Santa's sleigh. She let go of their leashes, slid to a stop and asked, "what's up, doc?"

Dr. Molly laughed. "I was just telling your big sister about the first time Cheryl came to stay.

Annie looked at Cheryl and asked, "why'd you stay?"

Her voice was just as gentle now as the first time I heard it. "I stayed because when Molly and I were sitting out on the front porch sipping iced tea, watching a storm pass over the lake, I knew I was home. I had never felt so certain about anything in all my life. But with Molly, I knew I was home."

WITH THE SWEETNESS of dessert still lingering, we piled into Cheryl's Chevy for the drive home. At the bridge over the McAllister River a truck pulled up behind us with its lights on bright.

"Why are they following so close?" I asked.

"Well, honey, I guess they're in a bigger hurry than we are," Dr. Molly said.

"I just can't go any faster. It's impossible to see out here. This fog is awful," Cheryl mumbled as she flipped her mirror up trying to get that bright light out of her eyes. Moving along that winding road was like trying to find our way through the feathers of a pillow.

"I don't like this one bit. Not one little bit." Cheryl sounded scared, and that scared me.

Molly reached over and touched her knee. "Honey, maybe you should pull over and let them pass. It must just be some darn kids out drinking."

Cheryl's voice shook. "There's no place to pull over for a mile."

Without saying a thing. Dr. Molly turned to us, "well now, the evening just wouldn't be complete without a little excitement on the way home."

She tried to make her voice sound calm and breezy, but the headlights lit her face. Her chin trembled, and I half expected tears to fall. She looked more sad than scared. That confused me. I reached over and squeezed Annie's hand until she wiggled her fingers loose. She scooched closer and looked up at me with eyes huge with worry.

Finally, Cheryl pulled over and stopped. The truck stopped too. Right beside Cheryl's window. The passenger window was open. Smoke billowed out.

"Scooch down back there, girls. They're just having their fun. That's all."

"I don't know what to do," Cheryl whispered.

"Now honey, you just wait for them to go on by."

The silence was broken when Annie whimpered. I pulled her down onto the floor of the car with me. "Can't you make 'em go away?" she pleaded.

Hiding in the back seat didn't hide us from the sound of his voice. Loud and clear he hollered through our closed windows.

"I know who you are! Yes, siree, I know! The flames of Hell are about to singe your sins! You better watch your back girlie girl, 'cause you never know who might meet you in the dark and show you what you're missing."

He laughed with the wickedness of the devil himself and raced down the road. It wasn't kids having fun. I lifted my head just in time to see red taillights through the storm of dirt and gravel that pounded the Chevy like hail.

When Dr. Molly reached her hand back to see if we were OK, we both jumped, and Annie's head bonked into my chin and I bit my lip something awful.

"I'm sorry," Dr. Molly said. I'm not sure what she was sorry for but the tears she had been holding broke her voice open, and she apologized again. This time for crying.

"It's not your fault–" I didn't know what else to say. I tasted blood.

"Annie? Are you alright?" Dr. Molly reached out again trying to touch her. But Annie smooshed her head into my sweaty armpit.

"She'll be OK. Won't you, Annie?" I tried, not sure that either one of us would ever really be OK.

In the quiet, I heard Cheryl crying too.

"Oh, honey. We're all safe and sound." Dr. Molly tried to comfort Cheryl while I was trying to comfort Annie who couldn't stop shaking. I knew she knew. The sound of the truck was gone. But my grandpa's laugh, as he raced away, was still roaring in my head.

"There you are. I was beginning to wonder if your grand adventure was going to last until dawn." The lines in Mama's face were soft, and she smiled as she held the door for us.

With Dr. Molly holding Annie in one arm and my hand with the other, we walked towards her. As soon as we stepped into the flood of light that spilled out from the kitchen door, Mama's face changed.

"What in the world? Molly? What's happened?" she accused. Daddy stepped into the room and then past her. He took Annie from her arms. "I trusted you."

"I know you did. Daniel, you have to let me explain–"

"I don't have to do nothing of the sort."

"Daddy–"

"Hush now, Ruth Ann. Dr. Molly has some answering to do," he snapped.

"But you won't let her," I said.

"I said hush," he repeated.

"No Daddy. No. It wasn't her. It wasn't her," Annie wailed.

"You go on in, Annie. You too, Ruth Ann." He put Annie down and swatted at her bottom to move along.

"It wasn't her," Annie said through sobs. I stood beside her and pulled her close. I felt so lightheaded that I think part of holding Annie was holding myself up.

"Please listen, Daniel. Please," Dr. Molly said then turned to Mama. "Elizabeth, please let me explain."

"Daniel, we are jumping to conclusions," Mama said.

He looked at her and back at Annie. "What happened?" Daddy demanded.

"Your children are scared. Please don't ask them to relive what they are still...please let them to go inside while I explain." I stepped away from Annie and over to Dr. Molly. Annie followed me and stood on the other side. I was scared but it didn't seem right to leave her alone with my daddy scowling and stomping.

"What happened?" Daddy folded his arms and stood with his feet spread apart waiting.

Dr. Molly spit the story out like she was trying to save herself from being drawn and quartered.

"Girls, is that what happened?" Daddy looked down and asked us both right in front of Dr. Molly like she'd be lying.

"It wasn't her," Annie said again.

"We understand that, Annie. What your father is asking is—"

"For the love of God, Elizabeth, they know what I'm asking. Is she telling the truth?"

"Yes, Daddy," we both said at once.

"Well then. I'm sorry for your trouble. You all had quite a fright. Your, uh, friend gonna be all right to drive you back home?"

"I'll drive us home. But yes, we'll be fine. Thank you, Daniel." Tears fell out with her thanks, she gave us each a squeeze and turned to go.

"Now, now. Not so fast," Daddy said.

Dr. Molly spun around and waited for the next blow. Her eyes and face were wet and shiny as she stood in the edge of the light.

"Girls, you thank Dr. Molly proper while I get my keys."

"Daniel, what are you doing?" Mama asked.

"I'm not about to let two ladies return our children and get back on the road alone with a lunatic out there." As he went to get his keys, he said, "I'll just follow behind. Simple as that."

Mama had her arms around us as Daddy pulled out behind the Chevy with Dr. Molly easing onto the road. They both swerved out of the way of Grandpa's truck as he turned into his drive.

CHAPTER 15

*A*nnie snored as I tiptoed out of the room towards the smell of bacon frying on Sunday morning.

"Where you going?" She bolted up as if her head was attached to the doorknob in my hand.

"Downstairs. Keep sleeping."

"No. I'll go with you." She jumped from her bunk so fast she just barely kept from falling.

"Annie, you're still so sleepy, you can barely stand up."

"Yes, I can. No, I'm not," she stammered.

"Well, I have to go to the bathroom first."

"Me too." She came into the bathroom with me.

"What's the matter? Are you still scared?"

"No."

"Well, it's OK if you are."

"I'm not…maybe a little bit. Maybe."

"Girls, what is going on in there? Why are you still in the bathroom?"

I opened the door.

"Morning Mama. We're hungry. We were just talking about breakfast and stuff."

"Well, speaking of *stuff,* your grandparents are coming for supper this evening." Mama was putting away a stack of clean towels when Annie and I looked at each other. "I know we have not spoken with your grandfather since that unfortunate debacle last week..."

She turned and looked at us. "Now, girls, please don't give me that look. They are family, after all. *Family comes before feelings.* I cannot expect that your grandfather will apologize for his misbehavior. And, quite frankly, he can be a despicable man, but that is neither here nor there."

"Mama, I was just telling Ruthie that I'm not feeling all that well."

"Now, Annie. If this is a stunt to get out of seeing your grandparents, I will not have it. If you really are continuing to feel poorly, then tomorrow, in lieu of school in the morning, we really must make a visit to Dr. White."

"That's OK. I'm going back to bed," she said. "But Ruthie, will you stay with me?" Her voice shook.

Mama let loose an exasperated sigh, folded her arms, and leaned back on the frame of the door. "Girls, he is your grandfather. Please help me to keep the peace." Mama looked at her feet and then up again. "And I know that you both were exposed to a vile creature on the road last night, but we really must leave that behind and concentrate on getting along with your grandparents, to the best of our ability."

"But Mama, you know how he is. Why do you make us?"

"Family. It is as simple as that. And I need your help. Your grandmother has a bag of pecans on her front porch. I thought it would be a nice gesture if the two of you make tonight's pie. How does that sound?"

"Horrible." I didn't care if Mama got mad at me, but I had to take care of Annie. "I'll do it. Just don't make Annie."

"But Ruthie, I need you," Annie cried.

"Annie, you do not need to be so fearful. Your father

drove the entire road and back again and never came upon the monster who screamed those foul things. In all likelihood, he is from another county and was on a drunken binge and will never be heard from again. Trust me, Annie."

Mama knelt down. "I promise to keep you safe. I would not let anyone hurt you. Don't you understand? That is why we proceeded with caution in regard to Dr. Molly. While we do not want to take gossip as gospel, I do need to pay attention to even those who are seemingly safe. And to my relief, she has proven herself to be entirely trustworthy. That example should give you some peace of mind and trust in my ability to care for you."

She didn't understand. She was wrong. I couldn't tell her that we weren't safe.

"OK, Mama. We'll be down in a minute. I was just getting ready to find a new book to read to Annie. Right, Annie?"

Annie nodded.

"Hurry along, then. Your breakfast will be getting cold."

"Annie, is it *him* you're afraid of?"

She nodded again. Her body started to shake.

"He can't hurt you. I won't let him."

"He can, Ruthie. You don't know. Nobody does."

"What do you mean? What don't I know?" I asked, glancing at the door, afraid that Mama would barge back in any minute.

"He said so. He said I can't tell."

"What are you talking about?" I thought we were talking about the road last night. I was wrong. What else is it?"

Annie's eyes went blank. I couldn't see her fear anymore. She was standing in front of me, but she was gone.

"Annie," I tried.

"We best eat breakfast, before it gets too cold." She walked out of our room and down the stairs.

· · ·

MAMA CHATTERED AS WE ATE. It was like the farm report on the radio. Background noise I didn't pay any attention to. And then Gertrude reared up outside the window. Annie dropped her fork and I screamed.

"Good grief, girls. I am sorry that you were frightened but this is a bit extreme," Mama scolded.

"Mama," my voice cracked. Annie looked up at me and pleaded with her eyes.

"Yes, Ruth Ann. Do help me to understand."

"It was scary. That's all," I said and watched Mama drift away.

Her voice softened. "Did I ever tell you the story of the bear in Alaska? Oh my, I was sitting on a pier and the tide was low…"

She may as well have been listing the price of corn and soybeans as she told the story again; the time *she* was afraid; the way that *she* was brave. The FACT that there was *nothing that could possibly be as scary as a black bear in the wilds of Alaska.* "Are you even listening to me?"

I wanted her to be the storyteller in the family. Just not now. I wanted her to listen to what we weren't saying so she would know the truth without us telling her. But it wasn't like that. Breakfast was over, and Annie and I crossed the road to get pecans for the pie.

"Ruthie?"

"Yeah."

"We need to tell."

"Tell who, what?" I asked, my heart beating like the wings of a bat trapped in the barn.

"I dunno. We just gotta tell somebody."

I thought about Dr. Molly as I bent over and picked up the sack of nuts. From the side of the house, Buddy charged, wagging his tail and barking. We both jumped back, and Annie hollered, "don't sneak up on people like that you stupid dog!" His tail went between his legs and the smile on his face was gone. He rolled to the ground, his belly up. "Get outa here. Git!" Annie yelled again.

"Annie! Stop it! Just stop it!" I cried.

She looked at me with the terror I felt. She dropped to her knees. I dropped the nuts. Buddy whimpered, got to his feet and slunk away. Annie sobbed without a sound.

"Annie," I whispered. "I'll take care of you. I'll do something. I don't know what, but something. I swear I will."

"He can get us. He can get us anytime he pleases. He said–…" Her words choked into silence by tears. The sound of Grandpa's truck roared like thunder. We both flinched like we'd been hit.

"He's home," I whispered the obvious. "Help me get the pecans back, quick." Snot and tears ran down both of our faces and we ducked like robbers, slinking into the shadows along the edge of the house.

I grabbed Annie's hand and stopped her. "Come on. Wait a minute. He'll drive out back and we'll make a run for it. Take your boots off so we can make a run for it." We ran.

"Ruthie!" Annie shouted in a whisper. I felt her pulling back. I kept running, nearly dragging her. "My boot!" she cried out.

"We can't stop now!" I yelled as we crossed the road. When we were safe in the shadows of our own house I said, "we'll get your boot later, when the coast is clear I'll go back for it." And then I asked what I was most afraid of knowing, "what did he say? What were you talking about?"

"Nothing. Nobody said nothing." Her eyes were wide and dry but tracks from her tears glistened like moon beams in the morning light. She was just as far away as Mama's Alaska.

We stared at each other listening for the sound of his breathing or his shuffling in our direction. But what we heard instead was Mama. The back door opened. We pressed into the wall. She blew the whistle. *Preet!!! Preet!!!* Nuts flew against the house as my hand flew to my mouth. The sack, now emptied yet again, floated down and landed on top of my head, and that's what Mama saw when she peered around the corner.

"What in the world are you two up to? A simple task of retrieving pecans for a pie becomes a comedic event in which Laurel and Hardy are given a run for their money. And Annie, I can see you hiding behind your sister," Mama laughed. "Re-gather your nuts and come inside. I've made a crust for you. Come along." With a shake of her head, she walked back inside.

"Help me pick them up and then you can go lie down. If he does come over, I'll tell him you're sleeping. I'll say you're sick. I won't let him get you, Annie. I won't."

"But what about you? He could hurt you too, Ruthie." Annie whimpered as we scurried about picking nuts out of the grass.

"He's not getting me. You don't need to worry about that." I believed my words with all of my being.

We stood at the edge of the porch and looked across the road just as Grandpa bent over and picked up Annie's bright yellow boot. He straightened, looked at our house, then back to his own.

Grandma stepped onto the porch and he slipped it behind his back, like a little kid hiding something from his mama. She said something we couldn't hear. He looked towards our house again. We pressed into the wall. With Annie's boot behind his back, he waited until Grandma stepped back inside, and tossed it into the bushes.

"I'll go get it," I murmured and took a step down.

"Girls, I asked that you come inside," Mama said through the screen.

213

"But Mama, Annie lost her boot over at Grandpa's," I pleaded. "I've gotta go get it."

Mama opened the door, looked over, and said, "is that it? The flash of yellow, in the bushes?"

"Yeah, can I go get it?" I asked stepping away.

"Let's get this pie in the oven and then I will retrieve it myself," she promised.

"But, Mama, Dr. Molly gave 'em to me. They're my good luck boots. I need it for the barns and she'll be mad that I lost her present. Ruthie could get it lickety split," Annie whimpered.

"No, Ruthie cannot get it *lickety split*. And, Annie, Dr. Molly will not be angry because nothing will happen to your boot. Wild hyenas will not carry it off in the next thirty minutes, I assure you. I am asking that you help to get this pie in the oven before your father comes home and then I will be more than happy to cross the road for your lucky yellow boot."

The pie was in the oven, and then there was this and that. When one thing led to another, Mama called over to Grandma asking her to bring the boot with her when she came to supper.

"Yoo-hoo!" Grandma called out in a sing songy voice. "We're here!"

"I'll be right there!" Mama hollered down the stairs and I ran past her to get Annie's boot back before Grandpa could make a ruckus about it.

"Hi." I said, trying to sound casual and looking around to see where it was. "Where's Annie's boot?"

"Ruth Ann Walker, a kinder request, please," Mama said from behind me.

"She didn't leave no boot on my property," Grandpa

muttered. "But I'll tell you what, me and Annie, we'll have us a looksee and see if we can't find that goldarn yellow boot. I'm sure it'll turn up."

"That's right. There wasn't anything in the bushes. I looked as soon as you called," Grandma said.

"Yup. Nothing there," Grandpa agreed. "Now, where's your sister? Where's my Annie?"

"Where's my boot? It was there. We saw it."

"Ah, there she be," he said to Annie who was standing in the doorway. "Now, I was just saying to your mama, you and me will find that boot. That's the truth of it. Mother, you tell Annie how you already did give it a look." But before Grandma could speak, he kept talking, "we're good at finding things, aren't we, Annie? You and me, we'll sort this out."

Out the window, dust from the drive swirled in the air, as Daddy parked his truck and started towards the house. Buddy lifted his head to listen and his tail slowly wagged against the floor, *fwip, fwip, fwip.*

"What's wrong with him?" Daddy asked ignoring his own mama and daddy. "Now Buddy, I count on you to make..." He bent down and rubbed Buddy's head, then asked, "was somebody shooting guns today? What's got him all *hangdog?* Right, boy, ya'll just *hangdog.*"

"Annie's boot is missing."

"What's that, Ruth Ann? What boot?" He lifted his face and kept petting Buddy. "I would think you might be more worried about this here dog than some ol' boot."

"Buddy had a scare, that's all. But it's Annie's favorite boot. Will you go with me to look for it, now? Buddy too?"

"Now, listen here. I just told you that me and Annie would find that dagnabbed boot. We're sitting down to supper, ain't that right, Elizabeth?"

"Please, Daddy, can you help us?" Annie begged.

215

"I said, enough!!!" Grandpa hollered, and Buddy crept out of the room.

"Can we please have a supper without stepping into another vat of displeasure? We can solve the mystery of the missing boot tomorrow. Perhaps Nancy Drew or Agatha Christie can assist us with clues. But tonight, it's suppertime," Mama scolded.

"That's right. Now ya'll listen to your mama and mind your manners," Grandpa said as he put his elbows on the table, tucked his napkin under his chin, and said, "get on with it."

"May I be excused, please?" Annie asked in a whisper just as Mama pulled the pie out of the oven.

"Lookie here, little missy. You can stick around and have a nice slice of pie with your old grandpa, now, can't you?"

"May I, Daddy?" Annie asked.

"I'm talking to you, Annie." This time, Grandpa was close to shouting.

"Leave her be, Dad. She's under the weather. Go ahead, Annie. That's fine."

"Pecan pie," Mama announced like she was presenting the queen, and turned around with her golden-brown pie. My hands shook something awful as I helped her serve slices round the table.

Grandpa had always been ornery, but now he was downright mean most times I saw him. And here I was serving him pie and he was serving up lies and bad behavior and Mama acted like it was fine and dandy.

"Well, I'm gonna have a smidge more pie before I go up and check on little Annie. Ruth Ann, serve your Grandpa another slice and put some of that whupped cream on top too. Don't be stingy! I reckon those pecans came from my tree and that cream from my cow so...that's right. Give it here!" he barked.

I wanted to push his face right into the pile of whipping cream that covered his pie, but I knew if I did, I'd be the next thing whipped. I may be a kid, but I know what's right and fair. And nothing Grandpa says is either.

"Walter, dear, that is your third piece of pie. You know what the doctor said about–"

"Shut up Mother! That's none of your gall-darn business! That's what."

Grandma wiped at her mouth, like she could wipe away the nastiness of his words with her own napkin.

"That's enough, Dad. Mother didn't do nothing to you. Keep your hateful words to yourself." Daddy wasn't one to speak up to his daddy, but here he was doing it again, and Grandpa didn't like it one bit.

"You wouldn't have a pot to piss in if I didn't–"

"Dad! I said that's enough!"

"Shut the hell up son. I'm gonna go check on little Annie. She's better company than the lot of you!"

Grandpa scooped the rest of that pie into his mouth and pushed his chair back and started to stand. I don't know what got into me, but I had had enough. And I wasn't about to let him go near my little sister if I had to wrestle him to the ground.

"Well now Grandpa, I don't think that's such a good idea." My hands were shaking but my voice was clear. "Like we already said, she's not feeling well." Slow. Steady.

"You see, last night, Annie and me, well we were headed home from a nice evening with our friends, Dr. Molly and Cheryl, and some crazed lunatic came driving up scaring the devil out of every one of us."

Nobody took a bite of pie while I was talking. Grandpa

stared at me with his cheeks so full of pie they were popping out like a chipmunk.

"Only some drunken old fool would be yelling like that. I bet God Himself heard the ruckus. And you know what I believe, Grandpa." I locked my eyes on him. I watched him swallow.

"I do believe that a person that crazy ain't sitting right with the Lord." Mama's fork touched the side of her plate and it sounded as loud as a blast from a cannon clearing the crows.

The quiet broke open when Grandpa started choking and coughing. Pretty soon he was bent over the kitchen sink puking up pecan pie with the cream on top. I didn't know what would happen to me. I didn't care. I said my piece even though I felt like I was caught in the threshing machine. I pushed back from the table.

"Goodnight, Grandma," I said on my way out.

"Ruth Ann Walker." Mama's voice was stern. "Where do you think–"

"Ruth Ann. Look at me," Daddy interrupted her. I turned. He stood with his hands on his hips. "You take care of Annie and tell her I'll be up to say goodnight real soon. And you tell her that tomorrow we'll find that boot." We looked into each other's eyes.

"I sure will, Daddy. I'll tell her that."

I glanced at Mama. Her eyes were fixed on Daddy. Neither one of them took much notice of Grandpa wiping puke and spit on the kitchen towel.

As I walked away, I heard Grandma scolding, "I told you three pieces of pie was too much. Look at you, you old fool. You just never learn, do you?"

And then to Daddy she said, "clean him up and send him home, Daniel. Or you can keep him for all I care." The kitchen door slammed.

CHAPTER 16

"Now there's my little sport. You feeling better today, Annie?" Daddy asked when Annie walked into the kitchen, sat at the table, and hung her head.

"I guess so," she murmured.

"Well, tell you what, I was thinking that what this family needs is an outing. A nice drive might do us all good. We could head on over to Okoboji. What do you think about that, 'Lizbeth?"

Mama was at the stove serving herself a bowl of stewed prunes. "I am not in need of a drive, but you can certainly take the girls out, if you'd like," she said into the sink.

"Now, I thought it might be nice for all of us to get away for a spell. Last night was a bit of a, what would you call it?" He slurped his coffee and stared at the back of Mama.

"Spectacle. Debacle. Embarrassment. Mortification. Oh, I don't know, any number of descriptors might do when a family comes entirely undone by inexcusable behavior."

Facing us, Mama huffed and put a prune in her mouth leaning against the stove, sounding like she was describing a bad movie she had watched.

"But Daddy, we need to go get Annie's boot back. I was hoping Heidi could come over and we could ride bikes or something," I sputtered past the pancake in my mouth.

"By gum, what's the point of even trying with this here family?" Daddy shouted.

"But, Daddy–"

"Ah, Annie, don't worry 'bout your ol' daddy. I'm going for a drive. The rest of you can sit around and wait for that old geezer to make trouble. I'm tired of it. That's all. Just tired of it." He stomped from the room, leaving his own pancakes half finished. "I'll get your boot back, Annie. Later."

Mama called after him, "Daniel! Wait! The girls will go with you." She turned to us. "Your father would like you to join him, as today he doesn't need to work or travel."

"Daddy, I wanna come! I do." Annie ran after him leaving her breakfast plate behind too.

"Well, that won't do. Dr. White said that the only thing wrong with your sister is appetite, and there she goes." Mama sighed, popped another slimy prune into her mouth and sat down at Annie's plate and picked up the fork, while she was still chewing.

"Why your father cannot understand something as rudimentary as nourishment baffles and infuriates me. Do as you will, Ruth Ann. It is neither here nor there."

Her fork scraped Annie's plate as Daddy lifted his keys from the hook.

"'Lizbeth, don't you let that son-of-a gun take Annie out on any–"

"Daddy, I'm coming with you!" Annie charged into the room with her shirt buttoned up all catawampus.

"Well, that's fine, Annie," he said and opened the kitchen door. "What's this?" He sounded confused. Annie gasped. Mama and I both jumped from the table. In his hand was Annie's yellow boot. "Looks like your boot went through the field plow. Did you run through the field, sport? Maybe you lost it there?"

"No! No!" she wailed and shook.

I thought of Shirley. It was just a boot, but it felt the same. The sweetness of the pancakes went sour in my mouth. I looked around. I looked for him. Nobody said his name. Who else could it be?

"Daniel, take it away." Mama's voice sounded like ice cracking on the pond in winter. I wasn't sure which one of us might fall through, but somebody was sure to go.

The shredded yellow boot sailed from Daddy's hand towards the barn. He knelt in front of Annie. "Ya know what, sport? You and me, we're gonna go to Okoboji and find you a pair of boots that fit you proper. You don't need no hand-me-downs."

I couldn't understand all of what Annie said, but I heard *Dr. Molly*, and Mama and Daddy did too. Daddy scooped her up and Mama reached out and rubbed her back.

"'Lizbeth, how 'bout you get on the horn and find out where Dr. Molly buys them boots and we'll get in the car and drive to Chicago if we need to and track down a pair for our girl here. How's that sound, Annie?"

"But, Daddy, what happened? What happened to Annie's boot?" I whimpered. "It's just like Shir–."

"Hush now," Daddy said, without being unkind. I was glad he stopped me. I didn't even mean to say it out loud. It flew out like spit.

Daddy drew in his breath and Mama's hand went still. Annie's voice came up from a place deep inside. "The same thing that happened to Shirley. That's what happened." I wasn't the only one.

Daddy exhaled. He put her on the ground. "Give that gal a call. And if she doesn't answer, well, we'll go searching. I'll be back."

"No, Daddy, no!" Annie shrieked the minute he turned towards the road. "Don't go. We'll buy new ones. Please, Daddy, please," she sobbed and grabbed ahold of his hand.

He looked from Annie to Mama, who nodded and then shook her head. I'm not sure if she was saying yes or no, or what the question was, but Daddy walked to the car with Annie and they drove off.

"Grandpa did it." I stared hard into the dust that rose up behind them, waiting for Mama to tell me I was wrong. She didn't.

"Your father will buy more boots." Mama's voice was as flat as the pancakes she scooped into the trash. I pushed Annie's empty chair up to the table. Her sailor hat was hanging on the back. I grabbed it and walked upstairs to find a hiding place. I would keep it safe. And as much as I thought I could keep Annie safe, I wasn't so sure.

It wasn't all that hard to keep an eye on Annie, being that she didn't leave the house much these days. Mama let her wear her new yellow boots in the house since they were still clean as a whistle. But today I talked her into going out for a visit with me. I just had to convince Mama.

"Can Annie and me go visit Dr. Molly and Cheryl and then go to Rexall's for a shake? That might help her put some weight back on." I didn't want to be mean, but I did want a shake, so I was playing to the part of Mama that was feeling like she failed in the fattening up of her child.

"Ruth Ann, it is not just a matter of weight. Nutrition must be taken into consideration also. But yes, yes you may." She walked into her bedroom where she kept her purse and came back with fifty cents and a warning. "Do not get underfoot at Dr. Molly's clinic. They are running an animal hospital not an amusement park."

"Thanks, Mama," I said as Annie and I raced from the house, hopped on our bikes and rode to town.

"Ruthie?"

"Yeah?"

"He could get us. Maybe he's gonna kill us too."

I stopped my bike so fast Annie almost ran right into me. "Who's gonna kill us?"

"He's real mean, Ruthie. I think maybe...maybe...Shirley." She couldn't say his name. I didn't need her to. Her voice tumbled into the rocks she was kicking. "Let's just go. I don't like standing here beside the road. I don't like it one bit. He might see us. He's bad. You don't know."

"Then tell me. You know it was him, right? The lunatic," I pleaded.

"That's what I'm saying. We're not safe...and he might k... He might hurt Mama and Daddy too," Annie whispered like he was hiding in the shadows of our bikes.

"We're telling Dr. Molly when we get there."

"You tell her. She might think I'm making it up and just being a baby. He said nobody would believe me anyhow." She looked around again. "Let's go. I'll use the bathroom and you tell her it was him when I'm in there."

I was just as worried as Annie when we got on our bikes and started to ride. I looked over my shoulder so much I was riding all swervy curvy.

When we got to the clinic, Annie saw the sign first. "It says they're closed."

"Yeah, but just for lunch."

"Hi girls." Dr. Molly's voice startled both of us something awful. She walked up from behind us. "You caught me taking a break."

"You surprised us," I accused and looked at Annie, whose face was wrapped in a mask of fear. "It's OK, Annie. It's Dr. Molly. We're OK now."

"What is it? What's going on?" Dr. Molly looked from me to Annie like she was trying to solve a riddle. And then she fumbled with the lock. "Fiddle sticks!"

Seeing her impatient like that made me believe we did have a reason to be afraid. Annie kept looking around, shifting from one foot to the other. I leaned my bike against the building, and then did the same with Annie's.

"Where's Cheryl?" I asked.

"Oh, she wasn't feeling well. She drove home a few minutes ago."

"By herself?" Annie asked, her facing losing all its color.

"Here we are, girls. Safe and sound."

I pushed Annie in ahead of me and shuffled past Dr. Molly wanting her to close and lock the door fast.

"If you girls are still shaken by that drunken ol' fool, you need to know that you're safe now." Dr. Molly looked between us.

"Can we lock the door?" Annie read my mind. "Just to be sure."

Dr. Molly turned the lock.

"Is that OK? Isn't anybody coming?" I wondered aloud.

"No, there are no appointments. I'm here to get some charts done." Dr. Molly bent down in front of Annie. "Now, tell me, what has you so shook up? You look like you saw a ghost."

"I have to go to the bathroom, right, Ruthie?"

"I guess so," I stammered, all of a sudden not wanting to be the one to tell the secret that I knew. After Annie left, I stared at my feet. "There's something we gotta tell you."

"What in tarnation is going on, Ruth Ann?" All the softness and singsong was gone from her voice.

I sputtered.

"That was fast," Dr. Molly said to Annie who was back before I got the words out.

"Yeah, I didn't poop or nothing."

"Oh, I guess I don't know what to say about that." It was Dr. Molly's turn to sputter. And she sputtered her way back to herself. "Maybe the two of you could give me a hand with some new arrivals."

"I'm a good helper." A magic curtain was pulled back, and Annie was herself again. Dr. Molly smiled, and I nearly cried with the relief of it.

"I just knew I could count on you. Now, it is a big job. And Ruth Ann, I'm going to ask you to do the dirty work. And I do mean dirty."

With every word, Dr. Molly, like Annie, wriggled into her old self, like a fish slithering back into the water. "Let me get Annie started, then it's your turn missy." Dr. Molly winked at me, and then knelt down in front of Annie. "For you, I have two puppies in kennels that need hugs and holding and feeding. And they each need their own turn."

"Oh, that's what I'm best at. I'm real good...you should see me taking care of my little..." She shoved her hands in the pockets of her jeans and kicked the floor before she looked up again and said, "I'm real good at that, Dr. Molly."

"Just as I suspected."

The two of them went into the back and I wandered around the waiting room straightening things up while I waited. When she came out, I took the broom from her hand and spit my story out like fels naptha soap.

"The lunatic was my grandpa."

"What lunatic was your grandpa?" Her face scrunched up in confusion.

"The lunatic who chased us! When you and Cheryl were bringing Annie and me home, the lunatic in the truck that was screaming all those hateful words."

The color in her face drained away. Her quiet scared me.

"Dr. Molly?" We both turned to look at Annie whose eyes

were as bright as stars when she walked out carrying a teeny, tiny Chihuahua in her arms. "I think Juan Valdez wants another bottle. He's real thirsty."

Dr. Molly's face lifted. Her laugh was soft. "Juan Valdez is always thirsty. How 'bout you give Barney his bottle first and then see if Senōr Valdez is still asking for more?"

"That's funny, Dr. Molly, Senōr. Hey Ruthie, when you're all done cleaning, maybe you could hold one of these puppies. They need lots of loving."

Annie looked down as Juan Valdez looked up, gave the funniest little bark and nearly fell from Annie's hands as he stood up and started licking her face. "He likes me a lot, I guess." Annie laughed and walked into the back to give Barney the beagle a bottle.

Just as soon as she left, Dr. Molly looked at me again. "Does she know?"

"Yeah, she's real skittish; afraid of everything. But Mama and Daddy don't know so they had Grandpa and Grandma over for supper and well, it didn't go all that well. Grandpa puked up his pie and Grandma got mad and called him an *old fool.*"

I wanted to finish my story before Annie came back, so words tumbled over each other and I was lucky they made sense at all. "And you know those boots you gave Annie? The yellow ones? Well, first, remember Shirley?"

"Slow down, I'm having trouble following. What do Annie's yellow boots have to do with Shirley?"

"Maybe he killed Shirley just like he cut up her boot."

"Killed Shirley? Cut up her boot? What in the world?"

"Well, Annie said it first. And she's scared that maybe he might try to kill us. I know it sounds crazy. But she dropped the boot you gave her in his yard and then, there it was on the stoop all cut up," I held my breath, "just like Shirley got killed. Nothing makes any sense."

With the broom in my hand, I held myself up, and caught my breath. Annie was back. She tipped her head to the side, and then looked down at the sleepy puppy she was holding. "OK, Barney's all plumped up too. Ruthie, come see his little tummy. It's just as fat as a baby pig. He's the cutest little thing."

I walked over and touched his fat, pink tummy. "He sure is." I turned to Dr. Molly. "Whose puppies are these anyhow?"

"Maybe we could have one!" Annie's excitement caught me in the face with a spray of spit.

"Buddy and Beets and Gertrude and Lizzy don't need any more competition for your lovin', Annie," I said as I wiped at my face.

Dr. Molly added, "they're already spoken for. They're just here to get looked after since they were taken from their mamas a little too soon.

"Well, I'll be their mama for now. I'll keep 'em safe," Annie whispered, and I could almost see a cloud pass by. The sun broke through again and she looked up and smiled.

WE RODE home under a sky that looked to be spilled with black paint. The darkness felt like it had settled in my stomach, and I couldn't sort out whether I was more afraid of what was behind me or what was in front. When we got home, Daddy's truck was in the driveway, but it was just Mama standing in the kitchen.

"Dr. Molly had puppies!" Annie called out as soon as we walked inside.

"That seems quite unlikely," Mama said and turned to smile at us.

"No, really, she did," Annie tried again.

"Annie, what Mama means is Dr. Molly didn't have puppies, she has puppies," I tried to explain.

"That's what I said. One's a little beagle like Buddy and the other one's Juan Valdez."

"What's there to eat, Mama?" I asked.

"I thought you were stopping for shakes at the Rexall?"

"We forgot," Annie said.

"Well then, I need my money back, Ruth Ann, and supper is only about an hour away so do not ruin your appetite. An apple will suffice."

"With peanut butter?" Annie asked.

"Surely," Mama said and stopped herself. I flinched and held my breath. "I mean, yes, that would be fine," she finished.

"That's OK, Mama. It's OK if you say Shirley. Loving those puppies made me feel lots better."

Mama walked over and hugged Annie. I let my breath out.

"I am so relieved to hear that. I know your father would like to visit with you. He was asking when I thought you would be home."

Annie ran from the kitchen yelling, "Ruthie, cut me up some apple too! Daddy, I'm home!"

I ate my apple and left Annie's on a plate with a dollop of peanut butter resting beside it. Mama worked on supper, and I figured maybe Annie was still visiting with Daddy, but he was sitting alone behind the newspaper when I walked into the living room. "Where's Annie?"

"She ran along. I'd like to visit with you too." Daddy rested the paper in his lap but kept staring at it like he was finishing up an article.

"Did I do something bad?"

"Nah, that's not it." Finally, he looked up. "I don't think them, uh, them ladies, the veterinarian and all are the trouble. I think maybe I was wrong about that." He cleared his throat, "What do you think the problem might be, Ruth Ann?"

I felt like I had a rock in my throat. It took a fair bit of trying to get the words to squeeze past it, and then they flew out like somebody slapped me on the back.

"Grandpa's mean. He scares Annie." Telling the truth turned that stone into a quarry. I looked down. "He scares me too." I was shaking. My hands dripped with sweat.

Daddy was quiet. I figured he was waiting for more.

"He's always been ornery, but that never used to scare her, or you. What makes you say that now, Ruth Ann? Is there something you're not telling me?" His voice was soft, like he didn't even want to hear his own words.

"Daddy, I'm sorry."

"I'm not asking for sorry. I'm asking what you're thinking."

I could feel the sadness pooling in my eyes.

"Ruthie, I think you may be right, but I just need to understand. That's all."

My tears fell. He put the paper off to the side, stood up, and hugged me. Right as he was losing his daddy, I was finding mine.

"I love you, Daddy," I whispered. He cleared his throat, stepped away from me, pulled out his hankie and blew his nose. He sat down and lifted the paper between us like a wall. The spell broke, but I stood in front of him, waiting, hoping he might reach for me again.

"You run along now, sport. I'll take care of things for you and Annie." Daddy disappeared into his paper like a genie in a bottle. There was no more comfort and no more questions. Worry crept along the edges of my spine and pulled my head down. I watched my feet carry me away. To Annie.

"You forgot about your apple," I said to the back of her head.

"Not hungry," she murmured from her pillow.

Daddy's *talk* was like taking a hose to fireflies dancing in the night. The light was gone. Annie squeezed herself tight into that same bottle Daddy disappeared into, and all the abracadabra's and belly rubs in the world weren't bringing either one of them out anytime soon.

I had to do something. I didn't have a better idea, so I asked, "you want a Lifesaver?" She didn't move. I stood holding out my precious butterscotch candies. This family did indeed need a lifesaver. But it wasn't butterscotch. It was me.

CHAPTER 17

*A*fter Grandpa puked up pecan pie, he and Grandma disappeared like cockroaches in the light of day. That was fine by me, but I wanted to understand. Not knowing what's what made my skin feel prickly and my imagination ran wild. One night at supper, I got up my gumption and turned to Daddy and asked, "did you tell Grandpa and Grandma to stay away or are they mad at us or are we mad at them?"

Mama asked me to pass the salt and then Daddy asked, "can anybody guess how much salt Hormel uses every day of the year?"

Annie pushed food around her plate not likely hearing my question or Daddy's. Mama stared at Daddy for a long minute then finally said, "isn't that interesting," even though there was nothing interesting being that nobody even gave a guess. That was that.

Going to sleep at night, I listened for the sound of Grandpa's shuffling steps coming in our direction. My dreams were riled up with worries about knives, and axes, and saws. After a while I tired out and started thinking about my birthday.

In the days leading up to it, winter came rushing in and threw a sparkly, silver blanket over the last of autumn's dry, brown leaves. Mama's rose hips looked like glittery gum drops hanging on their bare, thorny branches. On our way home from school, Annie stopped walking and picked one. "What are you doing? Those are Mama's roses." I looked around like she was stealing penny candies from the Rexall.

"I know what they are, Ruthie. Miss Barnes says you can make tea out of them and I want to see what they taste like."

"Ugh. You can't eat everything, you know. Even IF you can make tea."

"Well, Grandpa says..." Annie held the sparkly ball between her fingers. She threw it to the ground without saying more and walked ahead of me into the house.

I picked another from the bush and followed behind. "Annie, wait up!" I called out rushing to catch up. And then I heard something. At least, I thought I did. Holding my breath, I looked over at Grandpa and Grandma's place. *Did I see a shadow move? Did a curtain pull back?* I rubbed my eyes knowing that my imagination was getting the best of me.

"Yes siree, Hormel Meats may be able to drag a pig to slaughter but they ain't dragging me away from your birthday this year. You only turn twelve once, you know," were the first words I heard when I opened the door.

I was pleased as could be that, for once, Daddy wouldn't be traveling on my birthday. But right now, I couldn't shake my shimmy. I smiled at Daddy and looked around the kitchen. "Where's Annie?"

"Ruth Ann, please close that door, unless of course you are expecting *a band of merry men* to follow behind," Mama half joked, and half scolded.

I turned to pull the door closed and that's when I saw him. He was leaning against the side of the barn, tucked into the shadow. When he tipped his head to spit, the sailor hat he was wearing fell to the ground. He bent over, picked it up, and smiled, looking right at me.

I looked at Mama. Her back was to me. Daddy was looking down at a magazine lying on the table. I looked out. He was gone! Just like that! Maybe I was seeing things. Was he there at all? That shimmy got ahold of me again and rattled my bones.

"Well now, I guess I did expect a little more enthusiasm being that I'll be home for your birthday this year. Probably not be too late to go ahead to that meat packer's convention in Omaha. What do you think about that, Elizabeth?"

"Where's Annie?" The words pressed against the back of my clenched teeth.

"That does it, off to Omaha I go," Daddy said with a wink.

"No, Daddy. I want you home on my birthday. I just wondered where Annie got to, that's all." I squeezed my butt cheeks together to keep from shaking. My palms itched, and I started to scratch.

"Ruth Ann Walker, please stop that shaking and scratching. *Where Annie got to?* Hmmm, that's a mystery to be solved." Mama knew it wasn't a mystery and Annie didn't *got to* anywhere.

Panic and spit filled my mouth, the way it does before you puke. I couldn't be bothered trying to find the right words for Mama. I needed to find Annie.

"Annie!" I shouted.

"What's everybody looking at?" she asked from the doorway.

"Look, I have this for you." My hands shook as I pulled the rose hip from my pocket and hugged her. She looked at me like I was as crazy as I felt. "Mama, could you make us some tea with this? Miss Barnes told Annie it's good, right Annie?"

233

"Nah. She never said it was good. She just said you could drink it."

I looked out the window. Nothing.

"Ruth Ann, what is it that has you so agitated? What are you looking for?"

"Nothing, Mama," I lied. Now that Annie was found, I needed to find her hat. My brain spun like cotton candy. Find it. Now. Up the stairs. Annie behind me as I pulled it from my bottom drawer.

"Why do you have my hat? I've been looking for it." She snatched it from me.

"I was keeping it safe. Safe..." I murmured.

"Thanks. Are you OK, Ruthie? You look like you seen a ghost. And you're supposed to be happy. Tomorrow's your birthday." Annie tipped her head and waited.

"It's nothing." Useless words sloshed out like dirty water from a bucket. I didn't know how to keep us safe; how to be a lifesaver. I just knew I had to.

BEING that it was my birthday, I knew it would be the excuse Grandpa needed to show up, and Grandma wouldn't miss it. I watched, and listened, and waited. When it was time for supper, four plates sat in their usual spots, like any old day of the week. Mama made my favorite: mashed potatoes with hamburger gravy.

The relatives always showed up for everybody's birthday. None of them called. None of them came. I didn't know how to feel about that, and if Annie hadn't interrupted my daydreams, they would have kept thumping around like sneakers in the spin cycle, making a racket and going nowhere.

"I'm glad it's just us for Ruthie's birthday this year." Her voice broke the quiet. We all looked at her, waiting for more. "I just am."

"Me too." Daddy jumped in next, with his mouth full of mashed potatoes. "That means there's more for me." He smiled squishing potatoes out though his teeth.

"It looks to me like we have two twelve-year-olds at the table," Mama said but I could tell she didn't mean anything by it and Daddy actually gave her a wink as he loaded another forkful of glop and lifted it to his mouth.

I wanted to laugh and join in the fun. But shame sat like sludge in the pit of my stomach. I wanted to save my family from the evil monster, but it wasn't so easy. As much as I wanted Grandpa gone, I didn't want to lose our family.

It was my fault that nobody knocked on the door or sat around the table with us. But how could it be? He was the one scaring us. I was trying to save us. It's not that I didn't want family. I just wanted it to look different than it did. It was time for presents and cake.

"Me first!" Annie shouted and ran over to the Betty Crocker cookbook and pulled a card out from under it. Hers was drawn on a piece of light blue construction paper folded in two. I stared at it trying to make sense of what I was seeing when Mama said, "tell us about your picture, Annie."

"Well, see here, this is Buddy eating popcorn, and this here is me and you. You're the tall one." She smiled up at me. "It's the carnival, Ruthie. It's before–"

She got real quiet and then Daddy said, "looks like somebody's bobbing for apples."

"That's it Daddy! That there is Merle. I know it doesn't look exactly like her–"

"It's perfect, Annie. You're a great artist. I love it!" I hugged her tight.

"Look at the inside," she said, and reached over to open it.

"You are my sunshine. I love you, Annie," I read. The picture inside was of Annie and me standing next to each other holding hands. But in the place of my face was a round yellow sun with a big smile and beams of light reaching to the edges of the card.

"I love it," I whispered with tears in my eyes. "I love it so much. That's the best card ever." And now I didn't feel like a louse or lonely. I felt like the big sister I wanted to be.

"Well, Lizbeth, that about does it. No point in even turning ours in. The prize has been handed out." Daddy reached over playing like he was going to pull his card back.

"Hey! That has my name on it, not yours," I teased back as I wiped away my tears. My thoughts stopped running, and I was glad too that it was just the four of us.

"I didn't want to make you cry, Ruthie. I wanted to make you happy."

"Annie, Ruthie is shedding happy tears. Beautiful art and beautiful sentiment can bring us to tears," Mama said.

"Is that it, Ruthie? Are you crying happy tears?"

"You are my sunshine, my only sunshine, you make me happy..." I started singing and Mama and Daddy joined in.

"OK, OK, now open the others so you can do presents," Annie insisted.

"Thank you, Mama." I smiled knowing what to expect. Mama was funny when it came to picking out greeting cards. Not funny ha-ha, just funny. I always pictured her at the Ben Franklin rolling her cart past the cards, and without really coming to a complete stop, she'd spot the *daughter birthday* section and grab a card congratulating herself on making a snatch with the wheels still rolling.

"Thanks, Mama. That's a real nice card."

"Let's see it. Let's see," Annie said. "Oh. You gave that one to me too."

"Well, I am sure I did not."

236

Daddy laughed and put his hand over his mouth, saying all he needed to with the twinkle in his eyes.

"Perhaps," was all she said.

As I tore Daddy's card open, he stared down at the table.

"Read it out loud, Ruthie," Annie insisted.

"*Twelve is a magic number, as this daddy knows. There are twelve hours on a clock and twelve months in every year. There are twelve colors on the wheel and in the countdown to Christmas too. But most special of all, twelve is the number I think of, when I think of you. Happy Birthday to my 12-year-old girl!*" To myself I read the next part: *You're a good girl, Ruth Ann. I love you. Your daddy, forever.*

Daddy was still looking down when Mama said, "well now, *let them eat cake!* Annie, can you give me a hand, please."

"Let them eat cake!" Annie repeated throwing her fist in the air as one or the other of us did every birthday mimicking Mama. For now, Annie was back to herself and that was as much reason to celebrate as my birthday.

"Thank you, Daddy. That's a real nice card," I said when we were alone.

He was looking out the window and mumbled, "uh huh". Was he thinking about family and where everyone had gone? If we took turns filling the chairs with family, I had a feeling he would choose different than me. "You keep on being a good girl, now." Like a tumbleweed in the wind, I never could tell what direction he'd be going next.

WHEN ANNIE PASSED out slices of Angel Food cake slathered in whipped cream and strawberries pulled from the deep freeze, he said, "oh, no thank you Annie. But ya'll go ahead. I think I've had my fill. I may have had a bit much of that delicious hamburger gravy. That's the truth of it. Isn't it about time to open these here presents?"

"Yay! Open your presents, Ruthie!" Annie shouted.

I kept my eye on Daddy as I opened up a new diary, colored pencils, a sketching pad and two new Nancy Drew books. "Thanks. I love them all."

"When me and Mama were at the Ben Franklin getting your presents, Miss Suzanne said, *Looks like you got yourself a girl all set to tell stories with words and pictures!*" Annie beamed, and I was happy to see it.

"Before we know it, you will be heading off to college. Oh, to think of it…" Mama pulled her glasses off and wiped her eyes with her paper napkin.

"Now, Elizabeth, she's twelve, not twenty. Let's just keep the horses in the barn 'till it's time to ride. You know, Annie, maybe I will have a slice of that cake."

"Sure, Daddy, I'll get it!" Annie loaded up a piece of angel food cake with whipped cream and strawberries and put it down in front of him.

After his first bite, Daddy said, "you made a good choice, Ruth Ann. Angel food suits you best. We'll leave the devil to me," he winked, but his words gave me a shiver all the same.

"MAMA?" I whispered when I came into the kitchen the next morning. Kneeling on the floor, digging through old boxes, she didn't even look up. "Mama?" I said it louder this time and her head swiveled so fast I thought it might spin off like a top across the floor.

She pushed her glasses up and looked at me through an oily film. One hand pushed her catawampus hair back and the other smoothed the front of the blouse she was wearing last night for my birthday supper.

"I am looking for my clerical books. Could you please get breakfast for you and Annie and make lunches for the two of you, also."

"You all right, Mama?" I don't know why I even bothered asking, 'cause she wasn't listening. Turning twelve wasn't even worth it if it meant that Mama was just gonna throw her apron at me. I didn't need one more thing to worry about. But in this family, that's like asking not to fart after a bowl of beans. They just go together.

Annie walked in rubbing her eyes. "What's all that?"

"Mama's looking for her clerical books," I said, like it was a perfectly normal way to start off a school day.

Mama sat on her heels and looked at the two of us with smudgy wild eyes and said, "I began thinking last night over cake; I decided it is time for me to re-enter the work force. Before I know it, you girls will be off to college and I will have wasted the best years of my life."

Wasted? I thought. "You're getting a job?" I asked, trying to keep the sting from turning my voice to whine.

Without even giving her a chance to talk, Annie said. "but Mama, your job is being a mama! Ladies with kids are mamas. If you didn't have kids, you could be a doctor like Dr. Molly, but you have us, so you can't."

"Yes, Annie, but—"

"And right now, we need breakfast. Right, Ruthie."

"Mama said we can get it ourselves."

"Just this once, pour a bowl of cereal. We can make adjustments tomorrow morning." Mama went back to digging and sorting and Annie and I slurped down Cheerios watching.

"What's wrong with Mama?" Annie asked later as we walked to the barn.

"How should I know?" I snapped, wishing I hadn't. "I'm sorry. I wish Daddy was home. Maybe he would know what to do."

"Maybe he would have made us pancakes," Annie added. "It's not right, Ruthie. It's not fair."

When our school day was done, I didn't know what to expect as Annie ran ahead of me and was already out of sight when I came through the kitchen door. "Mama! Where are you?"

She didn't answer. I walked into the laundry room and saw her sitting in front of a typewriter where her sewing machine had been this morning. She took no notice of me standing in the doorway. Finally, the kitchen timer went off and Mama counted up words and mumbled, "damn!"

I had never, ever heard Mama curse. When she looked up at me, she didn't even have a look of being sorry. "Oh Ruth Ann, I'm glad you're here. I need your help."

"What are you doing? Why'd you change everything?" I asked, seeing the ironing board standing on end in a corner like a dead body propped up and waiting to be laid to rest.

"There is no need to be surly. As I said this morning, I am preparing for a return to work."

"Does Daddy know?"

"We have not had the opportunity yet to speak about the details, no. Currently, that is beside the point. I need your help."

"What do you need?" I chewed the inside of my cheek and held my breath. *Too much. Too much.*

"You can dictate a letter for me directly from this clerical book." I looked down, *The Ladies Guide to Clerical Skills: Intermediate, Book Four*, "Read the first one rather slowly as I will try to keep up and then as I improve you can read more quickly." A thought flashed in her eyes, like somebody turned a light on in another room. "Oh, but before you begin, could you please bring me a cup of coffee. The pot should still be warm."

For the next hour or so, there I was reading out loud, Mama typing and Annie running in with new pictures she was drawing and questions. *"Can I have a turn, Mama? I bet I could type real good. Look at that! It makes all the words for you. Will you make me a snack? What should I have? Can you call Merle for me, so she can come and color too? I'm still hungry."*

Mama never looked up. Until she snapped. "Annabelle Rose! Have you no ability to entertain yourself for a moment? Can you not see that I am working?"

"I'm sorry." Annie and Buddy slunk out of the room with their tails between their legs.

"Well, without interruption, we can begin to make real progress now."

"Annie wasn't doing anything bad."

"Nothing *bad*? Ruth Ann Walker, your grammar is dreadful."

"Dreadful. D R E A D F U L. Dreadful." Like a spelling bee contestant, I stared straight at Mama. She took no notice.

"For the love of Pete! What happens to my pens? Run into the kitchen and bring me a pen, please." I was back in a flash. "Ruth Ann, your task was a simple one. What did I ask you to do?" She wiped her glasses on the front of her dirty white blouse that had dabs of strawberry from my cake last night.

"I asked you to run along to the kitchen for a pen. Finally, you return with a #2 yellow lead pencil. You know that I only ever write with a fine point black Bic pen. Please return at once with exactly what I have requested."

"I'm sorry" *crazy lady* was what I said and what I thought as I raced back in search of her fine tipped black Bic pen.

I flew around the corner and crashed into a wall of Grandpa. "What are you doing here?" I accused. I should have kept my mouth shut. *Annie*, I worried.

"Where's your daddy?" Spit showered me with words he pushed past the wad of chew jammed into his mouth.

"I don't know."

"How 'bout your mama? Where's she?"

"In the sewing room." My voice shook.

Walking behind him, I held my breath, like I was moving through a tunnel. I wanted to honk my horn and let Mama know he was coming. But I didn't have a horn and my throat squeezed tight. I could barely swallow, much less scream.

I looked past him to Mama, who was tapping the eraser of her number-two pencil. Without looking up, she said, "Ruth Ann Walker, I will not continue to wait while you dilly-dally about."

"WHAT THE HELL?" he roared!

Mama's head snapped back like a BB gun caught her between the eyes.

"What the hell is going on, Elizabeth?" Grandpa growled, scarier still, as his voice was just above a whisper.

Mama's pencil dropped to the floor. "Well, I might be able to assist you if you could be a bit more specific with your question." She slipped behind her mask, and her voice came from the other side, like talking sweet to the bull, trusting he can't break down the fence. But Grandpa wasn't having it.

"You know what the hell I'm talking about, Elizabeth!" This time he shouted.

I crept backwards, hearing only bits and pieces of what he accused over the sound of blood rushing in my head: *Annie; pervert; good-for-nothing; family; so-called doctor.*

With the receiver pressed against my ear, I dialed the veterinary hospital, just as he shouted again at Mama, "and there you are, courting trouble like a frog sidling up to a snake for a game of cards. I tell you what, this here is MY family and I'll darn well take care of my own as I see fit, beings that nobody else has the sense that God gave 'em!"

Cheryl picked up on the first ring. "Ruth Ann, I can barely hear you."

"My grandpa's here and he's acting crazy. He's screaming at my mama in the sewing room." I tried to breathe. "I don't know where my daddy is, and Annie slunk off a while back. But Mama's...she's not right."

"Get Annie, and the two of you go outside and wait out of sight. Dr. Molly'll be there in a flash. I don't want you going back into the sewing room until she gets there. Do you understand me?"

I ran up the stairs to our room. My new colored pencils and paper were sitting by themselves in the middle of the floor.

"Annie, where are you?" I yelled in a whisper.

"Annie!"

"I'm scared," she whimpered, as she poked her nose out from under the bed. Buddy's nose poked out too.

"It's OK, Dr. Molly's on her way," I reassured Annie from behind my own mask. She and Buddy slunk out. I held her hand with my sweaty one and Buddy by the nape of the neck. We crept down the stairs out the front door and scooched into the bushes at the bottom of the stairs. Beets bolted out from the bush beside us. "Jiminy Christmas! You scared the devil outa me!" I scolded.

We crouched in our spot for what seemed like forever, listening to the shouting and silence until Dr. Molly came tearing down the road. She slowed to a crawl when she turned onto our driveway and stopped her car beside where we hid. We popped our heads out as she touched the first step.

Startled, she jumped back and asked, "are you OK?"

"We're fine. Right, Annie?" Annie just looked at her, not the least bit *fine*. I pulled her shaking body close.

"Is he still in there?"

We nodded.

"You girls wait here." She raced up the stairs.

We sat on the stoop waiting, like *Chicken Little*, for the sky to fall. The kitchen door slammed. We heard cursing and shouting, a jumble of sludge that I couldn't make out "Hide," I whispered and gave Annie a shove back into the bushes before her feet could catch her fall. I stood, pushed my glasses up and waited with Buddy beside me. His growl was low and fierce. Beets' stepped up beside us. Her tail flicked as she watched for her prey waiting to pounce.

Grandpa saw me and stopped. He bared his teeth. It wasn't a smile. "You and your friends is lying with the devil and them fires will burn you all to hell." His eyes fell to the bushes. "You give my best to your little sister now, Ruth Ann. You hear me?" Like the devil himself, he cackled.

I looked at him through the wall of hair falling over my face. I saw his smirk and heard his threat. Buddy lunged and barked. Grandpa kicked and swatted, and nearly lost his balance.

Panic broke me open, like a watermelon shattered on the ground. I hollered, "no, Buddy, no!" I jumped forward and pulled him back. With his hackles up and his growl deep, we watched Grandpa go.

"The fires of Hell little girlie! The fires of Hell!" His last words came from the back of his head, or maybe they shot out, like he was passing gas.

"Wait!" I shouted.

He turned and sneered.

"You don't get to keep on scaring us. I know what you did, and you know I do." My voice and hands shook. He took a step in my direction. He opened his mouth. Started to say something.

"I'm not done talking," I growled. "You leave us alone and leave our friends alone. Annie's done fishing with you and I'm done pretending that the way you act is normal. It's not. And it's sure not the way family's supposed to be!"

Grandpa came closer. And now Buddy growled. He looked at Buddy and stopped.

"You listen here, little missy," he started with his eyes narrowed and his evil grin. "I'll put you in your place and teach you respect for your elders. And your friends?" he sneered, "I've got plans for them." He cackled again, spit, and walked away.

"Annie, you can come out now." My voice came out stronger than I felt. "Annie," I called again, certain that I looked just as crazy as my mama, with my hair wild and my glasses sliding down. Not a sound. I jumped down and searched. She was gone. How could she have slipped away without either of seeing her?

I turned again to Grandpa. He crossed the road. She wasn't there. He climbed in his truck and, with a spray of gravel, was gone. Was she in his truck? Did she go there to hide, not knowing that he would drive away? Did she sneak into the house while I was trying to save Buddy? I felt the blood before I knew that terror split my lip.

"Oh, Buddy, where is she? Where's Annie?" He whimpered and ran towards the back of the house. I ran after him, believing, *knowing*, that he was *Lassie* chasing down *Timmy*. He stopped beside the old willow. He tipped his head back and yipped. And then I heard her.

Her whimper echoed in the stillness. She was nestled in the crook of the tree's branches. Relief flooded me with tears and then anger. Annie's own fear shook the last dry leaves that hid her. I took a breath. "You scared me. He's gone now. Let's go find Mama and Dr. Molly. They'll know what to do."

"He'll be back," she murmured.

"Come on," I pleaded. She jumped to the ground. I scooched down, and she rode me like a pony, with her own spirit broken.

When we got inside and walked to the door of the sewing

room, Dr. Molly was standing with her back to us, watching Mama flip through her clerical book just like she flipped through the hymnal on a Sunday, not taking in much, but avoiding what she didn't want to pay attention to.

"Elizabeth, can I make you a cup of tea? You're obviously upset. Let me help, if not for you, for the girls."

"I am perfectly fine. I have been rudely interrupted by *that* man, and now I must get back to the task at hand."

"I understand that. I really do. But look at yourself. Look at this room."

I looked around and saw what I'd heard from the porch. The ironing board was tipped over and laying against the edge of the table where Mama sat; her cup was broken, with coffee splashed out on the wooden floor; a shelf of paperback books were thrown into a pile, like a cord of wood dumped in the drive; and Mama and Daddy's wedding picture that used to hang on the wall, was shattered, with shards of glass catching the lamplight like diamonds spilled from a robbery gone wrong.

"I have to ask again, do you know where Daniel is?"

"I really do need Ruth Ann's assistance if ever I am going to brush up on my shorthand," Mama said instead of answering the question.

"Elizabeth, I want to take Ruth Ann and Annie home for the evening. Would that be OK with you?"

That got Mama's attention. She looked at Dr. Molly with a flat stare. "Well heavens Molly, you know, as well as I do, that Daniel will not agree to that plan tonight or any night. You know how he feels about *your type*."

Dr. Molly flinched, and I couldn't believe Mama's bad manners. Dr. Molly was a guest in our home and saved us from who knows what. Shame lit me up like a firetruck. But Dr. Molly acted like she was covered in Crisco, and all that nastiness slipped right off.

"I understand that," she stammered, "but I'll take them home, for now. When you've had time to get organized and uh, you're feeling a bit more like yourself, give me a call and I'll run them back to town. I'll feed them supper so you don't have to."

"Actually, Molly, you may take Annie home for supper, but I really do need Ruth Ann if ever–"

"I'll stay," I said, as I put Annie down and squeezed past Dr. Molly. "That might be best."

"Yes. That sounds like a plan. Taking Annie with you will get her out of my hair."

"I'm just here, Mama. I'm not in your hair." A waterfall of tears made trails down her cheeks.

Dr. Molly scooped Annie up and said, "I could use a helper and I can't think of a better one than you."

"Fine. That gives me some time alone with Ruth Ann. Ruth Ann, do you have my pen, so we may begin?"

"I'll get it."

As I left the room, Dr. Molly spoke to Mama slow and steady. "If you need anything at all, you just give me a call. Elizabeth, did you hear me?"

"Pardon me, Molly? Oh, yes, I will call when I hear from Daniel. Thanks for stopping by. Enjoy your afternoon."

I stood in the doorway, holding Mama's fine point black Bic pen when Dr. Molly turned around and almost got stuck with it. "This doesn't settle well with me. Call if anything at all comes up." After a quick hug, she started for the door, with Annie still in her arms.

"Ruthie?" she slid to the ground.

"Can't you come, too? Please. You could bring your pencils and we can make pictures. Please."

I gave her a hug. "I have to stay and take care of Mama. You get Dr. Molly and Cheryl and Sam and Wilbur all to yourself."

"And Scotty." She blinked the tears from her eyes.

"And Scotty, too." I smiled trying to make her feel better, even though I felt worse with every breath I took. Mama's words skipped like a scratch on a record: *your type*. What was that supposed to mean? What *type* was Dr. Molly, that staying with her was a bad thing?

"THERE YOU ARE. Finally. You really do need to work on punctuality. It is an asset in all aspects of your life. Now, where were we?"

Looking at Mama, I saw the damage that had been building. With curls stuck to her head, and one earring was dangling under the left wing of her frames, she looked like a tornado dropped her after the ride of her life. Splotches of coffee and strawberry made a polka dot pattern on her blouse, and her grimy fingernails gripped her pen like it was the only thing keeping her from flying away again. But none of that mattered now. I wanted to understand.

"Mama, what did Grandpa say to you? Why did he come over?"

She tipped her head back and laughed. "Oh Ruth Ann, you know that man is as crazy as a loon. Gibberish. That is all he had to say. Pure gibberish. He truly is a lunatic."

"What do you mean?" I asked in a panic. "Why'd you say *lunatic*?" My hands, wet with sweat, started to shake. Did she know that he was the one in the truck, who shouted and scared us? Did she and Daddy talk about it?

"Mama? Why'd you say that?"

"Say what, dear?"

"Why'd you say that Grandpa's a *lunatic*?"

"Well, for heaven's sake, is it not obvious? Did you not hear him ranting and raving like a mad man?"

"Sure, Mama, but you called him a *lunatic*."

"Must you repeat yourself? It's getting quite tiresome, and the point in having you stay was to be of assistance to me, not a drain on the bit of energy and focus that I have left. So, please, let's focus, shall we?"

"But, Mama, what are we focusing on? Why do you have all these clerical books out? I don't know why you're doing all this stuff now. And Mama, where's Daddy?"

"Oh, for the love of Pete, Ruth Ann! Must you pester me so! I am nearing the end of my tether with you! *Why this? Why that? Where's Daddy?*" she mimicked me in a whiny voice. "I kept you home to assist me, not confront me with endless questions and accusations."

"Mama, I'm just trying to understand..." I tried, but she started typing right in the middle of me talking. "Mama!"

"What is it?" she hollered back, nearly shaking loose a drip of sweat pooling just above her lip.

"I want to help you." I kneeled beside her chair. "I really do, Mama. You have to believe me."

"Believe you?" she shouted and stood, pushing me over as she did. "Don't you understand, Ruth Ann? There is no one I can believe! No one I can rely on! It's up to me! Only me!"

My sobs shook my shoulders. She stared. All I wanted was for her to reach out and touch me, and then she did. She slapped me across the face and screeched, "stop your sniveling! Stop it now!" I cried harder. She hit me! I couldn't believe it. And I could barely feel the sting of her hand, but her words, and the way she looked at me, broke my heart. I pushed myself up.

"I never before saw such a striking resemblance. You look just like your father right now." She sneered, and then her voice hardened. In a hoarse whisper, she pounded the last of her nails into me. "I do not need *him*, and I do not need *you*." Slamming her fist, she shouted, "GO! GET OUT OF MY HOUSE, NOW!"

I ran from the room and straight out the door. No coat, no shoes. Sliding the barn door open, I jumped on my bike and started riding, afraid for me and afraid for her. She never hit me before and never scared me the way she did this time.

Something rattled her loose from her bearings, and I didn't know what to do but ride. I was barely on the road when I saw a group of kids from school coming my way. They were all bundled up and laughing. And there I was, *unbundled* and not knowing *where* I was going, but I was going fast. The only thing moving faster than me was the blizzard I rode into.

A truck pulled up behind me. I panicked. Peddle faster! Go! Faster! I raced ahead of him with thoughts of Shirley and Annie's yellow boot. *Go! Go! Go!* My mind shouted. He honked his horn. I slid on the wet pavement and fell to the ground. Gravel dug into my knees. I closed my eyes and went limp. I waited. His footsteps.

Dr. Molly dropped to the ground beside me. "Where is he?" I shouted, bolting up and looking around. Her red truck was the only one pulled off the side of the road.

"Honey, it's me." Snow swirled around us as she pulled me into a hug. "It's just me." She helped me up, "Oh, you poor girl." The tears held back by a wall of fear broke free.

CHAPTER 18

"After I got Annie to the clinic, I called to check on you. Your mama assumed you were with me and, well, I didn't want her getting any more, out of sorts, so I didn't let on otherwise. I said I'd have you both back in the morning and she seemed fine with that. And then I went looking. And there you were, riding in this storm."

"I'm sorry you had to come get me. I didn't mean to cause trouble," I murmured.

"I know, honey, I know," she said and looked over at me. "Cheryl took Annie home with her, and we'll get those knees cleaned up when we get to the house." And then I swear she read my mind. "I guess your daddy called to say he was holed up in Chicago."

"Really? I thought maybe he left us. He's coming back?" Relief filled me up and tears spilled out. I didn't hear her answer. We rode in silence as we passed by cars in ditches and others spinning around in circles. We were about to cross the last bridge on our way to Cheryl and Annie when lights flashed in front of us, and we came to a stop.

Dr. Molly rolled her window down and called out to an

officer across the way, "we need to get through. Any idea how long it will be?"

He walked over to us. "Might be a bit yet. Some old coot, too big for his britches, had to be going mighty fast to land where he did down there. I don't reckon he'll be seeing the lights this Christmas. And, well, there's more trouble ahead. It'll be quite a spell, yes indeedy."

Dr. Molly closed the window and shivered.

"I'm really sorry about this. I didn't mean to be so selfish."

"Ah, Ruth Ann, you are anything but selfish. But you may have left your good sense sitting beside your shoes." She looked over and winked. Her kindness filled my eyes with tears again. We had just started moving when more sirens came screaming by. "My lord, what is ahead of us? So much commotion for the beginning of a storm."

Her breath shuddered. "I can't tell you how grateful I am that Annie and Cheryl are safe and sound at home. Cheryl would just want to park beside the road and wait for the storm to pass."

Her laugh was soft, but the weariness in her voice reminded me of Mama. I needed to be on the other side of feeling bad. I needed to be with Annie and Cheryl. But the road was blocked just as we were going to head down the lane by the lake. We stopped.

"Something's burning." The words tumbled out before I knew I was thinking them. Dr. Molly stared ahead. Silence. Another officer walked towards us. She rolled her window down.

"Well ma'am, there's a house burning up ahead. You'll have to U-turn just ahead and go back to town until we get things cleared up. Just take 'er slow and easy. Now that U-turn is…"

"I live up there, officer! What house is on fire? Is anyone hurt?"

"Well, I can't rightly say. You never can know for sure 'till the hospital or morgue gives us a name." He gave a little laugh. "Now, I'm just teasing ya'll. 'Tis a shame. Nice little community you have over here. The only thing I heard was that they may have lost a dog. But you know dogs; sometimes in situations like this, they run off. But ma'am, there's a car behind you so you just head up to that U-turn I was–"

"But officer–"

"Now ma'am, that's all I know. Your husband can probably give you a few more details when you get through a bit later tonight or tomorrow."

Dr. Molly pulled her truck forward and then off the side of the road. Without even looking over, she said, "I have to find out what's going on. You wait here. There are blankets behind the seat. I'm turning the engine off. I can't have you asphyxiated."

She pushed on the door, and it pushed back. Finally, she climbed out into the night that looked like a shaken snow globe. Before she headed off, she pried the door open just enough to look into my eyes and say, "I love you, honey." And then she was gone.

She was just out of sight when I opened my own door to run after her. "Dr. Molly, wait! Dr. Molly!" Within less than a minute, I lost sight of the truck and of her. "Dr. Molly!" I screamed into the storm, but snow blew back, and my words did too.

I ran without knowing where. I thought of Daddy's warning that tears turn to icicles, so I tried not to cry. *I should have stayed put. I never should have left home. Where was Annie? Was she OK?* My mind swirled like the white snow around me; the snow that Dr. Molly disappeared into. The wind howled, and I started to cry. I didn't care about icicles anymore.

"What are you doing?" Dr. Molly hollered above the storm.

"Dr. Molly, I found you!" I cried.

"What did I…come with me!" She grabbed my hand as we raced toward the flames. "Lord, have mercy," she said and fell to her knees. Flames laughed and danced, without a care in the world, as they devoured her little yellow house by the lake.

"We need to keep going. Get up! Get up, Dr. Molly!" It was like she didn't hear me. "Now!" I shouted. Pulling her to her feet, we ran. "Where are the lady and the little girl who were in the house?" I shouted at the firefighter who stopped us, keeping us from Annie and Cheryl.

"I can't say," the man shouted back. "All I do know is that an ambulance drove by with the lights flashing. The hospital can tell you who it was they were carrying. Not me. I'm just here to hold this line so nobody else gets in harm's way tonight." With that he shot a wad of tobacco slime into the white snow near my feet and declared, "For crying out loud, if that ain't the darndest thing I ever did see. Girl, you gotta use a bit of common sense. Common sense'll keep you from landing in the hospital too. Might have helped the folks that got caught in this mess, but who am I to say?"

I pushed Dr. Molly away from his words, looked at her, and shouted, "we have to find Annie and Cheryl. We have to go to the hospital and find them." She doubled over, broken in two with the pain of her worry. How would I ever get her back to her truck?

"Ruth Ann!" I spun around, looking for the voice that called out my name. "I thought that was you." Matthew Wright's daddy stood in front of us. He reached out and patted Dr. Molly's shoulder. "Now, now."

She straightened herself out. With one hand on her mouth and the other on her stomach, she held herself together. "What are you folks doing out here?" Tenderness shined in his eyes, just like Matthew, almost enough to make me cry. But there wasn't time.

"That house on fire is Dr. Molly's! Annie might be in there!" I choked back my worries and kept shouting, "we have to get to the hospital!"

Worry crossed his face like clouds blocking out the sun. "Where 'bouts is your car parked, Dr. Molly?"

"Her truck's parked back there," I answered for her and pointed.

"It's at the corner just before the lane. They wouldn't let us drive in any further," she finished.

"Let's go," Mr. Wright said and led us to his truck. I helped Dr. Molly in and pulled the door hard against the storm.

"Take good care on the road now," he said as we drove away from the flames. "This storm is a biter. No need to rush being that visiting hours are over and Ruth Ann, you're not old enough and Dr. Molly–" He tapped his fingers on the steering wheel.

"Now I'm confused; what was your little sister doing out here without your folks?" He asked as we pulled up to Dr. Molly's truck. There was no easy answer, so I didn't bother giving one before we were on our own again and headed for the hospital.

AGAINST THE BACKDROP of flashing red lights, the snow looked like pink cotton candy swirling and falling. At another time I might have talked about the county fair and snow cones, but every time Dr. Molly tapped the brakes, my mind shouted *Hurry, hurry, hurry*. But we didn't hurry.

We stopped just before the bridge. She sighed, broken by the weight of her worry, and my annoyance rose like spit before puke. She was the one person I wasn't supposed to take of. But here we were.

Her voice broke the silence that rested between us like a cat, curled and still. "No, no, no, we can't stop! We have to keep going!"

"Looks like they're getting that *old coot* out of the river," I muttered, hearing the sharp edge of my voice. A blue pick-up truck hung from a tow hook like first prize in the fishing derby. And then I gasped, "Dr. Molly..."

"Ruth Ann, please. We can't panic. We've got a long drive..."

"No. That's..." I threw the door open. *Annie! What if Annie...?* In a flash and with an iron grip Dr. Molly grabbed ahold of me and reached over and slammed the door shut.

"Ruth Ann, what in the world are you doing?"

"That's my grandpa's truck!" I sobbed. "Maybe he went to your house and got Annie! Maybe she went in the river too!" My resolve to be the strong one shattered. "Let me go! Let me go!" I beat my fists against her. She held tighter. Even though I could feel her start to shake, I couldn't shake myself free.

"Look at me!" she shouted. "Ruth Ann Walker, LOOK AT ME!" She held my face in front of hers. "Are you certain? Are you absolutely certain?" I nodded. Her hands that held my face instantly pooled with sweat against my skin. Her eyes darted from the truck to me and back again. "You must stay here. And *this* time, don't you *dare* disobey me." Her voice was colder than the night. "I will go out there and see if they can tell me anything." I nodded again.

Shaking with the terror that both of us felt, she pushed the door open, tucked her head down, and trudged toward the group of men huddled together. When moments later she pulled the door open, snow flew in along with her. I was too afraid of the answer to ask the question. I held my breath and my questions.

"All we can do is go to the hospital. They can't tell me anything." She gripped the wheel and traffic inched past my grandpa's truck, dangling and dripping, past the flashing lights. With the back of her hand, she rubbed at her snot and tears. "Oh, Ruth Ann, what a mess. If anything has happened to Annie, I will NEVER forgive myself." I believed her. It didn't make sense, but I wasn't sure I would either.

Sure that we could get there faster, if only we tried harder, we both leaned forward, like putting our weight into a game of tug-of-war. Finally, Dr. Molly turned into the hospital parking lot. I froze. "Honey, we need to get inside. Now." She looked at me. "Ruth Ann, I need to know."

"I'm afraid to know," I confessed through my tears. Splinters of fear poked the air right out of me. "I can't. I can't go inside." I slid to the floor of the truck.

"Standing in the unknowing will do us in. I'm going in and you're going with me." She got out, came around, opened my door, and carried me in her arms like a newborn lamb. Snow flew in our faces, and she nearly slipped and fell and then set me down on the ice-cold parking lot. Reality hit me when my feet hit the ground and together, we rushed through the sliding doors.

"There's been an accident..." Dr. Molly stuttered in broken bits of story. "...an emergency...chaos," she kept on. "We'd like to see Annabelle Rose Walker and my sister, Cheryl Malone."

"Dr. Molly, Cheryl ain't..." I started, recognizing the lie but not the reason for it. Without turning her head, I watched her set her jaw and knew to shut my mouth and stare at the frozen feet holding my body up.

"Can you please tell us what room they're in?" Dr. Molly asked, with certainty that they were there and alive. When the lady gave out two different room numbers, I grabbed ahold of Dr. Molly's hand.

"How old are you, honey?" The nurse stood up and asked.

"Thirteen?" I mumbled with spit shooting out with my lie.

"Hmm. Well, that won't do, because honey, you need to be thirteen today, not some day off in the future. Isn't that right?" She didn't care that my little sister could have died and we could have too. "You'll just have to wait over there," she pointed to a row of orange plastic chairs, "for your Mama to come back out."

"I'll get back with news quick as can be." Dr. Molly let loose of my hand and walked through the swinging double doors that the nurse pointed to.

Mama always said Annie's thoughts came like a rushing river and mine came slow and steady like an ocean tide. If I'd been faster on my feet, maybe I could be with her now. But I wasn't so I closed my eyes and before I knew it, it was summertime and Annie and I were lying down in the middle of the cornfield. The sun was warm, and the sound of the breeze set the tassels dancing.

"Why are you here?" I startled awake and jumped to my feet at the sound of my cousin's voice.

"Why are you here?" I spit back at Jimmy Jr., and shook my head, shaking loose corn tassels and confusion.

His little brother walked over, wiped away a tear and said, "Daddy says heaven's a lot better than this cold state of Iowa any day."

"What are you talking about?" I yelled. "What do you mean, *heaven?*"

"You know, the place where you go when you die. People die, Ruth Ann. They do," Jimmy Jr. added.

Words like *accident, God's way, Grandma, just won't be the same*, slipped through the fog of my brain and then I started to sob. Uncle Jimmy walked towards us with his head hanging down. "I just can't believe it. I just can't believe something like this could happen to me," he cried.

That last part found its way in and I couldn't hold myself back. I went crazy and started beating that man for every time he ever did say a cruel thing to Annie or was mean and disrespectful to my mama and daddy. Him pretending to care that my sister was dead was the last straw.

"Ruth Ann, stop! What are you doing?" Dr. Molly cried out as she ran over and pulled me away. She wrapped her arms around me and held me as I cried out.

"I can't believe she's dead. I can't believe she's dead."

"What are you talking about? Nobody's dead. They're both fine. They're just keeping them for a spell to make sure." She pushed me back and looked into my face and said, "honey, they're shaken, but they'll be fine. They got a little bruised up getting the animals out and all, but they'll be good as new."

As I caught my breath, she asked, "where did you get the notion that Annie was dead?"

I glared at my cousins and my uncle and they were glaring right back at me. "What the hell is going on here, Ruth Ann? You're just as crazy as your mama! You owe me an apology!" Uncle Jimmy spit.

"I don't owe you nothing! And don't you call my mama crazy you–" I lurched at him again.

"Ruth Ann, stop!" Dr. Molly shouted and pulled me back.

"But they said somebody died. I don't understand," I cried. Dr. Molly touched my shoulder and walked away. I followed right behind her.

"Excuse me, ma'am. Can you clear something up for us?" Dr. Molly asked the backend of a lady. She turned and looked at us with fisheyes and a frown. She was different from the one who was here when we came in. "We're confused. Can you tell us who died tonight?"

"Unless you're *family*, I can't say a thing." She went right back to working like we weren't even there. Finally, she looked up again. "If you could step away from the counter, we have work to do."

I turned to go when Dr. Molly called over to another lady who walked through the swinging door, "Mrs. Brown, it's me, Molly Hobart. I'm just trying to clear up some confusion."

"I know who you are." Her words curdled like sour milk.

"But Mrs. Brown, just yesterday–"

"We can't help you."

That lady wasn't wearing her black poodle slippers, but I knew her just the same. I looked from her to Dr. Molly, whose eyes filled with tears. "Why are you being so mean? Here she was taking care of those two little black dogs of yours and you–"

"Ruth Ann." Dr. Molly's voice was weak.

"But Dr. Molly, what's going on? Just yesterday you were helping her out. I don't understand."

"There is nothing to understand." I couldn't tell if she was talking to me or to herself. She walked over and sat in one of the orange plastic chairs.

I went to the window. I didn't know who died, but I knew it wasn't Annie or Cheryl. I exhaled. My breath steamed up the glass. I drew a question mark. *There is nothing to understand,* made me think of something that Heidi's mama used to say: *You can't make sense of things that don't make sense.* Maybe they were saying the same thing.

My anger and confusion melted into sadness, and I started to cry. Two faint beams of light moved like a snake, slithering towards me. Maybe it was Mama and Daddy. The soft lights turned harsh as they got closer, and my throat tightened up, knowing they would be angry.

Aunt Helen's car came to a stop. Fierce and snarling, icy

claws grabbed at everything in sight, taking the door out of her hand the minute she pushed it open. She nearly stumbled but caught herself, got the door closed and fell to her knees before she got 'round to the other side.

I expected Mama to open the other door. I would have rushed out to help, to walk her in. I wiped away my tears and waited. Aunt Helen was back on her feet and reached to take Grandma's hand. Hope and fear slipped out with my next breath, and I marched back over to Uncle Jimmy. "Who died?" I blurted out.

Dr. Molly was instantly beside me. "What's going on, Jim?" she asked in a voice so timid it was hard to hear.

He stood up, stuck out his chest. "What the hell do you think is going on, Dr. Molly?" He said *doctor* like it was a cuss word. "Why does the pervert doc show up at the hospital for family that ain't her own?"

"There was a fire. My family is here."

"My family's dead, Dr. Molly. My daddy dumped his truck in the McAllister River and now he's gone." *Grandpa's truck. The river. Lights. Snow.* "Maybe you had him so upset, he couldn't see straight on the road between here and the lake. Maybe that's what happened. Maybe *this* is your fault too!"

He snarled and spit his words. He spun around. But not before I saw tears standing in his eyes. Worrying about Annie and Cheryl crowded out all the room for remembering Grandpa's truck in the river. *Grandpa's dead? Grandpa's dead.* Pieces from a puzzle dropped into place.

Uncle Jimmy sat down with his head in his hands. I got shoved to the side from behind. Grandma's face, purple with rage, moved past me to Dr. Molly. "Get out! Get out!" she shouted at her. "You did nothing but rile him up! It's no wonder he ended up in the river! He was so worried about his little Annie, ever since you came along!" she roared.

Dr. Molly backed away and then ducked and leaned, as

261

Grandma hurled her handbag right at her head and missed. But Mrs. Brown wasn't quite so quick on her feet. She was heading our way, with a scowl on her face, when she got smacked upside the head and went down like tipping a cow.

Everything Grandma carried in that old bag flew every which way. Except for the hemorrhoid ointment. Can't say why Grandma was carrying it about or how it happened to get lodged between Mrs. Brown's teeth. But there it was. That tube of Preparation H was hanging out of her mouth like she was sucking a bottle, and every jaw in the room but hers was hanging slack.

A security guard came out from behind the swinging doors and shouted, "now hear me! You all settle down and behave like civilized folk." With his thumbs in his belt, he looked around at all the faces struck dumb. "This is not the place to carry on like the Hatfield's and McCoy's. Simmer down." He stuck a toothpick in one side of his mouth and opened the other and said, "that's better," and strutted away like he just shut down a fight at the OK Corral.

But then he looked down. "What the heck? Mrs. Brown? What are you doing down there?" We all stood still, like we were waiting for her to explain herself. Even my grandma was quiet as Mrs. Brown thrashed about like a beetle on her back. By gum, she was in a pickle. And wouldn't you know. Dr. Molly was the only one offering a hand. She knelt beside her, took the hemorrhoid cream out of her mouth, and put one hand underneath her head and took ahold of her arm with the other.

"Ruth Ann, give me a hand here." I scooched down on the other side. "Now, Mrs. Brown, we're going to help you up. Is that alright with you?"

Tears were running straight from her eyes to the floor. "That'd be fine. Yes. Thank you," she whimpered.

"One, two, three."

Up she came to sitting. Took a bit longer, but with the security guard's help we finally got her to her feet. She waddled away without another word. My cousins were crawling on the floor, like they were hunting for Easter eggs, gathering up the store of goods that were in Grandma's purse before she heaved it at Dr. Molly's head. I looked at her poured into her chair like old paint and walked over.

"I'm real sorry, Grandma." She held her face in her hands but didn't even look at me. Aunt Helen did.

"You best be going. Go home to your mama." If words were in color, hers were *icy blue* and filled my veins. I shivered and turned away. As much as I hated my family right now, I didn't want them hating me.

The next voice I heard was Dr. Molly's. "Let's get you home and let your mama know that you and Annie are OK." *But we're not OK!* My hurt turned to anger in an instant. She touched my arm and I jerked it away. Was this all her fault and everyone else was right?

I saw the bridge. The snow. Red flashing lights. Grandpa's truck in the river where he taught Annie to love fishing. And to hate it too. I didn't know I was crying until Dr. Molly reached out a tissue. I used my sleeve instead. How could I be right and everybody else be wrong? More family came through the door. Aunts and uncles and cousins. For all of them, I was already gone. Dr. Molly and I walked out of the hospital. I never felt so alone in all my life.

CHAPTER 19

By the time we pulled into the driveway at home, it was almost midnight. Mama was waiting. Rocking.

"This is unacceptable." She looked at me. "Ruth Ann, where is your sister?"

"Annie's–"

"Elizabeth," Dr. Molly interrupted, and walked over and kneeled down in front of Mama. "Annie is just fine. Truly, she is just fine."

"*Just fine?*" Mama stood so fast her rocker tipped back on its heels and nearly hit the wall as Dr. Molly fell flat on her bottom, tumbling at Mama's feet.

"The fact that you need to tell me that she is *just fine*, indicates otherwise. It is the middle of the night and my youngest child is not at home! Clearly, she is not *just fine*! Where is she Molly?" Mama hissed, and droplets of spit flew from her mouth and into the soft lamplight, showering Dr. Molly who still sat at her feet.

"There was a fire. Given the circumstances, yes, I would say that Annie IS fine." Dr. Molly rolled to her hands and

264

knees. She looked up. Mama looked down. They stood like boxers in a ring.

"Mama. Remember, you weren't feeling well and–" I ran over, wanting to claim my place again. Beside her. Before Dr. Molly. But she didn't want me either.

"Ruth Ann, I do not need a full recitation of the evening's events! Where is your sister?"

"She's at the hospital and Cheryl is too. Dr. Molly saw them and said they both just got scared and stuff."

"Why didn't you alert me sooner? Molly, this is unforgivable," Mama fumed.

"We tried to call. We tried lots of times. The line kept ringing busy." I ran to the phone in the hall. "Mama, you don't even have the phone hung up proper. That's why we couldn't tell you."

"Oh. Well. Yes. The incessant ringing was wearing on my last nerve. I simply decided to rest the receiver beside the cradle for a time. But that is beside the point, I must get to the hospital?"

"The roads are terrible, Elizabeth, and they're sleeping now."

Mama paused, like she was counting her knits and pearls, and finally saw the pattern they were making. "You mean to tell me that you and your *friend* had responsibility for my youngest child and she has now ended up in the hospital?" In the dim light, Mama's face glowed red.

I hiccuped. And then I did it again. I may as well have pulled a fire alarm. Both Mama and Dr. Molly stopped and looked at me. For the first time, Mama saw me.

"Ruth Ann Walker, where are your shoes? Do not tell me that you have been out in the cold, the snow no less, without shoes on your feet?"

Then she pointed her hot poker back at Dr. Molly. "Holy Mother of God, Molly, you clearly cannot be trusted to take proper care of my children and will never be placed in a position to do so again."

This was worse than watching Annie fight with Bud Fleeting, and the line I was supposed to be standing on got blurrier and blurrier.

"Mama, it's not her fault. Her house burned down." I remembered. Dr. Molly's not the enemy. Mama's not the enemy. And I needed to be in charge. "I'll just go ahead and make up the bed in the spare room for her." I didn't wait for Mama to answer and started for the stairs.

"Oh, I don't think so, Ruth Ann! The events of this night are unforgivable, and I must get to the hospital; I cannot be bothered making sleeping arrangements for Dr. Molly and her *friend*. Get your boots Ruth Ann; we are going now. And Dr. Hobart, please show yourself out."

Mama's words were barely out of her mouth when the air hissed through her teeth, she plopped back into her chair, and her head fell back. "God grant me your strength," she whispered.

"But Mama, their house burned down," I pleaded, not knowing if she was asleep or awake. With the letup of the storm inside my house, Dr. Molly and I both fumbled with apologies and offers.

"Elizabeth, I cannot tell you how sorry I am that your children got caught in all of this mess. I'd be happy to drive you both to the hospital, if that would be of any help."

"Mama, I'm sorry. We tried to call about a million times, but the telephone was busy." Suddenly I felt as frantic and confused as a coyote in the kitchen. Somebody must have been the one to blame, but who?

Mama slowly blinked her eyes open and looked at Dr. Molly. "Your *help* is no longer necessary."

"I'll let myself out," Dr. Molly whispered, and started for the door.

"Dr. Molly–" I wanted to stop her. I needed to let her go.

"It's best this way. Your mama will rest much easier with just family. Trust me." Her eyes swelled with tears, and she walked back into the storm.

"You heard Molly, it's best this way. We need to get to the hospital." Mama's words were as cold as the snow that blew in and settled on the kitchen floor like diamond dust.

I looked at my feet. "There's no point," I mumbled.

"No point in what?"

"Annie's sleeping and it's not even visiting hours, anyhow. There's no point in going now." Sorrow slid to the side and made room for scorn. "And Mama, you are acting just as hateful as everybody else. I am ashamed of you." I left for bed. I heard her huff and tsk, but she didn't try to stop me.

Buddy and Beets were curled up together at the foot of my bed. When I climbed in they smooshed up against me and the three of us spent the night tied like a knot, waiting for Annie.

I woke up to Buddy whining at the door. Beets was purring, and I was breathing through her fur. I wiped stray bits from my mouth and walked over to let Buddy out. The hall light was on. I followed the sound of typing. "Mama, what are you doing? What time is it?"

"Oh, well, I guess I don't know. I was not able to sleep, given the sound of the storm. I decided to use the time to brush up. Speaking of which, could you be a dear and pick up that clerical book and do some dictation for me."

"Mama, it's not even light out yet and when it is, we've got to go to the hospital and bring Annie home."

"Yes, of course. But given the early hour, I thought that we could use this time–"

"Mama? Are you OK?"

"I don't know." She told the truth and dropped her head. Her hands disappeared into her dark curls streaked with gray. "It is all too much. It is simply too much," she murmured.

I stepped closer and touched her back. Her bones rippled underneath my hand. The smell of stale coffee rose from her breath.

"I have such a headache," she moaned.

I went into the kitchen for Anacin. I passed by the telephone, still resting beside its cradle. I put it back. It rang.

"Hello? My daddy's not here. May I take a message, please?" The voice was familiar but distant. "Oh hi. I don't know where he is. Sure, just a minute."

"Mama, it's Aunt Alice. She needs to talk to you."

Mama hollered back from the sewing room, "take a message. I will call her back later in the day."

"She's busy. She said she'll have to get back to you…OK, just a minute."

"Mama, it's real important and it can't wait 'till *later in the day*."

I left the phone sitting beside the cradle. Finally, Mama wandered in.

"We have to get to the hospital. Annie is there, and your grandfather is dead," Mama said as she rushed to grab her coat and shoes. "Ruth Ann, how could you have kept this information from me?" she accused.

"But Mama–"

"Do not, *but Mama* me. What is Annie to think not having had me come to her aid?"

"Where's Daddy? He needs to come with us."

"If I knew your father's whereabouts, he would be here with us. Clearly, I do not. Therefore, he *is* not.

"But he'll be back home tonight, right?" I pleaded.

"Get dressed immediately. Annie is alone, and Daniel doesn't even know that his father has passed. What a terrible mess this has all become," Mama moaned.

When we pushed the hospital door open, Dr. Molly was sitting alone. "Dr. Molly, did you spend the night here?" She looked nearly as bedraggled as my mama.

"Come, Ruth Ann. We are here about Annie." Mama hustled away from me.

"Did you?" I asked again as Mama walked away.

"I slept at the office for most of the night. I just got here and thought I'd try again to see Cheryl. Oh, there's Dr. Wallingford. Excuse me, Ruth Ann."

She rushed away and called out to Dr. Wallingford who, just the other day, had been in the clinic with Miser. "Dr. Wallingford, hi. Could you help me? I'm here to see Cheryl."

"Now, Dr. Molly, much as I'd liked to...you know I can't do that. You best get in touch with her family. Now they'd be welcome here in the hospital. I've got to get to my rounds. You best go home and rest. But call her family. That'd be best."

"But Doctor, I'm the only family she has in the state. I thought I could just pop back with fresh clothes for her. Just a couple of things before she's released."

I heard her pleading and watched Dr. Wallingford shuttle about and stare at his shoes. That's when my own mama breezed past on her way to see Annie. Dr. Wallingford smiled and held the door open for Mama to pass through.

"This is ridiculous!" Dr. Molly shouted and tried to follow my mama back, but his arm blocked the door.

"Now, listen here Doc, we don't want to be making a scene, now do we? You make the rules in your clinic and I make them here. That's just how it is. Rules are rules. If you're not gonna head home, sit for a spell and I know that your friend will be out in no time."

Dr. Molly walked over and sat beside me. Her head was propped up in the same pair of hands that saved and soothed dogs and cats and cows and goats all throughout the county.

But here in the Emmet County Hospital she was treated like a nobody. Like she didn't matter. Family that couldn't be troubled to cross the state line for Cheryl was welcome. But family that was made by love and caring wasn't. I felt ashamed to be standing on the side of the line that counted.

We waited in the orange plastic chairs for more than an hour, before Mama came walking out with Annie who bolted into the both of us as we stood up at the sight of her.

"Ruthie, there was a fire. Dr. Molly, your house caught fire and burned down."

"I'm so glad you're OK!" I said into her hair as I hugged her tight.

"And Dr. Molly, Cheryl's coming out real soon. How come you didn't come back? She was waiting and waiting; me too." Annie tipped her head in confusion.

"That's a long, boring story," Dr. Molly said but I knew she didn't mean those words exactly. "But I'm so happy to see you now!" And then I watched Dr. Molly's eyes look back at the door. I looked too. No Cheryl.

"Well, I need to get you girls home. This has been quite the fiasco." Mama said.

"Fiasco, Elizabeth? My home was burned down, our family–"

"*Our* family? There is no *our* family, Molly." She took Annie by the hand. "Girls, we need to be getting home."

"But Mama, I wasn't done telling Dr. Molly how me and Cheryl was in the kitchen making supper when we smelled smoke." She turned to Dr. Molly, "before that, the dogs were barking and barking. We figured there was an old 'coon riling them up. When she opened the door the neighbor came running...right then...right at the same minute."

"Thank you, Annie." Molly reached out and touched Annie. Your mama really needs to get home. It's been quite..." She looked at Mama, "a *fiasco* for all of us."

"Yes. Molly is correct. That's enough. Now you've told her. I am grateful to see that, at least, *you* have shoes and a proper coat on."

"But I didn't tell her about Mr. Lincoln and the old tomcat. I didn't tell her those parts yet...or about how Cheryl ran back in even when she knew the fire–"

Nearly breathless, Annie turned to me again and asked, "did you see the house, Ruthie? It's all burned up. I never did see nothing like it."

"No, I didn't see it." It was hard to hear Annie's story over the roar of my anger at Mama and my brain bouncing around trying to decide if I was mad at Dr. Molly too.

"Enough, Annie. Enough of this talk." Mama's cheeks filled up with air, and she blew it out with her final words. "Girls, we are going home now. Goodbye, Molly. To the car, girls. At once."

"But Mama, what about Dr. Molly? She's all by herself waiting for Cheryl," Annie moaned.

"I'll be alright." Dr. Molly looked as lonesome as could be.

We walked into the snowy morning, "It's the first snowfall Annie," I tried.

"I know." She kicked the dry white powder at her feet.

I turned back. "Look Annie!" Cheryl was easing her way across the room to Dr. Molly. Whatever confusion I felt was gone. I saw our friends and remembered. That's what love is.

"I wish we could go back," Annie moaned.

"We'll see them later," I said.

"Well, I don't know about that," Mama sputtered.

"What! What do you mean by that?" Annie cried out.

"We need to focus on *family*. Our family."

"Why can't they be our family too?" I asked.

"Family is defined by...by birth and by law," Mama explained, not sounding like she was too sure of what she was saying.

271

"But why?" Annie asked.

"Annie, please; I am exhausted."

"That's why Dr. Molly couldn't go back to see Cheryl. She's not *family*," I explained to Annie, wanting to sneer at Mama as I said it.

"Sure, they're family. They do all the stuff that families do, don't they, Ruthie?"

"For the love of Pete, Annie. Drop it!" Mama shouted as we were getting into the car.

"There they are!" Annie exclaimed from the backseat.

Dr. Molly held Cheryl's hand and walked her slow and steady to their truck. "They sure look like family to me," I said as Mama slammed her door shut and started the car before I even pulled both legs in. Next thing I knew, Mama pulled up to my school.

"I will be taking Annie home with me while you go on to school, Ruth Ann."

"How I'm supposed to concentrate on stuff when I barely got any sleep at all."

"Please, Ruth Ann. Make this easier on me. Please."

"Make it easier on *you*?" I snapped and threw the door open.

"But Mama, I need Ruthie." Tears spilled out from the deep blue pools of Annie's eyes that used to sparkle like the lake in summertime. But Mama plunged ahead.

"And she will be home just as soon as she finishes with her obligation to school. There has been enough disruption with all of this nonsense." To me, "off you go. The day will end before you know it."

I sat in my classroom staring out at the snow falling, when a fat, red-breasted robin landed on a branch laced with ice. We stared at each other. With a flutter of wings, she crashed into the window. *Poor thing, she wants in.*

I thought about Dr. Molly. I watched her *crash* into the

glass door at the hospital; the glass that kept her out; the rules that said she wasn't family. Half the time, I wanted out of the craziness of my family, and all Dr. Molly wanted was a chance to get into hers.

Mrs. Puddle walked over. "I know you've experienced a terrible tragedy." She touched my hand. I pulled it to my lap and looked around the room. *This is so embarrassing.* "The loss of family is our greatest loss." She teared up. "If there's anything you need, anything at all..." Pat, pat.

My face burned. I looked out from under my hair. *Maybe they know; maybe they all know the truth.* Or maybe I'll blurt it out; the truth about how I wanted my grandpa dead. Maybe that makes me the monster. I'm not sorry he died. Not one bit sorry. But I'm supposed to be. Another pat, and she walked away.

Wind picked up handfuls of snow and threw it in my face the minute the last bell rang. I shoved my hands in my pockets and waited for Mama. I had to get back to Annie. But there was no sign of her, so without a hat or mittens, I started walking.

I was about five minutes from school and fifteen from home when a car pulled off the side of the road ahead of me. I knew that my hair must have looked like spun cotton candy, but I was so happy to see Mr. Wright. I smiled and ran to his car just as Matthew opened the passenger door. They both stepped out.

"Well, aren't you a sorry sight dragging yourself through this blizzard," Mr. Wright winked and put his arm over my shoulder. "Now, if you don't mind riding along with that scalawag, we could give you a lift."

Matthew sat in the back seat with me, and his daddy whistled along with the music on the radio. Hot air blew from the car's heater, and as my hair begin to thaw drips of water fell on my face like rain. Real quiet like, Matthew said,

"I'm sorry about your grandpa, Ruth Ann." I looked at him and nodded, wondering what he knew and wasn't saying. Silence sat between us like a pond frozen over in winter.

"I'm real sorry too about Dr. Molly's house burning down. My daddy says they might never find out who it was that set that fire."

My head snapped around like I'd been caught in a lasso. "What are you talking about? What do you mean *who* set the fire? Someone did it on purpose? Matthew, what are you saying?" I knew I wasn't giving him one minute's chance to speak but my blood ran cold and my mind ran in circles like a dog after its tail.

"Calm down, Ruth Ann, nobody knows nothing for sure." He touched my hand that rested on the bench between us. I flinched. He snapped back, away from the hot coals of my anger. "Every time I try to say the right thing, it's the wrong thing," he muttered.

That was the truth of it. I was tied in more knots than a piece of macramé. I felt bad about snapping, but I couldn't find my way back to kindness. If somebody set the fire, and if my grandpa died on that road on the same night...

"You've been through a lot. Anybody can see that." Looking at me in the rear-view mirror, Mr. Wright's kind words filled me with sorrow and shame. But how could I ever make sense of what they were saying?

"Mr. Wright, you were there. Did somebody do it on purpose?"

"Now, nobody knows for sure, but I'm sorry to say, some folks think it might have been arson, all right. It's a sorry and scary world these days."

"Arson?"

"Do you think they'll find the lunatic who did it?" Matthew questioned his dad. But when he said *lunatic*, I wondered if he was thinking of my grandpa too.

"Well, I can't say I know that. Truth is, even if I heard rumors, I couldn't speak up just yet with the investigation going on." Then to me he said, "now, honey, I am might sorry about your grandpa. Can't say that I ever did get to know him well." He stared at the road ahead. "Your grandma must be broken-hearted."

"Uh huh." *Lunatic*, echoed in my head. When we pulled up my drive, I thanked Mr. Wright and Matthew, and stumbled towards my house, barely even noticing the blowing snow that iced me over again before I got to the kitchen door.

Annie was waiting. Outside. "Ruthie, Grandpa's dead." Her voice. Flat. "He crashed. He crashed into the river, Ruthie." She shuddered as breath blew the rest of her words away and icy trails of tears froze on her blotchy red cheeks.

"How long have you been out here?" My words sounded scolding. I didn't want them to.

"I've been waiting...a while...for you," she whimpered as I pulled her into a hug. Sobs shook loose the last of what was holding her together, and she cried out, "Grandpa's dead! It's all my fault! It's all my fault!"

"No, it's not, Annie. You didn't do anything wrong. Where's Mama?"

"She's resting, and Daddy's gone and his daddy's...oh." Annie choked and coughed and wailed.

Holding her up with one arm, I pushed the door open with the other, and walked her into the kitchen. "You didn't do anything, Annie. It's not your fault," I whispered again.

"I made him mad and hurt his feelings, Ruthie. He told me bad things would happen. But I didn't know he would die. I didn't know." She slunk to the floor, with her head in her hands.

"None of it is your fault." I kneeled down next to her and rubbed her back. "Annie, look at me. Grandpa crashed his truck, that's all there is to it. He drank his whiskey and crashed his truck. You weren't even there. It can't be your fault."

Buddy followed behind whining the whole way as I helped Annie climb the stairs to our room where she could be safe and warm. Buddy jumped up beside her, and I wished that I could lie down beside them and wake up to this whole mess being fixed. But I knew it wouldn't work that way so I went looking for Mama.

CHAPTER 20

"Hey, Mama," I said feeling shy and unsure as I turned her bedroom light on. It was half past three and she was curled in a ball on the side of her bed. "You alright?"

"Certainly, everything is just fine. My father-in-law is dead in a drunken wreckage on the road from Squam Lake. Apparently, rumors are circulating as to his reason for being there. My husband is missing. The daughter I have always been able to rely on is traipsing about the countryside with miscreants. And my youngest child has fallen asleep after upchucking to the point that nothing more can rise up from the depths of her. Of course, I am just fine."

My heart raced with every new word she spoke. But she wasn't finished. "Oh, and did I mention that, currently, there are no funds, whatsoever, with which to pay the bills if your father does not make an appearance with his paycheck?"

I sat down on the bed and looked straight at her. "I'm here now, Mama. And Annie's tuckered out but she's up and moving. She's had a scare and she feels real bad that Grandpa's dead. I know Daddy will be back soon and everything really will be fine."

"Ruth Ann, things were not *fine* when he was here, and they will not be fine *if and when* he returns. This is not the way life is supposed to be. This surely is not what I bargained for," she said with a bitter laugh.

"Mama, things will be *fine* 'cause that's how we'll make 'em." I stood up and said, "I'm gonna check on Annie, and why don't you wash your face and see what we can fix for supper. And Mama, Dr. Molly and Cheryl will be having supper with us tonight. Their house burned down, and they don't have a stove to cook a pot of beans on, and they need our help right now."

Until I said it, I hadn't even thought about Dr. Molly. It was like the words came out before I thought them. And when I heard them, they made sense to me. I turned and left the room without giving Mama time to say no.

"Ruth Ann Walker, you are not in charge!" She shouted at my back. How many times did I hear Annie say the same thing? And this time? The quiet that followed me down the hall told me that I was.

"Wanna help Mama and me make some supper?" I asked the blanket covered lump that Buddy was snuggled up to. Annie peeked out with a blank stare. "Annie?" I asked.

"I miss Grandpa."

"You miss him?" I stammered. She must have heard my confusion, and maybe even disgust, and slid back under the covers. "Annie, I'm sorry. I'm just surprised you miss him, that's all. I thought he did bad things to you?" Here we were, having the talk I never wanted to be having and couldn't stand not to. "Annie, talk to me."

She started to cry, and I scooched down beside her, kept my mouth shut and waited.

"It's not the *bad* Grandpa I miss. It's the *good* one, Ruthie.

278

We used to play cards and go fishing. And now he can't be good again 'cause he's gone. I must have done something to make him like that. I just don't know what. And now I can't even say I'm sorry," she sobbed. And shook.

I rubbed her back and waited. Thinking. Then my thoughts turned to words. "Maybe with Grandpa gone, we can...oh I don't know. I'm just thinking..." I felt Annie hold her breath waiting for me to keep going.

"When Dr. Molly and I were waiting for you and Cheryl, I got to thinking. Maybe Mama and those folks at the hospital are wrong. Maybe family isn't just the folks who are related to us. Maybe sometimes it's the folks who love us. I closed my eyes and waited for Annie to make peace or find sleep.

Lying next to her, I knew that I could finally keep Annie safe. Grandpa was gone, but were we really rid of him? He would still be in the shadows. He would be there in the next storm. Every new litter of kittens would bring Shirley's memory back; and she would bring Grandpa too. I didn't see how our family could ever step foot in our house again, or us in theirs. We needed a new family more now than ever.

I was staring into space when I saw Mama standing in the doorway. With the little bit of light there was, I could see a trail of tears left behind like streaks on the window after a storm. She walked away, without saying a thing. There was nothing she needed to say. Right now, it was up to me.

When Mama was the best of herself, the self that threw her head back and laughed, she reminded me to be the best of myself too. She told me that my imagination was a good thing. And right now, it's all that I had. I had to imagine that family could heal; that family could be different, be new. I imagined a family that was made up with love and kindness. The kind of family that lived in a yellow house beside a lake and sat around a dining table and talked and laughed.

· · ·

I WALKED DOWNSTAIRS EXPECTING to find Mama. I didn't. On the counter was a box of dried noodles, and a jar of stewed tomatoes from the garden. I traipsed through the snow to the cellar door. From the deep freeze, I pulled out a package of ground beef wrapped in butcher paper. As I reached up to turn the light off, I looked around at all the pickles and preserves that lined the walls. That got me to thinking. With the meat in one hand, and a jar of canned cherries in the other, I started making plans.

The snow had stopped, and stars winked between the clouds when I left the house and walked two doors down to Matthew's. He opened the door and his mama stepped up behind him.

"Now what in the world brings you out in the dark? Everything OK at home?" Mrs. Wright asked, with worry carving deep lines in her forehead. Against the sound of a crackling fire, and the smell of cookies baking,

I told her bits and pieces of my story. Matthew stood by listening. For the first time, I wasn't ashamed or embarrassed. Words tumbled free and with them I did too. Mrs. Wright nodded and took my hand. Matthew bent down to pet Sage and give me space for talking. His mama already knew that my grandpa was dead and that Dr. Molly had a fire. If she knew my daddy was gone or that my mama was sad and acting crazy, she didn't let on. By the time I went home empty handed I knew that things really would be *just fine*.

And then, even though I felt shy about doing it, I called Dr. Molly. "I'd like to invite you and Cheryl to have supper with my family."

"Honey, your mama has been very clear. We need to respect her wishes. I'm sorry, Ruth Ann. We just can't right now."

"But wait," I blurted before she said goodbye. "My mama's

coming and going out of her mind. She's just not thinking right these days. But I am." I took a breath as I listened to hers and waited.

With her answer, I let my breath out and threw the frozen meat and tomatoes in a pan, turned the heat on low, and walked into the living room. I got busy cleaning up the pigsty that was our home. In all the commotion of fires and death and typewriters and sorrow, our house was just as out of control as our lives. I did my best to make the house *presentable* and then did what I could to look presentable too. And now for Mama.

"Mama, you gotta get up now. We need you," I said and flicked on her light. She was back to lying curled in a ball on her bed. "We're gonna be having company for supper and I thought you might wanna take a quick bath and change your clothes."

She looked up at me like I was speaking Swahili. "That blouse is filthy. And Mama, you are too." I didn't bite my tongue or shout. I just told her the truth. "There's not a lot of time."

"What do you mean, *company for supper?*"

"*Company for supper.* And Mama, right now you look like a hobo." She flipped on her back and reached a hand up to her dirty, matted head. "You get in the bath, and I'll look in your closet."

"Ruth Ann, I do not understand. I do not need *company.* I need rest."

"You can rest after supper." My heart pounded in my chest when I looked at the clock and saw that folks would be here in no time, and Mama was still lying prone on her bed. And there was no saying if she was going to do what I told her to. But I kept right on like a runaway train. "That's all there is to it, Mama. Upsy daisy."

I can't say that I know exactly how it happened, but she

got in the bath because I told her to, and I went looking for something clean for her to wear. When I opened the closet, I couldn't even see what was hanging there, because all I could see is what was missing.

Half of Daddy's clothes were gone. Did that mean he was gone too? I stood staring at the emptiness. Mama's voice filled my head. How would the mortgage get paid if he didn't show up with a paycheck? I could clean the house and organize supper, but I couldn't pay the bills. Panic nearly shook me loose from my hinges, and then Mama's voice broke through to me.

"Ruth Ann, I have a pair of navy-blue trousers. Do you see those?" she called from the bath.

He never said goodbye. What would I tell Annie? Where would we live?

"Ruth Ann!" Mama called out again.

"I'm coming, Mama." I could hear my own voice, steady and calm. Even I couldn't hear the tears that I swallowed; the worry that choked me. Was he really gone this time?

I pulled out the trousers and a blouse I'd never seen Mama wear. It smelled musty, but it would have to do. While Mama bathed, I cleaned her glasses and laid out her clothes with my sweaty, shaking hands. I searched through her drawer for a pair of underpants that weren't all torn up but I couldn't find even one. What I did find I put on top of the trousers and called out to her, "Mama, I'm going downstairs. Your clothes are on your bed. You come on down when you're ready." Despite everything that was happening, I trusted that she would.

I pushed away sadness and tears and pulled open cupboards and drawers. Daddy's face was everywhere. I searched through Mama's special occasion stuff in the breakfront and remembered when we were *family*, all of us, Grandpa and Grandma too.

But now it was a different family I was planning for. When I thought about it, a feeling crept into my stomach. For a minute I stopped. It wasn't the feeling I was used to when I knew that *family* was coming for supper. I knew what to do with bad feelings. I was accidentally doing the same with good.

I let myself smile as I laid out a tablecloth with red poinsettias and green holly. The cloth napkins were red and green to match. In the middle of the table were two Scotties wearing Santa hats and filled with salt and pepper. Red candles sat on either side. There was a minute, but just that, that I wondered if I did it wrong. The only way I knew to make things special was with Mama's Christmas things. Red and green and gold filled all the spaces that I could find.

Then I remembered Daddy walking towards me. I remembered him holding Mama and me. *How could he go? Where is he?* I didn't feel just one thing or the other. Like the wheat and the chaff it all came together from the same stalk. And tonight I would gather the wheat. I was ready. It looked just right. Just right for family to gather 'round.

I finished lighting the candles when headlights turned into the drive. Dr. Molly, slow and steady, walked towards the front porch, with Cheryl on her arm. I opened the door and Dr. Molly opened her arms. "You're sure this is OK? We don't want to make things harder for you girls," Dr. Molly asked, still holding me in a hug.

"I'm sure," I said completely unsure of anything but this moment. I wanted to tell her everything but couldn't say a word. The spell would break if I did, and I would lose the thread I was holding; the one that held me together. Over Dr. Molly's shoulder, I saw Cheryl who looked like a scared puppy. How could she not? You can't have a *lunatic* burn down your house without it burning a hole in your heart, too.

Her voice cracked with the first words she spoke. "Elizabeth, you're beautiful."

I turned. Cheryl was right. Mama was beautiful. She didn't put on the clothes I laid out, but an emerald green dress that hung in her closet instead. She fixed her hair and wore stockings and shoes. Her smile was shy, as she came into the kitchen and turned to Cheryl first.

"Cheryl, I'm so sorry about your home. What a time you've been through. You must be completely worn out." And then to Dr. Molly. "Molly, I'm sorry. I haven't been myself recently. I am truly sorry if I added more pain to your situation."

"It is so good to see you, Elizabeth. I've missed you terribly," Dr. Molly said choking back tears. "It's been, quite a…"

"Fiasco," Mama and Dr. Molly said together and smiled.

And then Mama looked around. "I must say, I am a bit embarrassed. I know that you are here for supper, but, Ruth Ann, I haven't the foggiest notion what we are feeding our guests."

"Well, Mama, I don't altogether know either." I smiled at her worried look and said, "mostly, it's a surprise. But I could use some help with a pan of meat and tomatoes on the stovetop."

"How 'bout you and I take a look at your pan while Cheryl and your Mama get better acquainted? That alright with you two? And then we can let your surprise unfold, as it will."

Mama was all goodness and hospitality and took Cheryl by the elbow and led her into the living room. "My goodness, Ruth Ann, did you do all of this?" she called out.

"Yeah, I guess I did." I stepped in behind them and took a look at what they were seeing. Candles were lit all around the room and Mama's collection of Nutcrackers was on the mantle. A green ceramic yule log, that Mama made before I was born, was sitting on the coffee table with three red candles. Her little Nativity set was laid out real pretty on a piece of red fabric covering up the sofa table by the window. I walked closer.

Mary's reflection was in the window as she looked down at baby Jesus in the manger. For the first time in my life, I thought that maybe Jesus was looking down on me. I could almost feel Him breathing a breath of peace into my home and heart.

When the doorbell rang, I spun around, tripped over Buddy, picked myself up, and felt that moment of peace get shoved aside by shame. "Good thing your daddy isn't...I am so sorry." Mama swallowed her words, and pulled me into a hug, and didn't even try to push me away.

"It's OK, Mama. Daddy's right, I never will be *dancing with Fred Astaire.*" I smiled to make her feel better and she smiled too, remembering Daddy before he left. The bell rang again.

"For heaven's sake, who might that be?" Mama asked as I walked across the room and opened the living room door. Standing on the front porch was Matthew and his whole family. Every single one of them was holding a pot or bag or plate of something to eat. But when I opened the door they didn't come in. They started singing.

"*Silent night, holy night, all is calm, all is bright...*" They sang the chorus and every one of us stood watching and listening, too surprised to interrupt.

"Ruth Ann, you didn't tell me that you invited the Von Trapp Family for supper," Mama joked. "Come in, come in," she said as she swept her arm back like she was making way for the queen.

"We've been practicing. Right, Matthew?" Little Laurie said looking up at her big brother. They were all lit up like a choir of angels.

"You born in a barn? All the heat is going out and the cold

coming in. Get yourselves in here and close that door behind you," came a voice from behind us.

Daddy! I pushed past Dr. Molly and Mama and crashed into my daddy's open arms. His words brushed past my ear, "like I said, come on in." The Wrights filed in, with smiles and hellos, and walked past me and took supper to the table.

While we were all busy facing the front of the house, Daddy had slipped in the back. I stepped away from the commotion. "What are you doing here? I thought you were gone for good," I accused. And then, not sure if he knew, I whispered, "your daddy..." My anger and my sadness got all wrapped up in a sputter of words and a flood of tears.

"I know, Ruthie. I know." He sighed and whispered back, "we'll talk about my daddy later." I saw a flash in his eyes. I didn't understand. " But what made you think that I was gone for good?" He asked like it hadn't even occurred to him.

"Your clothes. They're gone," I whimpered, hoping the commotion around us would keep others from hearing.

"Nah. I just did some sorting. And I've been doing some thinking."

"Thinking 'bout what?" I asked more perplexed than relieved just yet.

"Well, two things. For one, going places." He reached into his back pocket and pulled out a map of New York state. I must have looked horrified. "All of us. A vacation," he said with a smile.

"What's the other thing?" I asked, not sure I could feel relief yet.

"What I forgot." He looked down at me and must have seen my thoughts racing around the corners in my brain. "Don't you want to know what it was?" The side of his mouth turned up, trying to smile.

I just stared.

"Ruth Ann, I forgot what matters most: you and Annie and your mama. I've been heading in the direction of nowhere for years. It's time that I turned back. I'm here and I'm not leaving." He laughed softly, "not without the lot of you, anyhow." He pulled me close again, and whispered, "I love you, sweet Ruthie. There's a world out there. And I want to see it with my family."

"You expecting more company?" he asked when the doorbell rang again.

Stepping out of his hug, I walked over and opened the door. "Heidi, what are you doing here?"

Her smile was as bright as the North Star. "We just thought you might like a hot meal after your cold walk home. And we were hoping you wouldn't mind some company."

"Dr. Molly gave a call," Mr. Hansen finished. "She thought it'd be OK if we crashed the party. I hope it is."

"This is the best day of my life!" I cried out. As they filed past on the way to the table too, I turned to look back at Daddy. His map was lying on the table beside him.

He turned from me to Mama. "You are the beautiful girl I married," I heard him murmur. "The most beautiful girl in the room

"Later, we will need to talk about all of this, *all* of this, Daniel." She tapped the map. "But this is not the time. Our daughter–" Mama turned to me, tears filled her eyes, and she reached out. Her hand was so soft and frail, but her grip was like steel.

"I was wrong, Ruth Ann Walker, apparently, *you are in charge*. And such a capable charge you are." Pride and joy filled my cheeks with a hot red blush and tears welled in my eyes again.

Heidi came up beside me. "Did you do all this?" She didn't wait for me to answer. "It's beautiful, Ruthie. It looks just like

Christmas." Leaving my folks alone, we walked, arm in arm, into the dining room.

The table was laid with ham and scalloped potatoes, cornbread stuffing and fried chicken, fresh bread and tater tot casserole, Jell-O salad, a plate of pickles and olives. On the buffet, the cherries from the cellar bubbled through the top crust of the pie that Mrs. Wright made. A little dough hatchet rested on top, just like Mama always did, remembering George Washington, *who could not tell a lie.*

I stopped to wonder if maybe my family would be done with secrets and lies. "That smells great!" Heidi exclaimed, interrupting my thoughts, as Cheryl came in from the kitchen with a steaming casserole.

"Is that the hamburger and tomatoes?" I asked in awe.

"You got a good start, Ruth Ann. And then Molly gave it a go and I finished it off. It just needed a few spices and a little loving." I saw Cheryl *really* smile for the first time since before the fire. And then her eyes grew misty as she looked behind me. Every one of us turned to see Daddy in the doorway.

He was holding Annie in his arms. Like two blue sapphires, her eyes sparkled with life, as she looked around the room in her fuzzy jammies with the feet still attached, and her old white sailor hat resting on top of her head.

"Is it Christmas, Ruthie?" Annie's soft voice broke open the stillness and faces lifted up with smiles.

"You've been sleeping for a couple of hours, not a couple of months," I said with a laugh. "But today's kind of like Thanksgiving and Christmas."

Dr. Molly stepped away from Cheryl and walked over to Annie, who was still in Daddy's arms. "Today we get the very best of both." She reached out and squeezed Annie's toes. "You know why?"

"Why?" Annie asked, with her head tucked into Daddy's

neck, and a smile growing bigger the longer she looked at Dr. Molly.

"Well, I reckon today's even better because the gifts we're sharing are so enormous they won't fit inside a cornucopia, or under the biggest Christmas tree in the *whole* world. And these are the kind of gifts we'll be keeping forever and ever."

"What gifts are you talking 'bout, Dr. Molly?"

"Friendship, family, and love, sweetie. That's what I'm talking about."

Daddy passed Annie into Dr. Molly's arms, as he pulled out a hankie and wiped his own tears away. Annie burrowed in close, and Dr. Molly closed her eyes and teardrops squeezed out from the edges. Matthew cleared his throat and called out, "let's eat!"

Folks laughed and clapped, and all talked at once. We got more plates and chairs, and everybody scooched into place and bowed their heads, as Mr. Wright said a blessing. There were no doors or windows that kept anybody out. Laws and blood didn't matter. We sat at the table passing food and laughing and talking. The truth came down, like the curtain at the end of a play: *This* is family. And nobody's going to tell me different.

ACKNOWLEDGMENTS

Thank you to all of the people who have inspired me and believed in me as a writer. A special thanks to my writer friends Pam Hays, Andrea Gabriel, Rick Rogers, and Laura Kalpakian. Each of you, in different ways have propelled me forward. And thanks to the dear members of the writers' group who read countless drafts of this story.

A special thanks to all of those who have shared stories with me over a lifetime. Friends, family, clients, strangers. All of you have added to the treasure trove from which I draw.

My biggest thanks goes to my sweet family. My children: Autumn, for your insights and kindness as an early reader; Sam, for your expertise and skill with cover and website design. You, your spouses and your children fill me with love. And special thanks to my sweet wife, Laurie, for reading drafts and for endless support, encouragement, and love. All of you bring light and joy to my life. Thank you.

ABOUT THE AUTHOR

Mary Ann Boyle lives with her wife in a community on the edge of the Salish Sea. In her 30-year career as a licensed mental health counselor, she was privileged to join clients in the unfolding of their individual stories, and gather groups together to explore life through literature. When not hunkered down writing, she enjoys reading great stories, riding her bike, going for walks, hiking in the Pacific Northwest, and traveling the world. But most of all, she loves spending time with friends and family. She is a ridiculously obsessed mom and grandma.

Please visit her website: maryannboyle.net